One Summer in the Sun

Sienna Santerre

Arachis Press 2022

One Summer in the Sun
©2022 Sienna Santerre

ISBN 978-1-937745-81-3

Arachis Press
4803 Peanut Road
Graceville, FL 32440
http://arachispress.com

JUNE

Chapter One
Kris

"I wish this summer would never end."

"Not me. There are so many things I want to do with my life!"

"Sheesh, Ronnie, can't they wait a while?"

"Time and tide wait for no man. Nor woman." Ronnie sat up and looked out over the nearly motionless Gulf waters. "The tide is coming up, isn't it?"

"I think so," mumbled Kris, turning over on her beach towel. "What difference does it make?"

"None. I just wondered." Her eyes swept the white sand before she, too, settled back onto her towel. "We'll need a few good high tides to wash away all the seaweed Abby brought in."

"Our very own graduation hurricane. Weren't we fortunate?" There was at least a trace of sarcasm in Kristine Greene's voice. Her friend might have missed it, as she had been doing since the pair were in first grade together.

"It certainly made things more interesting!" The ceremony had been held amid rain squalls and wind gusts. But Hurricane Abby had only brushed by Naples and caused no great damage there. Nothing needed to be postponed.

Honey began playing on Ronnie's tiny, tinny transistor radio, tuned to WQAM out of Miami. Kris was tempted to make a rude remark about the song but held her tongue. She knew Ronnie liked it. Maybe she would not admit to the fact but her friend knew.

The Q was about it for listening to pop during the days. At night, the local station played contemporary music but would broadcast 'easy listening' through the daytime. By afternoon, the summer storms out over the Everglades would fill the signal from Miami with bursts of static, making it impossible to listen. Those would grow worse, more common, as the season progressed.

As Bobby Goldsboro faded, she asked, "Working today?"

"Noon to five. Mister Brooks thinks I should be able to fit my schedule into any hours he has open, now that school is out."

He was probably right. Ronnie would try her best to accommodate her boss, even if she came complaining to her friends after. "He'll miss you, come fall."

"I s'pose."

If the old man and his wife remained in business. Their little book store cum gift shop was located on too valuable a piece of land. Kris's dad had assured her of this, that another piece of 'old Naples' would soon come down and two or three stories of the new one would rise in its place. She might not be here when it happened. None of her friends might, off to college or to jobs in other towns, some off to the military.

Jumpin' Jack Flash on the radio. That was better. "I guess, guess, guessss!" someone sang along, almost in key.

"Hi, Joey. You're blocking the sun."

"You're brown enough. Well, in spots." The girl plopped down beside them on the sand, not bothering with a towel.

Spots was a reference to her freckles. Kris turned her head to look at her, shielding her eyes from the sun. In shorts and tee, not a swim-suit. There didn't seem to be a suit under the tee, either, nor anything else. Joey could get away with that.

"Someone drop you?"

"Nope. Rode my bike."

That was a long way. Joey's family didn't live as close to the beach as hers or Rhonda's. At least they were inside the city limits. "You'll need a car someday."

"So people tell me."

"Another lie from the establishment?" asked Ronnie.

"Isn't everything?"

Neither was the least serious, Kris knew. She also knew not to join in. They would gang up on her, the little rich girl. Rich she didn't mind; little was not quite as much fun.

"I understand the Kennedy funeral will be televised tomorrow," Joey said of a sudden. "I'll be working."

Kris almost quipped, *I'll be sleeping*, but thought better of it. "They'll show some of it on the evening news, I'd think."

"That's so," agreed Ronnie.

"I'd probably have to come watch at your house. No chance of tuning it in at mine."

"Sure. Drop by just before Prince Charming gallops up to whisk me away."

"So another Saturday night without a date?" asked Kris.

"Seems that way. How 'bout you two?"

"Not sure," replied Joey. Her gaze was toward the water, the sparkling Gulf spreading beneath an intensely blue sky. "Tonight, yeah."

"Me too," said Ronnie.

"Me three," said Kris.

"If tomorrow night doesn't pan out, we should get together. Watcha say?"

"Sounds good, Joey. So does getting in the water again." Ronnie rose from her beach towel. A reasonably modest two-piece swimsuit, with a floral pattern of pink and yellow and white, neither flattered nor detracted from a lean but unremarkable body. "Then I have to go home and clean up for work."

"I'll go in too." Both started toward the water, then began moving faster, finally sprinting, racing to dive in. Kris made sure all the strings on her bikini were securely tied and followed at a more leisurely pace.

Bill Biddle intercepted her before she reached them, already splashing beyond the sand. "Why don't you come up and join us on the pier?" he asked, nodding his head in that direction. She looked up to see a handful of classmates lined up along the railing. Make that former classmates.

"Get her up here, Bill," someone called. "I want a closer look at that bikini." The girl next to him punched the boy on the arm.

"Then buy binoculars," Kris shouted back. All athletes, some of them guys she had dated at some time. The girls were faces and names but little more to her, most of them. Barely that without her glasses.

"We're going to have a party," Bill informed her. "A going away party."

"I think this whole summer is a going away party," she told him. He didn't seem to get it so she went on. "Who's going this time?"

"Arnie. Off to the navy this weekend."

"Poole?"

"Yep. We'll have a keg tonight. Up at the pass."

If she didn't have a date she might have accepted. "Hey, Arnie!" She waved toward the lanky boy. He always looked goofy. Maybe that would change. "Take care of yourself, okay?" she called. "Bye, Bill," said Kris and made her way to the water.

Chapter Two
Ronnie

Saving herself for marriage seemed terribly old-fashioned to Rhonda Deerfield, yet that was just what she had been doing. She had no illusions that her best friends had done the same. Rhonda would not change her habit this night. No. If it were going to happen it would not be with Daryl.

Daryl was trustworthy. She was pretty sure of this. Oh, he could be encouraged. Couldn't all guys? Daryl Sterne was no one she intended to encourage. He was someone to go out with, just to have someone to go out with. She felt she should have that someone on a Friday night and assumed Daryl saw her the same way.

They wouldn't see each other after this summer, anyway, would they? She'd be at the University of Florida, he was bound for Florida State. That should make them mortal enemies the rest of their lives!

At least during football season. She wouldn't see any of her friends, not the real friends. Everyone was headed a different direction. Or in Joey's case, staying right here in Naples while the rest of them left. Joanna Varney was bright, maybe even the brightest of them all. She could do better than the local JC. She deserved better.

Pink lipstick? If she got much tanner it wouldn't look quite right. She finished her makeup and stood to look herself over. Maybe she should have gone more casual. It was only dinner and a movie with Daryl. Oh, chances were he'd have on a jacket and tie. It was so stupid of them both.

More so when the weather was this hot. Ronnie almost wished she'd been the one invited to a keg party on a deserted beach, dancing to car radio music by headlight illumination, wearing shorts and slapping at mosquitoes. She wasn't sure she would enjoy it, she knew she would feel out of place, but maybe just to do something different. Instead, an evening in a white dress, neither boring nor exciting. Just an evening.

The doorbell rang. That was almost certainly Daryl. Yeah, there was his dark blue Falcon in the drive. Did someone let him in? "Hi, Ronnie. Ready to go?" Mom was at his side, at the door.

Mom liked Daryl, of course. He was solid and bland and polite and was going to be an engineer. Big and sort of good looking too, but slow-moving, not athletic. Dad, of course, made jokes about him, the same sort Kris made. Those two were kindred spirits.

Yes, he was in a jacket, gold colored, with a striped tie. He might have worn both last time they went out, for all she knew. "Bye Mom," she said. "Home before midnight. We don't want Daryl's car to turn into a pumpkin." That set a time without her mother awkwardly attempting it. Mom had become unsure about curfews now she was officially an adult.

With a polite goodbye to her mom, Daryl followed her out the door. He held the car door open for her, being painfully polite as usual, a robot gentleman. Before turning the key in the ignition, he turned and asked, "*Blackbeard's Ghost?* Or should I drive to Fort Myers? There are better movies playing up there." Daryl did not sound eager.

She wasn't that eager to spend an hour riding north either. Not to mention coming back. "Don't bother. It's just a movie." Maybe neither would enjoy it much but it was something to do on a Friday night, an excuse not to sit home. "We can catch the first show, can't we? And eat after."

"Sure." He cranked the engine and eased away from the curb. Even were they a little late, it wouldn't matter any. Was this going to be her summer? None of it mattering any?

"Huh?" Daryl had said something.

"I just asked about work," he said.

"Oh, it's okay. How about with you?"

"A pain. But it's college money." Daryl was actually working construction, working for his father's company. It felt odd to think of him in work clothes, doing whatever he did.

"What does your dad have you doing?"

"Digging, mostly. Trenches for concrete footers."

Hard manual labor. It did feel odd. She tried to picture Daryl shoveling dirt in a sweat-stained tee and found she couldn't. Did he sit and talk with the other guys on the job? Did he use the same profanities, maybe drink a beer—maybe more than one—at the end of the day? Ronnie had seen construction workers and thought she knew a thing or two about them.

"I hope you showered well after a day of that," she quipped. Why did she say that? It wasn't the sort of thing she did. Daryl only chuckled. She didn't seem to have embarrassed him. Not as much as she embarrassed herself.

"Lots of cars," he mumbled. "I'll see if there's a parking space on Broad." He pulled into one about halfway up the block. Only a block and a half from the beach. Ronnie thought she might prefer to walk that direction instead of back toward the theater. She got out before Daryl could come around to get the door.

It wasn't quite dark yet. A glow came from the direction of the Gulf, the just-set sun. Black silhouettes of coconut palms stood against a smoke-purple sky. They lined both sides of Broad Avenue, had as far back as she could remember, tall when she was still a little girl. They clipped the nuts off before they matured these days but once one could drive about in the early morning and pick up freshly-fallen coconuts.

Too many had fallen on people's cars. That wouldn't do as more and more took up residence in town and in the developments beyond, northerners who didn't understand a few dents from fallen coconuts were part of the price of life in paradise. That was what Dad said, anyway.

There were kids standing around the theater entrance, and at the drugstore next door. The venerable *Beach Store*—it was older than she was, in a town where very little was old. The theater was old too and located in a Quonset hut. That definitely would be torn down soon. Everyone knew that. Some would miss it, eyesore though it was.

"Just a coke," she murmured to Daryl when he paused at the concession counter. She didn't really want that, even. She just thought she should let him buy her something, so he wouldn't feel awkward if he got something for himself. How dingy this place was, its dim tiled and stuccoed walls, the dark red ragged carpet, littered with bits of popcorn and ticket stubs. Up a couple steps from the lobby; to the right was the gallery where black people would have sat only a few years ago. To the left, the main seating. It was a reasonably large place, really, with just as big a screen as any theater in Fort Myers.

Unless one counted the drive-ins. She was glad Daryl didn't suggest that. The opening credits were running. Perfect timing. Enjoy the movie, she told herself. It will be okay. Even enjoy Daryl's arm around you and don't mind if he kisses you later. It's something to do on a Friday night.

Chapter Three
Kris

"Let's not go all the way to Fort Myers."

Mackie slowed down. Without looking toward his date, he asked, "Where then?"

"Turn on the Vanderbilt Beach road," Kris told him.

Even in the dark, she could see the boy shrug. "You aren't going to ask me to get my car stuck in the sand, are you?"

Kris had to giggle. "Maybe."

Mackie took a left off the highway, toward the Gulf. He was driving an older Dodge this evening, another used vehicle from his father's car lot. One never knew what he might show up in.

"The sandy roads should be firm enough with all this rain," he remarked. "You do intend to go to the party at the pass, right?"

"Does everyone know about it?" Kris asked.

"Let's hope the cops don't." The beaches at Wiggin's Pass were remote and well outside city limits. A deputy might cruise by but would be unlikely to drive his patrol car in. But he could and that could become a disaster for an athlete like Mackie, headed off on a scholarship. Even then, though, there would probably just be a warning to clear out.

And a confiscation of any alcohol, of course. They turned at the beach road and headed north. Saw palmettos lined the way, low, dark masses in the dusk, with a spindly pine rising from them here and there. Here and there also stood a house. This area was finally beginning to fill in, after long being on the fringes of Naples's development.

"Somewhere along here," muttered Mackie, apparently to himself. There was more than one unpaved road toward the beach and the inlet, and each was probably as good as another. "Yeah." He turned the big Dodge carefully into the sandy way, splashing through a shallow puddle. The palmettos were close now, a wall on either side of them.

Not for long. They gave way to clumps of tall grass. Kris could hear music from somewhere ahead. It sounded thin. A car radio most likely.

"More than I expected," said Mackie, as his headlights revealed the crowd. Some of the other cars had their lights on, motors running, radios playing. There was a driftwood fire, not very large. Not much wood was left around here to pick up. Moths could be seen darting through the light.

There would be mosquitoes and sand flies too. That was a given. Her date pulled the big Dodge into an empty space.

"Hey, Mackerel," someone called.

"Hi, Doughnut," Mackie called back. "Wasn't expecting you here."

"Wasn't expecting me either. What the heck 're we doing in this place?"

Doughnut. William Booth had picked up the nickname on his first day at Lake Park Elementary, when his mom had packed him a doughnut in his lunch. Jelly-filled, she remembered. Red jelly. That was what, third grade? The schools were just becoming integrated and Kris had never known a black kid before.

His parents and everyone else in their neighborhood off Goodlette Road called him Willie. She'd never liked to use that name; he was always either Doughnut or William to her. Most of the guys from the football team had taken to just calling him Booth.

Mackie was one of those guys. He might be William's best friend. His best white friend, maybe she should say. Or not. Kris simply wasn't sure about it. She was a bit on the outside when it came to these guys—these athletes—despite dating more than one of them. They were a tight-knit team.

A team no longer. They would be going their ways now. Harold Macklin off to—where? Some college up north. He might have told her which one. William had been offered scholarships. Recruiters had come and visited. Not from anyplace big. Small colleges, offering a partial ride. He was a pretty impressive athlete but just a bit on the small side. Not that there was anything wrong with being small!

There was beer but the vaunted keg was not in evidence. Coolers with cans. That was just as good. Better maybe. How would they have kept a keg cold on a hot Florida summer night? It was a pretty good night. All the afternoon's clouds had blown away to rain on someone else, leaving only the stars. Kris thought she'd like to walk down to where she could see them over the Gulf.

Ha, she was already bored by this party and she'd just arrived! Mackie had a can in his hand, standing with a bunch of his buddies. He wouldn't even notice if she disappeared. Any one of those pathways through the grass would take her to the beach. They weren't that near to the pass itself, were they? It was hard to sure of that in the dark. Things looked different.

Someone was behind her. Her heart might have tripped just a little faster for a moment. Running. Not attempting to be sneaky at all. She turned around to see William jogging after her.

"I don't trust some of these guys so much, Kris," he said, almost apologetically. "You mind if I come with you?"

"Sure, Doughnut. You can make the Mackerel jealous." Not that she cared. For all she knew, this might the last time she ever went anywhere with Harold Macklin.

He ambled along at her side for a few seconds. "This party's for Arnie, right? Poole?"

"You didn't know?"

"We just heard there was a party and came. Didn't know who it was for." William hesitated. "Wasn't invited, either."

Kris snickered. "Are you afraid someone's gonna throw you out, Doughnut?"

The boy only laughed at that. Then, "Arnie's going into the navy before the draft gets him. I've been thinking of signing up for the marines myself. Get ahead of things and choose my path."

A path to getting shot, thought Kris. "Going to college would work just as well."

"If it was just me." She waited for him to say more but that was it. If he expected Kris to try prying it out of him, William Booth was mistaken.

Instead, she said, "I wouldn't want you to end up like Donny."

Donny Weeden's flag-draped coffin had come home this winter. All the kids had known Donny and remembered him dropping out to join the army. All the kids knew Donny's mom too; she taught civics and business classes at the high school. Donny had never been a good student. It had been his opportunity to prove himself.

Damn. Kris felt a sudden anger and wasn't completely sure why. It was all just such a waste.

They were at the edge of the beach, proper, where grass ended and only white sand extended to the water. The Gulf was dead-calm, the sky completely clear, the nearly full moon rising at her back. There were the stars she'd walked over here to see, extending down to the barely visible horizon, black sky meeting black water.

"Do you think there are sharks in the water?" she asked. "I'd like to go in."

Doughnut's expression clearly showed he thought she was crazy. "This near the pass? No way, girl!"

"Hmm. Okay, I'll just go down and get my feet wet. If there are itty-bitty sharks they can attack my toes." Kris had left her shoes in Mackie's Dodge. Flats for the intended casual date tonight, though she wore heels when she could get away with it, being such a runt. Her dress was as mini as she felt comfortable wearing, cotton, and floral patterned. She could have swam in it. Or even doffed it.

That would certainly have scandalized Doughnut! He was a pretty strait-laced guy. He peeled off his own sneakers, worn without laces on his bare feet. There were holes worn through the ends of them by his toes. Kris couldn't see that here but had noticed it before.

They went in only to their ankles. Without thinking about it, she reached over and took her friend's hand. Had she held it since they were little kids?

"Whatcha doin', boy?" asked someone. Two guys approached them. One of them Kris knew from school. Knew his name and that was pretty much it. Hadn't he hung out with Joey sometimes? The other? No idea. "This boy botherin' you?"

"No, but you are," she shot back at once. Probably she shouldn't have, she realized at once. She often had second thoughts of that sort.

"Ditch the nigger," the other one said, the one she didn't know. "We can show you what real men are like." Both snickered at that.

"Maybe we should show him he shouldn't be messin' with white girls," said the first. Jim something, wasn't he? "Should we teach you a lesson, boy?"

In better light, they might have seen Doughnut's muscles and been less belligerent. Admittedly, he was not a tall guy. We short people are always underestimated, Kris thought.

"Get lost," came Mackie's voice. "You're bothering my friends." Her date did look large, looming out of the dark.

"Okay," said one or the other. "We didn't mean no harm. Let's go get another beer," he told his buddy. Both disappeared into the night.

"This is what you get for stealing my date, Doughnut," said Mackie.

"She stole *me*, Mackerel. Forced me to come down here!"

"It's the truth. I intended to ravage him right here on the sand."

Both boys laughed at the absurdity of it, but Doughnut looked a tad embarrassed. "It's a good thing you did come along," he said, as they headed back to the party. "I had friends with me and they wouldn't have thought twice about jumpin' those red-necks."

A part of Kris thought she might have liked to see that.

Chapter Four
Joey

She had seen Ronnie and Daryl last night but hadn't said hello. No sense in intruding, as long as Ronnie hadn't noticed her. Steve was keeping her pretty busy in his car anyway. Joey didn't think she would go out with him again. She was tired of greasers, even cute ones. Damn, she was tired of just about everyone.

Tired of this job too. Yeah, the convenience store had 'seven' right in its name so what had she expected? If it had to open early, she had to get up earlier. Saturday and Sunday. She'd done it for months now, through her senior year at Naples High. Maybe it was time to graduate to something better here too.

George was inventorying or something, over at the coolers. Maybe he was just malingering. As manager, that was his prerogative but he liked to look busy anyway. "Kandy," he called to the girl straightening out the snack shelves, "you take the cash register. Joey, with me."

Kandy cashiering? Joey wasn't sure she could count beyond ten and then only if she used her fingers. "Whatcha need Gee-oh?" she asked. That's what George told them to call him. She hardly thought of how stupid it sounded anymore.

"You should've been here earlier this morning," he told her, leading her into the back room. "You're my oldest girl on this shift. It's up to you to set an example."

Joey had to laugh. "It would be wasted on Kandy."

"Don't smart back, Miss Varney. Maybe I'll just dock you half an hour."

She bit back a retort. It wouldn't do her any good and be just as wasted on Gee-oh.

"But we'll let it slide this time, okay?" George's voice became ingratiating. "There's no reason you and me can't get along, is there Joanna?"

Joey cautiously nodded. He thinks he has an advantage now, after backing off on his threat, she thought. He expects me to be grateful!

"I'll get back to the counter then," said the young woman.

A hand on her arm. The grip tightened when she instinctively attempted to pull away from Gee-oh's touch. "I think we can get along really great," he went on. His voice had taken on more of an edge and he was—what? Panting? Breathing hard, anyway. Joey twisted out of his grasp.

George was quick to anger. "Hippie slut!" he hissed. "Think you're too good for me? I'll bet you put out for any long-haired freak who comes along."

The absurdity of it hit Joey first. She laughed in the man's face. The snarl of rage that erupted from him brought a moment of fear but that gave way to her own anger. Anger at herself as much as this pitiful convenience store manager, standing here red in face and bulging at the crotch. She had put up with this for too long. Joey turned and marched from the room, through the store, and out the front door. Her apron was tossed into the parking lot.

Good thing I didn't carry a purse, Joey told herself. I'd have to go back and get it and that would ruin the effect. A few minutes later she peddled her bike up her own uneven driveway.

Her stepfather looked up from the couch as she entered, without a great deal of interest, and turned his eyes back to a fishing show on the television. Mom stepped out of the kitchen.

"Home already? Is something wrong?"

"I quit. George pawed at me one time too often."

"What?" Wayne half-rose from the couch, his face dark. "I'll go down there and teach—"

"No need. It goes with the territory."

Her mom didn't say anything but she knew all about that. Wayne was a good guy, a much better guy than her dad had been. But he had a temper.

"It was time to get a better job anyway," she went on.

A grin came to her stepfather's broad red face. "Why, I can give you one right now. Why don't you go out and mow our patch of sand spurs so I don't have to?"

"Why not?" she said, taking a place on the sofa beside him. "What are they catching?"

Chapter Five
Ronnie

It was usually her house. In part because it lay between Joey's and Kris's, in part because her parents made the three feel more comfortable. They'd been hanging out here forever, it seemed.

Ronnie sometimes referred to the three of them as 'the Triumvirate.' When did she start that? They might still have been in grade school. Her best friends had accepted it in time, though not without jokes at her expense. Now they used it naturally themselves.

They watched scenes from the funeral on the evening news, on the little black and white set in Ronnie's bedroom. Only she had seen any of it earlier. She heard the phone ring and her mom answer it.

"Ronnie! It's Mister Brooks!"

Couldn't Mom have come to tell her rather than hollering? She went to see what was up. Her boss hardly ever called her.

"Wants you to take more shifts?" asked Kris when she returned. "Tell him to give 'em to Joey. She needs the work!"

"I wish I could. Brooks called to tell me he's closing the store. I'll only have a job for two more weeks." She kept her voice as level as she could. Ronnie hurt some, inside, not for herself but for the Brooks couple. She wished they could have kept their little shop open forever, that this town would stop changing so quickly.

"That sucks," said Joey.

"Sucks? I've never heard that before. It sounds kind of dirty," Kris said.

"Oh, the surfer guys say it. I don't think it has anything to do with you-know-what."

Ronnie wasn't sure she did know what. It didn't matter. "I'll miss getting discounts on books," she said. "But, hey, I was going to be gone in a couple months anyway."

"You have enough books," stated Kris. "Now you'll be free to play with us the rest of the summer."

Joey snorted. "Easy for you to say, with your allowance. But we're all free tonight, huh? What'll we do?"

"There's the old standby," said Kris. "Cruise around town."

Ronnie had to laugh at that. "And wave at everyone else doing the same. Your car or mine?"

"Joey's!"

"It's been a long time since I was able to haul the two of you anywhere on my bike," said their friend. "We should all ride around together sometime, like we used to."

"But tonight it's my Bug—"

"Shotgun!" called Joey at once.

"Kris is the smallest," objected Ronnie. "She should be in the back."

"But my arms are too short to reach the wheel from there."

There was no arguing with that. It was undoubtedly better to ride in Kris's new car than in her old cramped Simca, even if she did end up in the rear seat.

The three trooped out into the living room. "We're going to go sample the exotic night life of Naples," Ronnie told her mother.

"Do you want to eat first? I can fix something."

"We'll stop somewhere for burgers. *Chris's.*" Her friends nodded in agreement. They were heading out the door before Mom could say anything more. She hadn't told her about the store closing, had she? Tomorrow would be okay.

Moments later she was clambering into the cramped back seat of the black VW. Kris had insisted on that color even though it would get hot in the Florida sun. I'll park in the shade, she had told anyone who brought it up. She hadn't today.

Not that it mattered any. They had the convertible top down quickly. Who needed air conditioning? The familiar, noisy engine rasped and started up, and Kris eased out of the Deerfields' old fash-ioned oyster shell drive. The house itself was kind of old fashioned and the land here was likely to be worth more than the house sitting on it. That was true of a lot of places in town. *Brooks Books and Looks* included.

The Bug turned on Seventh and headed toward the beach. "We're taking the scenic route," Kris informed them.

"All the beach accesses will still be crowded," said Joey. "Even this late. All summer."

"If we want to watch the fireworks show on July Fourth we'll have to come early and find a space," Kris replied. She turned right on Gulf Shore.

"It would be simpler to walk over," felt Ronnie. Or ride bikes, like Joey had suggested. It had been ages since the trio had wheeled around town that way, hadn't it?

Past the *Beach Club* and its golf course. The oldest in a town now riddled with golf clubs. The oldest still in operation. Her dad said there had once been one downtown. She should look that up sometime. On northward. It was filling up more and more on either side of the road, apartment buildings mostly. Condos.

The beach still lay over there, somewhere to their left. It used to be visible along this way. They could have seen the sun setting over the Gulf. She didn't want to think of that right now. There were enough things to be depressed about.

"So," she said to Kris, "who do you support now? I know Joey's still big on McCarthy." She and Kris had both been enthusiastic about Kennedy. That was over.

"Does it matter? Oh, McGovern, I guess."

"Yeah. Me too."

Joey had once accused them of choosing their candidate on his looks. It would not be a good idea to bring that up again.

"Lowdermilk Park," announced Kris. "Close to closing time." She turned into the parking lot and did a circuit before pulling back out onto the street. It was one place the water could still be glimpsed, up at this north end of town.

Almost a month earlier, a farewell party for the Class of Sixty-eight had been held there, one sunny day to remember each other by for the rest of their lives. They would never see some of those kids again, some of them kids they had gone to school with for twelve years.

The band had been good, hadn't it? Cute singer. Why didn't she date guys like that instead of Daryl? Good ol' Daryl, as she might forever think of him. For all Ronnie knew, she might never see him again either.

Around a curve, over a bridge, through the burgeoning Moorings development to the highway. Directly across, a couple blocks back, was Naples High. Never again their destination.

What was? Well, *Chris's Gourmet Castle* tonight. It would be packed and that was okay.

Chapter Six
Joey

Ronnie did read a lot. So did she, for that matter. Pay attention, Joey scolded herself. She could think about that after mass.

She liked coming to this earliest of services, riding her bicycle through the still-dark streets. That hadn't been possible the last few months. Her job had gotten in the way. No more. Joey usually attended alone; Mom had become reticent about going to mass since her divorce and remarriage. But Joey came. Oh, now and then she ended up at the beach instead of Saint Ann's, but no one was perfect. That's why they had church, right?

She knew she couldn't use Ronnie's discount at the book store forever. Or past the end of this summer. The Sanctus. Holy, holy, holy. Time to kneel. Everything was in English now. Joey had grown up with Latin in church, had learned to sing the Latin mass when she went to school at Saint Ann Elementary, catty-cornered and up half a block or so from the church. Four years only.

She'd missed going to school with her best friends during those years. Mom and Dad—her birth dad, not Wayne—thought it would be good for her. Mom had kept her enrolled after the divorce. She'd needed her friends even more then. Joey joined the line for communion. A short line.

A short service too. It never took more than half an hour at the early morning mass. Father Al might have come close to making it twenty minutes now and again. He almost always said this mass.

Her blue bicycle was chained behind the church. The chain probably wasn't necessary but there was no reason to tempt either people or fate. She would hurry right out and ride down to the pier. There might still be overnight fishermen leaving with their catches. The final blessing and—here we go. She followed the others out into the dawn.

At least there would still be the library. Her friends were leaving but that refuge remained. There would be the library at Edison College too. Losing her job—okay, quitting her job—had convinced her the junior college in Fort Myers was her best choice now. It was cheap and she could live at home and there was even a free bus to take her there.

The bike's metal and seat were wet from the dew. She folded the beach towel she carried and sat on that as she peddled toward the pier. Too bad she couldn't peddle somewhere far away. There was a tiny bit of wobble in the rear, wasn't there? She'd have to check it when she got home. Probably the nut just needed tightening. It was a good bike, a dependable single-speed with twenty-six inch wheels to go with her long legs.

Joey had attached commodious baskets in the rear so she could do the grocery shopping. The *Sunshine* was a just a little way down the highway from their house. When she was little she could see the Trail —Highway Forty-one, that was—from the yard, with only vacant sand spur-filled lots between, but construction since had hidden it.

She stopped in the shadows of the huge banyan tree a block east of the pier. A favorite hangout of kids as far back as she could remember. Probably before that! Its roots had buckled the sidewalk, stained brown from the rains that had dripped through its branches longer than Joey had lived.

Ronnie loved that banyan. It was like the epitome of that old Naples she was always going on about. Joey peddled on to the pier but only went around the circle at the entry and headed back east. She wasn't going to walk out there this morning. She felt like riding. She felt like pushing herself. The damp beach towel went into one of the baskets and she started pumping.

Maybe she'd buzz by Kris's home. The Greenes lived south of the pier, but close to it. Close to the city docks, too, which was good since her dad had a very nice boat. Kris should invite them to go out on it more often. A right, a left a couple blocks up. Joey felt like peddling all the way to Gordon Pass and back. Maybe up and down the streets of Port Royal too! Nah, she wouldn't go that far.

Nothing was doing at the Greenes' house. Even Kris's little brother wasn't up or at least not outside. Lazy bunch. She drove herself on, peddling hard, down past the docks. There were early risers here. Early enough. Boats were already out, surely.

Yeah, two years at Edison and then what? She had no clear idea of a 'career,' as she was ever being advised to strive toward. Everything suggested sounded tedious. Joey wanted to write. How did one go about that?

Maybe she shouldn't go to college at all. That thought had swirled around in her head more than once but it couldn't be flushed all the way down. She should have a career. Something to depend on, right? She sure couldn't depend on anyone else.

Except Mom to have breakfast ready by the time she'd peddled home. She could hang out at the docks some other day.

Chapter Seven
Kris

"No one cares about experience and references when you're our age," felt Ronnie.

That was probably so, thought Kris. She hadn't had a reason to think about it. "So you're both looking for jobs?"

"Not right away," Ronnie said. "I should help close down the store. It's going to be busy for the next two weeks." She shrugged. "After that? I don't know. It won't be long till I'm gone—" She glanced toward Joey before adding, "And you too."

"Yeah, everyone but me," said Joey.

"You still thinking of going to Edison?" asked Kris.

"Not thinking any longer. I'm going to borrow my mom's car and drive up to enroll for the fall semester tomorrow. There's no point in putting it off any more."

Of course, Joey would be accepted. Edison took just about anyone and her grades were exceptionally good. Better than those of her friends. Yes, even better than serious, hard-working Ronnie's.

It wasn't fair that Joey was being sent to Fort Myers, just as it wasn't fair that all those boys were being sent to Vietnam. There wasn't anything she could do about any of it, though. Nothing at all.

"The moon will be full tomorrow night," Ronnie announced of a sudden.

Joey nodded. "It was pretty full last night. It was still in the sky when I got up this morning."

"I wouldn't know. I slept in," replied Kris.

"Me too," Ronnie said, "but it did shine in here when I was trying to sleep. I wouldn't mind having a nap right now." She flopped back onto her bed. It was neatly made, of course, with a pink bedspread. Feminine without being frilly. Understated. Something like that. Kris suspected her friend of consciously trying to project that image.

The whole room was understated but no one would think a guy slept here. Lived here. Of course not in any other sense. It was a small room too. The house was small, with stuccoed interior walls. That was very old-school Florida. Kris had made the mistake from time to time of brushing against their sandpaper-like surface, over the years she had visited. Maybe she would never remember to always be careful.

Maybe she wouldn't have to. "Do you think you'll get home much?" she asked Ronnie. "It's a long drive from Gainesville." She couldn't help snickering. "Even longer in your car."

"That depends on how many times it breaks down per trip," observed Joey.

"Well, one thing I'm not going to miss is you two ganging up on me!" sniffed their friend. Then her tone became—wistful, maybe? "But I am going to miss seeing you. Both of you. I don't think I'll be making many weekend visits home."

"Joey will ride her bike up now and again."

"I wouldn't put it past her."

Joey only grinned at that. Kris was not entirely willing to put it past her either, even if it had been a joke.

"Well, it's months until any of that matters," Kris stated. "And we'll see each other at Thanksgiving and Christmas, right?"

"Shouldn't that be Hanukkah?" asked Joey.

"Then too. And I might see you some weekends if there aren't any parties in Miami—oh, wait, there are always parties in Miami!"

"We should make the rest of this summer a party," Joey declared. "Starting with a celebration of the full moon. Let's go out and howl!"

"Tomorrow?" asked Ronnie.

"Right. We'll all meet at the beach. Ride your bikes!"

Why not? "Third Avenue. Sunset." The two girls nodded agreement. "Okay. So what do we do tonight?"

"Sleep," responded Ronnie, at once.

"Me too. I'm bushed."

Kris scowled at the pair. "Aw, you guys are no fun. It's not like it's a school night!"

"You'll have to wait until you get to University of Miami to party all night, every night," Joey told her.

"Anyway, we need our beauty sleep."

Joey turned and confided to Ronnie, in a stage whisper, "It's too late for Kris to worry about that."

Damn, thought Kris, she got in the one-liner first. And she had a good one in her head, all loaded up. "Okay, rest up then. I expect no excuses tomorrow."

"I do have a full shift," began Ronnie, a little hesitantly.

It was Joey who jumped on it. "No excuses! We're all committed now. Committed to partying the rest of the summer!"

Ronnie laughed at that. "Won't we run out of things to do in this town? I mean, I love Naples and all but it's not that exciting."

"We'll go somewhere else if we get bored," Kris decided. "Hey, did you know the whole Summerlin family is in town? Even Lin." She'd heard it from her mom earlier that day. Mom was up on all the gossip.

"We aren't likely to be invited to any of their parties," said Joey. She sounded quite certain about it.

"So we invite Jelly to ours. Or Jam."

"He's cute," opined Ronnie. It was rare for her to express such an opinion. Kris was inclined to agree with it.

Joey made an unappreciative noise.

Chapter Eight
Ronnie

"Are we going to see the moon at all?" Ronnie asked the sky.

"It'll clear," Joey assured her. "There are already stars showing out over the water."

But that was the opposite direction from the rising moon. Ronnie turned back to the west. There were still clouds out that way too, lightning flickering along the horizon. Closer, rose the pilings at Third Avenue, the tallest anywhere along the beach. They were thick wooden posts, gray from exposure to the elements, during the day; now that gray was becoming black as the light faded.

Some of the guys liked to surf here sometimes, because of the sandbars that built up around the pilings. These and other groins were meant to protect the sand of Naples's beaches. Her dad said they were useless and a waste of the town's money.

Mostly the surfers stuck to the pier or went up to Doctor's Pass. Neither at this time of year. The Gulf was a sheet of glass through most of the summer.

"Did you remember your chain?" asked her friend.

"Uh-huh." Ronnie wouldn't mention how long it had taken to find it. She hadn't needed to lock up her bike in months. She *would* ride it more this summer. Maybe she would even take it with her to Gainesville, if she could figure out how. Strap it to the top of her little Simca?

Both bikes secured to the metal signpost, the girls turned their attention back to the beach. An angler could just be made out, wading and casting beside the pilings. "After snook," said Joey.

Ronnie had fished for sheepshead around these pilings during sunlight hours. She couldn't see herself wading out in the dark for a snook or any other fish. The ringing of a bell, faintly, brought her back from her contemplation of the black water.

That bell was fastened to a small bicycle being pedaled toward them, Kris straddling its white banana seat. It looked green in the illumination of the street light but she knew it to be sky blue.

"About time," commented Joey.

"I had to ride further than you," Kris complained. It wasn't really much further. Maybe not further at all than the distance from Joey's home. "And my legs are shorter."

That was most certainly true. Kris chained her bike with the others. There wasn't room for another against the post so she ran her chain through the frame of Joey's bike. "It's awfully dark," she said when finished with the chore.

"Joey guarantees a clear sky," Ronnie informed her friend.

"Well okay then. Joey's word for it is all we need. Wanta walk down toward the pier?"

That was nine blocks south. They could readily see its lights from here. "Might as well," said Joey.

"It would have been easier if I'd met you there! Let's go." Kris set off down the beach. Ronnie and Joey followed. In a few seconds, the trio were walking side by side on the sand. Pallid ghost crabs, little more than shadows, scuttled out of their way now and then. A pair of older beach-walkers passed, giving the girls friendly nods.

"There's no phosphorescence yet," Ronnie noted.

"Give it a month," responded Joey. Beyond that, none of them seemed to feel much like talking. The moon broke through the clouds, turning the beach to silver.

A month, thought Ronnie, and then another month and soon this summer would be gone. They would be gone, each on her own path, leading away from each other. It seemed unlikely that any of them would even live here again. Naples would be a place to visit. Not home.

Lights shone in only some of the houses along the beach front. Many of those who lived there did not summer in Florida. Naples wasn't really their home either. That wasn't true of the Summerlins. Preston Summerlin was a lawyer with a practice here, a man who had long been a figure in local politics. They would pass their house shortly. It was an old place, and not particular large—another of those that stood on a lot that was worth far more than the house itself.

There didn't seem to be much going on at the Summerlin home

either. The girls strolled on past it. They were close to the pier now.

"Dad says that twenty years ago the tallest Australian pine on the beachfront rose right in front of the Summerlins' house," Ronnie said. "People who came to their parties by boat used it as a landmark." She looked toward the house again. "The tree's gone now. Blew down in Hurricane Donna."

"Wouldn't the pier have been enough?" asked Kris.

"It would certainly get them close, wouldn't it? I heard that a seaplane flew in and landed here once, using that landmark."

"Flying boat," Joey corrected her. "Sea planes land on pontoons, flying boats land on their hull." Her smile could be made out by the lights from the houses. Joey loved to show off her knowledge of things the other two considered unimportant. "I've heard the story too. And it was the Salas house then. The Salas widow married Summerlin."

"Oh, yeah." Kris became enthusiastic. "Her husband was gunned down by the mafia."

All three had heard some variant of the tale. Old news in a town that was busy forgetting its past. They walked on to the pier.

Chapter Nine
Joey

Walking all the way to the end of Naples pier was like entering another world. Before one lay nothing but the dark Gulf of Mexico and the darker sky. The lights of Naples seemed far away behind them.

A few fishermen leaned on the railings; it was still a little early for many of the all-nighters to show up. Joey's father had been one of those. When she was little, she had just thought he enjoyed fishing. Now she was aware that he had been avoiding being at home.

Eventually, he chose to avoid it permanently.

"So, do we go any further?" she asked.

"All the way to Mexico!" declared Kris. "You jump in and lead the way."

Instead, they sat and looked out over the water for a couple minutes, wordless. At last, Joey said, "That's enough of being awestruck for this evening. What now?"

There was no answer. The trio began walking back toward the beach. The snack bar and bait shop, located halfway out the pier's length, were closed and dark, but a light shone down onto the water there. They watched fish, mostly bait-sized, swim in and out of its illumination, before moving on.

Down the stairs to the sand they went, the same white sand on which they had stretched many a sun-drenched day. Now the full moon shone on it, still low enough in the sky for long shadows to extend across the beach, the shadows of palms, of Australian pines, of the old two story homes that had stood here for decades. They didn't look like the homes people built in Naples these days.

"Back to the bikes?" asked Ronnie.

None of them seemed to wish to walk further south, beyond the pier. "Might as well," Joey said.

A couple blocks north they could see the tiny glow of someone's cigarette, someone seated in the sand a little further up the beach, almost at the edge of the sea grape bushes that grew there. They paid no attention; it was common enough, night or day.

"Hey, Joey!"

She turned toward the voice. All three did. "And Kris! And—um."

"Ronnie. Ronnie Deerfield."

"Really? Damn, you've changed."

"You haven't seen her in years, Jam."

The young man laughed but declined to rise. "Only in Naples do I get called that. I guess I don't mind any." He took another drag on his smoke. They all could tell from the smell as they drew closer that it was not tobacco.

Ronnie looked like she might panic. She was not the sort to be calm when someone was breaking the rules. Even more so when they were breaking laws that could land them in prison.

Kris sat down beside James Summerlin and held out her hand. He passed the cigarette to her. A long pull and she gave it back. Joey was tempted to take a seat and share, too, but decided it was not the time nor place for it. Moreover, she had decidedly mixed feelings about the boy she knew as Jam.

"So, do your folks know you sneak down here to smoke dope?" she asked.

"Probably. They haven't told me I can do it in the house, anyway." He smiled somewhat beatifically. "You know, it was fairly common in the part of the world Mother hails from. Though perhaps not exactly legal."

Ronnie smiled at that. "The lawyer's son."

"Oh, God, is that what I sound like?" He passed the joint to Kris again.

After handing it back, she said, "Your mother? She's from Cuba, right? Did she leave when Castro took over?"

Both her friends had to laugh. "Long before then," said James. "Her family was big stuff there." A shrug. Almost a smile. "Until they got on the bad side of Batista."

"Oh. Okay, so Kris is stupid. Is Angelica here?" she asked, rising.

"Yeah, but over to Miami tonight, with the rest of the family. They're picking up Lin." His gaze slowly passed over the three, not settling on any one of them, and then beyond, to the darkness over the Gulf. He took another pull on his smoke and said, "We'll have a party on Saturday. You have to come. All of you."

"Afternoon?" asked Kris.

"And on into the evening. Show up anytime."

"Okay," said Joey, though she doubted she would. "We'd better get Kris back to her bicycle while she can still ride."

"A little more of that and I can fly home!" declared Kris. Exaggerating, of course. One had to tolerate a bit of that from ones friends.

They were barely out of James's earshot when Ronnie said, "His hair is really long. He would have been kicked out of Naples High."

"He hasn't been in any school this past year," Kris informed them. "He finished up a year early and spent the time since goofing off. So my mom says."

"He'll have to do something now," said Ronnie. "Go to college or be drafted."

"Or go to Canada," added Joey.

"Or even where his mama comes from."

The Summerlin kids filled Joey's thoughts as they walked north. Lin wasn't a Summerlin. Her father was Enrique Salas, the man who had been gunned down in the streets of Havana. Some said by the mafia, some said by agents of the Batista regime. He was just as dead either way. Lin—Linda Salas—was six years older than her half-siblings, the twins Angelica and James.

Angelica had become 'Jelly' at some point and, inevitably, 'Jam' had attached itself to her brother James. It is unlikely their parents could have foreseen this. Both had attended St. Ann's for a while, before being sent off to separate boarding schools—that was why Joey knew them.

They must have all had their own thoughts for nothing much was said until they reached the Third Avenue pilings. The fisherman was gone. No cars were parked at the end of the street; nothing was there but the three bikes.

"This might have been a bit of a bust if we hadn't run into Jam," said Kris, unchaining her little bicycle from the other two.

Joey disagreed. "It's a beautiful moonlit night," she said. "That's

enough for me." She removed the chain from her own bike and straddled it. "Be careful riding home," she said, and pedaled away. She was
to the corner before thinking she should have waited for Ronnie and
ridden along with her.

She stopped and waited for her friend. Both pedaled on.

Chapter Ten
Kris

"Oh, we have been invited too," said Marge Greene. "There will be a barbecue."

Kris was not overly surprised to learn this but had to comment, "Don't lawyers see enough of each other on weekdays?"

Marge turned to her daughter. "They need weekends to discuss politics," she deadpanned.

Kris fell into the spirit of it, gravely shaking her head. "And on the sabbath, yet. I just hope he sticks to the kosher hot dogs."

She realized at once maybe she shouldn't have made the joke. Her mother did make an effort, at least now and then, to have her family be more observant. David Thomas Greene and daughter were probably hopeless causes.

In truth, Kris didn't quite know what she believed. At times she thought maybe she was an atheist. She didn't think about any of it very often.

"I think I'll ride the bike again," she told her mother. Marge seemed comfortable with the change in topic. "As long as I got it out I might as well use it this summer. Maybe I'll even take it with me to Miami!"

Marge had to smile at that. Both knew well that Kris was given to sudden enthusiasms. "It might be nice to have an adult bicycle instead."

"When I'm adult sized! See you later, Mom."

"Dinner?"

"I'll try."

Her mother was right, decided Kris, as she pedaled away from their house, west toward the beach. She didn't need a larger bike but the Stingray was for kids. Did anyone ride around the Miami campus anyway? Or the city?

Stingrays had been brand-new when she was thirteen and Kris had insisted she must have one. Not this one. It was newer and not used much since she got the Bug.

She wheeled past the pier. Pretty crowded for a Tuesday. A hot Tuesday with the noon sun beating down. Kris felt the perspiration running down her back under the tee she had thrown on. It would be soaked soon.

Those clouds building out to the east promised everyone a soaking soon. She didn't stop but took a right up Twelfth Avenue, lined with parked cars, and past the big banyan. There were kids standing in its shade, as usual. No one she recognized or wanted to admit to recognizing. She turned left at the next corner; the old *Naples Hotel* site kept the street from going through. Back and forth, left and right, she zigzagged through the older part of town, heading toward Cambier Park. Can-of-Beer Park as they had always called it. It was close enough to easily walk from her home but Kris hadn't bothered in a long time.

When she was younger, the rec center there had practically been a second home. She would walk over after the junior high let out—it was only a few blocks away—and kill time. It was better when she could get her friends to come too.

Up Eighth Avenue to the front of the center, a not particularly large building, tan stucco and tall, narrow, tinted-glass windows. Oh, there was Donny's bike. The last thing she wanted to do was hang with her brother and she was sure he felt the same. If he had any sense—which she doubted—he'd be inside, in the air conditioning. Playing ping pong maybe. She chained the Stingray and wandered around toward the rear of the building. A few seniors were on the shuffle board courts. Some guys out in the heat playing basketball, and deserted tennis courts beyond them. Who would be crazy enough to be shooting hoops in this heat?

Well, Donny, she realized as she got closer. Two other guys, both bigger. Guys she knew. They were playing one of those stupid games where you try to hit the other guy's shot. Horse or whatever they called it.

She leaned against the high chain link fence, hanging with her fingers through the mesh, a little while before they noticed her. "Now we can have teams," said Harold Macklin. "The Greenes against me and Doughnut."

"The two of them put together are barely as tall as you, Mackie," replied William. "Hi, Kris."

"Hi. You all go on playing. I'm just killing time."

Mackie stood in one spot, slowly dribbling, one hand and then the other. "I'm ready to quit. At least for a while. And I need a drink."

It took a while to fill three hot and thirsty boys at the nearby drinking fountain. More so in that they felt the need to splash a good bit of the water on themselves and each other, not to mention time also spent pushing each other aside. Then all four plopped down in the shade of one of the ficus trees planted around the center.

No one felt like saying anything for a minute or two. It was enough just to cool down. Then Donny asked, "Gonna play anymore?"

Mackie only shook his head. "Think not," said William.

"Think I'll go inside then. Get a Coke." With that, he was gone.

"He's being discreet," observed Macklin. "He knows he's a, um, fourth wheel."

"Yeah?" asked William. "I wouldn't have thought of that. I mean, the kid gettin' out of the way."

But Mackie was quite possibly right, thought Kris. Donny had a lot of sense when it came to social situations. She sometimes wished she had a pest for a little brother, as girls always seemed to have in stories.

"I'm invited to a party at the Summerlin house on Saturday," she said. "Want to come? Either of you."

"You mean it's one or the other?" asked Mackie. He sounded so serious Doughnut might have believed he meant it.

"But of course. I can't show up with two dates, can I?"

"Why not?' Both grinned. After a moment's hesitation, William did too.

"Unfortunately," said Mackie, "I, uh, already have plans. Booth here can escort you. You're not working, right?"

"Nope. No plans either." He turned to Kris, decidedly hesitant. "Sure you'd want me to come?"

"Sure!" Why not?

"I'd recommend skipping the barbecue and waiting till it gets dark," said Mackie.

"Right. All the adults will be a bit sloshed." She laughed and shook her head. "I forget we're adults now!"

"Not till fall. We got one last summer to be kids," Doughnut announced.

One summer. One summer to say goodbye to being kids, to the world in which they'd grown up. To everything.

"I need to get going," said Mackie. "You riding with me, Doughnut?"

"Um, yeah, I'd better." His eyes, perhaps inadvertently, flicked for a second to the police station across the street. Even these days, it probably wasn't best for a black kid to be walking through downtown Naples. He'd have been hesitant about coming to the park by himself. Kris recognized this when she thought about it.

Maybe she didn't think about things like that often enough. "I could ride him home on my handlebars," she offered.

"I'll have to depend on that on Saturday. Let's go, Mackerel. Good to see you, Kris." The pair rose and headed to the parking lot.

Kris sat a while longer, leaning back against the tree trunk. Dark clouds were piling up out over the Glades but the sun still shone overhead. There would be more sunny days but summer would end. Their last summer.

One summer in the sun and then life would change for all of them.

Chapter Eleven

Joey

"Are you sure you want us along?" asked Ronnie. "We don't know anything."

"Neither do I. So we'll know three times as much nothing."

"We should have borrowed Harold Macklin from Kris."

"Mackie's not mine to lend," said Kris. "He's certainly not my boyfriend. We just go out together sometimes." She said nothing more for a few moments, her eyes on the road ahead. "He's never seemed all that much into me."

Joey said nothing to that. She'd noticed. Ronnie had too. It was to be expected that the two had gossiped about it.

"This our turn?" Kris asked.

"Ridge Road? I think so," said Joey. "Never been here."

"It's a good thing I thought to bring a map," Ronnie told them, holding it up. "Pine Ridge is confusing. The streets wind and are not numbered." They could hear the rattle of the paper as she unfolded her chart on the back seat. "Hmm, was that Center Street? Keep going."

"Your brother knows Russ, right?" Kris asked over her shoulder.

"Uh-huh. Take the next left."

"I've never met him," said Joey. "Alan told me about the car. I ran into him when I was up at Edison." Neither Kris nor Ronnie was likely to have ever had a conversation with Alan Wesolowski, despite being classmates for years. A word or two at best. He was a quiet sort. A daydreamer. "He was enrolling too." A late decision, like her own.

"And Russ just graduated. There are still a lot of empty lots in this neighborhood, aren't there? Big lots, too. Here we are." Kris pulled her Volkswagen into the drive. "And that must be the car. God, it's ugly."

"If it runs, I don't care. Russ only wants seventy-five dollars for it." According to Alan. She couldn't afford much more.

"I wonder if the surf racks are included," said Ronnie, squeezing out of the back seat. "You'll have to get a board if they are."

"There are *loads* of cheap surfboards around," Kris told them. "Everyone suddenly wants the new short boards and they're practically giving the big ones away."

"That's for sure," said a tall, blond young man stepping out of the shadows of the open garage. "In fact, I have one of those I'd be willing to sell, too. Hi, Rhonda. And Kris, right? So you must be Joanna."

"Joey." Had Alan called her that when he spoke to his brother? Of course, it *was* her name. She looked over the Corvair. It definitely was ugly on first look, but that was mostly the oxidized green paint.

"It's a Sixty-two," Russ informed her as they walked over to it. "It runs fine but, um, it's a bit of a dog with its two-speed automatic. You won't win any drag races."

"Unless they're against Ronnie's Simca," said Kris. "You wouldn't stand a chance against the Bug."

"We'll all have rear-engine cars if you get it," Ronnie said.

Kris snickered. "They'll call us the Unsafe at Any Speed Gang."

"Yeah, yeah, sure. Can we take a test drive?" Joey asked. "You and me, not these two."

"Sure. The keys are in the ignition." Russ slipped into the front passenger seat without further words.

It took a few seconds for the engine to catch. Joey scanned the dash in front of her. "Where's the shifter?"

"That little lever there." Russ pointed it out. It looked more like it belonged on a toaster than in an automobile. "Despite the two-speed tranny, it does have pretty good power. More than your friends' cars."

She nodded. Joey knew the Corvair had a bigger engine. Hmm, noisy, but not as noisy as Kris's car. Smoother, too. She backed out of the concrete drive.

"You have a new car?" she asked as she put it into drive and gingerly gave it some gas.

"Yeah." Russ chuckled. "A new old car. A van, actually."

Joey had seen the Econoline in the driveway. It was green too, a darker green. "For surf trips. Can I turn here?"

"Yeah, Hickory will loop back around." He waited until she went around the corner. "Surf trips, right. I can camp in it. I took this

Corvair to the east coast more than a few times."

Then at least it was dependable. Or had been at some point. Russ had been driving it back and forth to Edison too. "Now you'll be going to college over there."

He only nodded and looked out the window. Houses stood here and there among the vacant lots of pine and palmetto. The lots to the right were quite large. Some had fencing and pasturage. Horses, maybe? Joey didn't see any.

"Take the next left, if you want. Or drive more."

"Nah, that's enough. Seventy-five is definite?"

"It seems like a reasonable amount to me." Joey almost laughed at his nonchalant drawl.

"Me too. Consider it sold." She knew there would be more expenses. Insurance. That could be worried about later on. There was the Wesolowski house. Not just a house. A sign out front said something about it being a veterinary clinic. She wasn't sure it was actually in Pine Ridge, strictly. A couple spindly pines stood in the front yard and there was a separate parking space over to the far side. For people and their pets, Joey figured.

Her friends stood at the front of the open garage, looking at something on the floor. Oh, a surfboard. Ronnie came out to greet them. "What do you think?" she asked.

"The deal is done. I just need to slip this guy some greenbacks."

"And sign some papers so we can change the registration," added Russ. "Hey, how's your brother doing these days? I don't hear much from him."

"Neither do we. I guess the navy's keeping him busy."

Russ nodded slowly. "He never said a word to me before enlisting."

"He didn't say much to his family," said Joey. Ronnie had confided at the time. Two years ago.

"No, he didn't," Ronnie agreed. She didn't seem to want to say more.

"You serious about selling your surfboard?" asked Kris, emerging from the shade of the garage.

"I am. Alan wants to strip off the fiberglass and cut it down into a short board but I'd rather not let him!"

"Alan surfs?" asked Joey.

"I've never seen him," added Kris.

"That he does. We usually go to Doctor's Pass 'cause it's nearer, so you wouldn't see us much at the pier. If you're serious, fifteen bucks and you can have both the board and the surf racks. I don't feel like bothering to remove them anyway."

"We'll all chip in," said Ronnie. Kris nodded agreement.

Of course, the racks would stay on her own new old car, Joey realized. She'd be the one carrying the board around. "It is long, isn't it?"

"Nine-six. The square-ender is, um, not the best to learn on, maybe. It's designed as a specialty board. A nose-rider." Russ let out a small, quick laugh. "Something that's gone out of style all of a sudden." He went to pick it up. "It's in good shape and not all that heavy. Gordon and Smith makes good boards. Officially, this is known as the 'Stretch' model."

Joey could see where the square-ender nickname came from. The nose of the surfboard was squared off. Well, so was the rear but that was common enough. She'd seen enough surfers and boards to know the rudiments even though she'd never tried it herself. Kris had, but not seriously, just borrowing boys' boards.

A few minutes later, money had changed hands and signatures had been scrawled. The board was atop Joey's new car. Her new old car. "I'll ride with you," said Ronnie. "You can drop me at work." She seemed hesitant to speak any further but she turned to Russ and said, "We're all going to a party at the Summerlins' house tomorrow night. Want to come?"

Was she asking Russ Wesolowski out on a date? Well, she had said 'we,' not 'me,' hadn't she? Still, it surprised Joey. Kris looked a tad bemused too.

The boy frowned. "Tomorrow. Ah, no, I'm going to be heading out of town. For most of the rest of the summer, actually. That's why I wanted to get the car sold right now."

"Then tell your brother," Joey said. "He's invited too." She wasn't quite sure why she made the invitation. Just because she'd run into Alan? She hardly knew him, really.

"I'll tell him but it's unlikely he'd go. You know how he is."

"Yeah. He can just show up if he doesn't want to call one of us or anything. Good to do business with you, Russ!" She got into the Corvair and cranked it. Her own car. Maybe she didn't really need it but she did need the feeling of freedom that went with it. Ronnie slipped in on the passenger side.

They were only a little way down the street when Joey asked, "Do you have a bit of a crush on Russ?"

Ronnie stifled an embarrassed giggle. "I used to, when he hung out with Rick. They'd go snake hunting together, of all things."

"He's into that naturalist stuff, huh?"

"Yeah." She looked out the window and didn't speak again until Joey turned onto the highway. "He's going to study biology at Florida Atlantic. Marine biology."

"If he doesn't spend all his time surfing."

"I wouldn't put it past him."

Chapter Twelve
Ronnie

The 'going out of business' sign hung on the door of *Brooks Books and Looks*. One more week. There were plenty of signs inside too, offering discounts on this and that. Those discounts would deepen this coming week.

And what would happen to what was left? Ronnie didn't want to ask. She was curious, to be sure, but thought she might not like the answer. Be that as it might be. Next weekend, whatever was left would be inventoried and packed up and that would be an end of it. For her.

A few browsers wandered about. Fewer bought anything before wandering out again. A going out of business sale would have been more successful in December, when there were tourists and winter residents. But if the store were more successful, it wouldn't need to go out of business, would it?

Suellen Brooks kept going back and forth, apparently unable to decide whether she needed to be up front or helping Stuart in the back. There wasn't really much to do, not yet. It was the anticipation of what was to come, the final closing of their shop, that was keeping her on edge, Ronnie decided. Her nervousness was catching.

"We're going to take another ten per cent off everything on Monday," said Missus Brooks. "Maybe we should have from the start."

"Umm-huh," murmured Ronnie. She had no idea how to express her sympathy, other than to listen. Suellen was a stout woman, in her later middle age. Not that far from retirement? "Are you and Mister Brooks going to retire now?"

Surprisingly, a smile came to the older woman's face. "We're leaving Naples and setting up elsewhere. Our house is on the market." She looked out the window toward Fifth Avenue, the slowly passing cars, a few pedestrians. "It was the cost of doing business here, you know. We sold enough to do okay, really, but the rent was high and now this old place is going to be torn down. If we're being forced to relocate anyway, we decided to do it in another town."

Ronnie might have asked more but someone came to the register at that moment with a stack of souvenir tee-shirts. As she rang up the sale she noticed a slight young man somewhat hesitantly come in and look around. He headed toward the books. She knew him from school didn't she?

Suellen Brooks had gone back to the store room again when she was finished. She gave the boy another look. Oh, of course. Alan Wesolowski. Was it just by coincidence he came in this morning?

Ronnie walked on over. "Hi Alan. Come here often?" She knew it was a stupid thing to say well before it left her mouth but she let it out anyway.

"Um, yeah. It's, uh, kind of far from where I live." He stood there, seemingly embarrassed, before blurting, "I did buy a music box here once for my mom."

His eyes went back to the books. Alan was probably just as aware as her that they were saying stupid things. They might as well keep on at it.

"Books are all fifty per cent off," she said. He had undoubtedly seen the large sign. "Your mom's a veterinarian, isn't she?"

He nodded. "Both my parents." Nothing more was offered.

"That must be interesting." Ronnie tried to sound enthusiastic.

Alan gave her a lopsided grin. "I suppose. I just get to clean out cages and mop poop and puke off the floor."

At last. Ronnie laughed, not very loudly. "Are you coming by the party tonight? Russ did let you know you were invited, didn't he?" It was as good an opportunity as any to ask. She suspected that might have been why he came in. Scouting. Making sure of the invite. Maybe he even meant to come by the party. Or at least drive by and take a look.

"Um, yeah. I don't, uh—know the Summerlins."

"That doesn't matter." She considered that fact a moment. "You should officially be someone's date, I suppose. Not that you're likely to be quizzed about it!"

"Oh? Umm."

"So you're with me, okay?" She hurried on before he could say anything. "In fact, you can pick me up. Come by the house at like four or five."

He nodded. Ronnie wondered if he actually would. She'd find out! "Russ can't come, right?"

"Russ headed off early this morning for an extended surf trip up the east coast. All the way to Hatteras. He'll be gone for weeks."

"Oh, so that's why he got the van!"

"It is." Alan sort of grimaced. It might have been meant as a wry smile. "I wish I could have gone too."

And avoided going to the party with her tonight? Alan probably didn't mean it to sound that way.

He gathered up four books, science fiction novels. "I'll be getting these."

Chapter Thirteen

Kris

"Whose clunker is that?" called Donny, peering out the picture window. "Oh, Doughnut."

Kris had no idea what sort of vehicle William Booth drove. She went to stand by her brother. A pickup truck? Maybe it was his father's. He was a painter, right?

The kind that made money, that painted houses. Not the kind Kris had dreams of being. She *was* going to study art and design, though. The University of Miami was as good a school as any for that. Better than many.

"You gonna come along?" she asked. Their parents were already at the Summerlin place. They might even be ready to head home.

He shook his head. "Not for me. Have fun."

"Okay." Kris wasn't surprised. Donny wouldn't really want to hang with his family tonight. She stepped out of the front door to greet Doughnut. It was still light out. Not much longer.

"Ready?" Booth's clothing was casual but maybe a little too nice for hanging out on the beach. That was likely to be where they would end up.

She gave the old truck a looking over. Yes, there were lots of paint splashes in the bed. "We could walk," she said. "It's only seven blocks. Or eight, maybe. Not very far!"

"Well, if you're embarrassed to be seen in my pop's truck—" He gave her a grin.

"I'm short. Nobody will see me if I scrunch down a little. But it is a nice evening to walk."

It was. It was clearing now but the typical afternoon rains had come through to cool the air some. The sun was near to dipping below the horizon. Kris thought she wanted to see the Gulf before it disappeared completely. "No," she suddenly decided. "Get in my Bug. Oh, let's get the top down first."

"Yes, ma'am." Doughnut helped fold it back and slipped into the front seat as Kris started up the Volkswagen. She drove straight to the water, south of the pier. The sun had just touched the horizon; there was an illusion of its bottom edge bulging to meet the water.

"I'd like to watch that every evening for the rest of my life," she proclaimed.

Doughnut raised an eyebrow. "You won't be able to when you're going to college on the other coast."

"Hmm, that's true. I'll have to get up early and watch the sun rise instead!" They watched for a minute or so more before Kris put her Beetle in reverse and turned around. "I'll leave the car in the pier parking area," she said. "We can walk the rest of the way." There wouldn't be any good place to park near the Summerlin house, most likely. "Oh, and we should put the lid up again."

Over a couple blocks and a right off First—or Gulf Shore Boulevard, if one preferred that newer, fancier name. She swung across the street to claim a parking spot on the north side, a little way down from the big banyan. She wouldn't want the moisture dripping from its foliage to fall on her Bug. They were putting the top up when an older white station wagon pulled alongside. There were surf board racks on the roof.

Joey leaned out a rear window. "It's ugly, isn't it? Even uglier than the Corvair!"

"I am not trading," came the driver's voice. A male voice. Kris couldn't make out who was behind the wheel but Ronnie occupied the shotgun position. The wagon pulled into the next space up.

"Oh, that's Alan," said Doughnut. "I'd know that Rambler anywhere."

The younger Wesolowski brother emerged from the driver's side. "Hi, Will. And you should know they call it American Motors these days. This fine station wagon is an American Motors Classic." He seemed slightly embarrassed after making this seemingly uncharacteristic announcement but went on. "It used to be my parents' and is evidence of their eccentricity."

Alan and Doughnut knew each other? Sure, they had gone to school together but Kris would have thought the two unlikely to interact. And she'd never heard anyone call him Will. It was Doughnut or

Willie or maybe William.

Her friends had emerged from the wagon and Alan was going around it, locking each door. "I was already at Ronnie's house when he showed up," said Joey, "so I claimed a seat. Otherwise, we would have risked driving one of the Unsafes."

"We were both waiting to see if he would come," added Ronnie, with a little bit of a giggle. Kris was also surprised by that. Ronnie Deerfield was not one to tease anyone, especially a shy boy like Alan.

"I sort of knew where Ronnie lived," said Alan. "The neighborhood. I looked in the phone book to be sure. Hey, Will, I picked up some new books at the store where Ronnie works. Let me know if you'd like to borrow them. There are some Asimovs."

"Will do." It was Doughnut's turn to seem a little embarrassed now. He was a science fiction fan? Kris had never suspected that.

"Let's get going," she said, and fell in beside Doughnut as they started toward the pier. To him, she whispered, "Wesolowski calls you Will. Do you prefer that?"

"Um, well, yeah." There was a slight hesitation. Maybe he didn't want it to seem he was no longer the kid nicknamed Doughnut, the friend she had grown up with. "It's a name for an adult, you know?"

"Then Will you are, from now on," Kris decided, as they walked on into the dusk.

Chapter Fourteen
Ronnie

She hadn't even thought of saying anything to Daryl about this party. Ronnie hadn't thought of him at all until her mother seemed surprised by Alan showing up at the Deerfields' door. Daryl wouldn't have wanted to come to this party anyway, she told herself. Maybe it was true.

But then, he hadn't called her since they went out last week, had he? Daryl Sterne was the past now. She had expected that to happen, but not now, not so abruptly. Not that she expected to start dating Alan Wesolowski. Ronnie barely knew him. He might have no interest.

They progressed up the sidewalk along Gulf Shore as a group rather than in pairs. Maybe there was a subconscious desire not to seem like couples. Or unconscious? Ronnie was not sure of the difference. Definitely self-conscious.

Of course, Alan wasn't her date. Not really. Or was he? Neither one had actually asked the other out. Well, maybe she sort of had. And what of William and Kris? No, they were all just friends going to a party together. Joey was evidence of that. Ronnie was glad—relieved, might be the better word—she hadn't come attached to someone. A pang of guilt told her she shouldn't judge the redneck boys Joey sometimes dated. She shouldn't call them rednecks either. She only did that in her head, to be sure. Ronnie would never say something like that aloud.

Unlike William, Alan had not dressed up at all. He wore a white surfer tee with jeans. *Gordon and Smith* it said on the tee-shirt, the same as the board they had bought from his brother. Ronnie wondered what sort of surfboard Alan had. Hadn't Russ said something about him making his own?

There were lights. Lights around the old stuccoed house, lights strung between the palm trees. "Ouch! Damn" Joey swatted at her arm. "A big ol' gallinipper."

"At least the sand flies aren't out," offered Alan.

"Just wait," came Doughnut's response.

"I'd rather not," said Joey. "I hope the Summerlins will be handing out repellent as party favors."

There was a crowd, mostly adults, in the yard. Yes, thought Ronnie, we're adults too. She needed to remember that! A few younger kids darted in and out. She could see more party-goers on the back porch. There was music playing there, swing music, but no one danced. Most of those outside were congregated toward the rear of the lawn, closer to the beach, or where Preston Summerlin manned a massive brick grill. Ronnie understood the man had built it himself after marrying Maria and moving in.

"Is Linda here?" she whispered to Kris. She was uncertain she would recognize the young woman.

"I don't see her. She should stand out. She's even taller than Joey. There's Jelly. Angelica."

"And her brother," added Joey, ignoring the mention of her height. "I half-expected him to be on the beach smoking weed again."

"Give him time. The night is young."

Angelica was the one to come over and greet them. The girl wore a white blouse and striped bell bottom trousers, riding low on her hips. Those had only begun to show up on anyone's fashion radar here in Naples. A headband restrained long waves of dark hair. "Kris! I am so glad you could come. Your parents are here somewhere." Her eyes swept over the rest of the little group. "And Joanna."

"Hi, Jel," mumbled Joey.

"You'll remember Ronnie," spoke Kris. From the look Angelica gave her, Ronnie doubted it. "And this is Will. And Alan."

"Pleased to meet you," said William. Alan only nodded. But both boys had eyes for Angelica Summerlin, try though they might not to show it. Ronnie knew. Her friends knew.

And Jelly certainly knew. She would believe she outclassed the trio they had arrived with and she was probably right. Ronnie knew it didn't matter any but she began to understand Joey's feelings about her sometime friend.

"Did they finally let you graduate from somewhere?" Kris asked. She was one person Angelica was unlikely to overawe. "Or just kick you out again?"

"Oh, they got tired of doing that." She said this with such a straight face Ronnie wasn't sure whether or not she was joking. "I have an actual diploma. Signed and everything!"

"Forged, undoubtedly. Where are the drinks?"

"Oh, around. Seek and you shall find. Daddy has a whole tub full of three-two beer on ice somewhere here, just for us young 'ns." That had recently become legal for eighteen-year-olds in Florida and most considered it a joke. But it was like Mister Summerlin to think of providing it.

"So where did you get this purported diploma?" Kris was asking as they made their way across the grass. "That place in Massachusetts?"

"No, no. That's ancient history. I finished up in a school in Switzerland. I had to brush up on my French pretty quickly."

Kris only snorted at that. Jelly giggled.

"Do you think she really speaks French?" Ronnie whispered to Joey.

"Spanish, too. Her mother's people are a sophisticated bunch. Her dad claims to be a simple small town lawyer."

She knew there was some truth in that. Preston Summerlin came of an old local family, had grown up in Naples, where his father had practiced law before him. Maybe he still did. Ronnie had met the elder Summerlin once, as a little girl, when her father had some business with him. All she remembered, really, was his pronounced southern accent, spoken with a deep musical voice. His son had something of that voice himself. Conrad Summerlin was unlikely to be here tonight but she thought she could recognize him if he was.

Ronnie came out of her reverie to see that she had separated from her friends. No matter. They were only a few steps ahead of her but there was no reason to hang with them all evening. And she wasn't Alan's date, she told herself again.

Then she told herself she was being too insistent about that and smiled at the thought. Let things go as they will tonight and don't dwell on them. Let things go as they will the rest of this summer.

"I brought you something to do drink," came Alan's voice, He was at her elbow, holding a couple cups of punch. Probably punch. It was red so it seemed likely. "I didn't know if you cared for beer."

She felt slightly bothered that he would be paying her attention. She almost told herself again he wasn't her date, but took the cup with a 'thank you.'

"There are hot dogs and burgers and stuff if you're hungry," he said.

"Okay. We should say hi to James." They were only a few yards from where he stood, apparently by himself, gazing toward the gulf. "Do you know him?"

"Hun-uh. He's the brother of the girl we just met, right?"

"Right." Ronnie realized that might not be the best recommendation. The Summerlin boy turned to them as they approached. He might have already noticed them earlier and expected it. He wore an Hawaiian shirt, blue and white coconut palms on crimson. The buttons could be real coconut shell. It would be hard to be sure anytime and impossible in this light.

A loud voice broke in before they could say anything to each other. "My god, Jammer, pull that aloha shirt outa your pants. Only fags tuck them in." It was Gordon Rhein, one of the local surfers. Grubby, as his friends called him.

The boy at his side, a couple years younger maybe, added, "And old farts like my dad."

Grubby snickered. "Yeah, we've gotta give the parents some leeway."

Jam looked like he was uncertain whether to believe them. He might suspect they were pulling his leg. Alan spoke up. "It's true. No self-respecting Hawaiian would wear it like that."

"Oh, it's a matter of tradition, then," said Jam, pulling the shirt from his white shorts. "We can't go around breaking tradition."

Sarcasm? Maybe. Amusement, certainly. "James, this is Alan. Alan, James."

"Call me Jam. It's my special Naples name."

Grubby and his friend had moved off. Ronnie was glad of that. She'd never cared for him, even though he had dated Kris for a time. Maybe because he had dated Kris for a time. He seemed too full of himself. Too likely to put his hands on someone without asking, too. Not aggressively—just like it was no big deal. Kris had told her he had plans to be a photographer. Maybe the idea of him being a fellow artist had appealed to her.

She wondered what sort of plans Alan had for a career. They might be as nebulous as her own.

"Where did Kris and Joey go?" asked Jam.

"I think they followed your sister somewhere."

"Never a wise idea. It happens a lot anyway." He glanced at Alan. "But usually with guys. It *was* a good idea to get your date out of her clutches."

Okay, she might just as well accept that Alan Wesolowski was her date tonight. He probably thought he was.

"Oh, here comes my other sister. She's not much safer." Linda was very tall. All the Summerlins were though, strictly, she was a Salas, not a Summerlin. Hadn't she gone back to using her birth name in New York? "Hey, Lin, this is Ronnie. She's a friend of Kris Greene. And Alan. He's some surfer she's letting follow her around."

"I saw Kris. She's grown a lot since I saw her last—but not taller!" She only smiled slightly at her quip before going on. "Wasn't that your old friend from school with her? Joanna?"

"I'm surprised you remember her."

"She stands out. She could be a model. Maybe I'll tell her so if I run into her again."

Jam turned to them. "Lin was a model, you know. We were very, very proud of her."

She gave Jam an amused look. "By now, I am sure you know my little brother is an idiot. It is a burden we must bear."

"The reason she ran off to New York," broke in Jam. "Couldn't take the shame any more."

"Ah, you figured it out at last! But, yes, I modeled. Not seriously. It proved an entree to the publishing world."

Ronnie was very much aware Linda Salas was on the staff of a glossy magazine. And she had known she modeled for a while. Lin was not what most would call a beautiful woman. Striking, maybe, slender and with a definite fashion taste. Tonight she wore white slacks that accentuated her long legs, and a deep blue sleeveless top exposing tanned arms. Lin was naturally dark even without exposure to the Florida sun. "Joey might be more interested in your current job. She wants to write."

Lin only nodded. She probably heard a lot of that sort of thing. Ronnie wasn't sure what to say to someone like this sophisticated older woman. She knew she wasn't the best at that sort of thing, at picking up social cues. She gave Alan a sidelong glance. He was even worse, wasn't he? A fine pair they made.

"It was nice to meet you. Enjoy yourselves," said Linda and went off to talk with grownups. That's how it felt to Ronnie, anyway.

"Let's go down on the beach," suggested Jam. It seemed as good a thing to do as any. Ronnie was already tired of all these people.

Chapter Fifteen
Kris

Grubby was still nice to look at, thought Kris. Cute, with his blond hair falling over his eyes, and he had a lean athletic body. They had dated a while, back in the fall—nearly a year ago, now—and he had been the first boy, the only boy, with whom she had gone all the way. He seemed to lose interest in her after that.

That was okay. She had to admit she'd lost interest herself. There wasn't much to Grubby Rhein below that pleasing surface. And there was nothing to regret.

"Are there any more of those little sausages, boy?" an older man holding an empty paper plate asked Will.

The 'boy' seemed uncertain how to respond. Kris did it for him. "Will isn't a server, Mister Gambell. He's my date." There. She had said it and that made it official.

"Oh. My apologies, young man." The look he gave the two hovered between embarrassment and disapproval. Gambell turned and walked away—taking care to move neither too quickly nor too slow—without further word.

"You dressed too nicely," Kris told Will as they watched him disappear. "It confuses people."

"I'm sure my color had nothing to do with it."

"Why, of course not! Don't you know Mister Summerlin's guests are far too sophisticated for that sort of thing?"

"The Summerlins are friends of your family?"

"My dad and Summerlin argue over politics but they're pretty good friends. You know Preston Summerlin quit his country club when they wouldn't let us Jews in."

"I forgot you're Jewish," said Will, his voice lowering almost to a whisper. "You get some of the same we do, don't you? I mean, blacks."

She had to laugh, despite his seriousness. "Not when people forget we're Jewish!" Then, after a moment of thought, "It's not just us, you know. Catholics like Joey used to have a hard time, and not just here in the South."

"Everybody needs someone to hate, I guess."

"Isn't that a Dean Martin song?"

"If you say so, Miss Greene. Here comes Joey."

Joey had a stacked plate in each hand. "Why aren't you two eating? There's loads of food over there and nobody will notice if you take the wrong kind of beer."

"I'll get you something," volunteered Will.

"You'll be mistaken for a server again," Kris called after him. "See anyone interesting here?" she asked her friend.

"Mm-mmph, nope." She balanced both plates on one arm while she bit into the hamburger in her hand. "These burgers are really, really good. Someone should hire Mister Summerlin as a short-order cook. Where's Ron? I'll bet her and that boy are off smooching somewhere. It's always the quiet types. Mm-mmph-mm-mm."

"I hope that quiet boy is driving you home. No more beer for you, my girl." Joey's giggle only supported her suspicions. "Ronnie and Alan followed Jam down to the beach."

"Ah, so now Ronnie's not only making out but smoking pot with my old friend. Maybe she's making out with him, too! And she used to be such a nice girl."

"Yes, Joey. We'll always remember her as our sweet innocent Ronnie. Here comes Will with some food." She looked at the plates her friend was balancing. "I guess you don't need any more."

"Hmm, yes." Joey peered at both plates and then dumped the contents of one into the other. "Now I'll only need one hand. Hey, William, run and fetch me a drink, will you? No beer. Kris disapproves."

"Don't mind her," Kris told him.

"I was going back for punch for us anyway." The young man hurried away.

"It's nice to have someone at your beck and call," observed Joey. "You just snap your fingers and he comes running. With food." She tried to snap her own fingers but no sound came. "Too much hamburger grease."

A couple minutes later, drinks in hand, they ventured past the fringe of sea oats and sea grapes between the Summerlins' lawn and the beach, in search of their friends. "It's dark down here," muttered Joey. "We're liable to trip over them."

"Not if we see the little bitty lights from their smokes," Kris assured her. But no tiny orange glows could be spied. As her eyes adjusted, she made out three forms, silhouetted by the lights of the pier, reflecting across the calm Gulf water. They sat on a ledge of sand where high tide had lapped not long ago. "There they are." Whether Joey or Will saw them or not, they followed her.

The three were sitting, talking, and only glanced up when they approached.

"Hey, Jam," said Joey, and plopped down on the sand next to him.

"Joey's been boozing," Kris reported, taking a spot beyond her.

Jam gave her a casual look. "Seems sober to me."

"I only had two beers," claimed Joey, "and I didn't even finish the second one. But I think I drank 'em down too fast."

"That will do it."

"Yeah. Alcohol just hits me fast anyway. Quick metabolism or something. And then it's gone just as quick." Her voice lowered to a whisper. "But now I really need to pee."

"Wade in the water," suggested Alan.

Joey eyed the dark Gulf. "What about sharks?"

"They won't mind."

Alan must have had some beer too. Even the low alcohol kind can have an effect.

Joey waded out as far as her knees, took a look at the dark water beyond, and sat down. "You know, there are restrooms right over there at the pier," said Ronnie, peering out into the night at their friend.

"And even closer in the house," added Jam. No one felt a need to comment.

A minute later, a dripping Joey returned to them. "Now I've peed in the pool, no one can go swimming," she told them. She looked at the sand. "I'm too wet to sit down."

Jam got up. "Let's walk then." He gave William a look. "Who's your friend, Kris?"

"Call him Doughnut," said Joey. "It fits in with Jam and Jelly."

Kris did have to smile at that, but said, "I'd rather you didn't. This is Will. Will Booth."

"Hey, Will. So which way are we going?"

"South," said Kris.

"North," said Joey.

"The directions of your respective homes, huh?"

The girls looked at each other. "They are, aren't they?" Joey remarked. "Okay, then south."

"North," said Kris, giggling though she attempted not to.

Jam looked toward the Gulf. "As long as it's not west. Though maybe that would be as good as any." His voice didn't exactly die, in approved dramatic fashion, but it did fade a bit toward the end. He stood staring into the darkness for a moment. "South," he decided and started in the direction of the pier.

Kris held up a hand to stop the rest of them, grinned and pointed north. It took a few seconds before Jam turned around and saw them all headed the other way. "You guys are mean," he announced, after running to catch up. "I can get that sort of thing from my sisters!"

"Are they staying long?" Alan asked.

"Lin's hanging for a month, unless she gets bored and runs off to Miami. It's her vacation time but she says she's going to write while she's here." He gave the slightest of shrugs. "We'll see."

He didn't offer anything about his younger sister, nor about himself. Kris felt maybe it would be better not to pry. Some other time, maybe.

"Will you all be around on the Fourth?" Jam asked. "You should come to the house to watch the fireworks. Best seat on the beach."

The girls had already made some nebulous plans about meeting at third. This sounded better. "All of us?" Joey asked.

"Sure. And if you have new boyfriends and girlfriends by then, bring them too."

"We'll bring one for you too," stated Joey. "Who could we set Jam up with?"

"You're here on your own tonight," Ronnie pointed out.

"Yes," said Kris. "We hereby appoint you Jam's official Fourth of

July date."

Joey did not seem overly pleased how her statement had backfired on her, making a wry face. But she did chuckle then.

"What street is this?" asked Jam, after they had walked some distance, speaking little, only taking in the night, the dark Gulf, the stars thick above.

"Avenue," corrected Kris. "It's Fifth. Take a right for stylish shopping in the heart of Naples."

"Some other time. Let's turn back. I could have another burger or two if there's any left. Or even a beer."

"But none for Joey."

"I'll keep an eye on her," he promised, "now she's my official date." Joey snorted in an unladylike way.

It was, in fact, Joey and Jam who had done most of the talking as they had strolled along through the night and continued to as they headed back south. Reminiscing about things they'd done as kids. Kris was willing to just listen but soon found herself and Will falling a little behind and falling into their own private conversation.

After a while, her hand found his. "We haven't had much time to ourselves," she whispered.

"There will be other chances. If you want."

She thought she did want. Oh, dozens of other confusing thoughts came tumbling into her head on the heels of that one. Seeing more of Will? Dating him?

Why not? He was worth twice any other guy she'd ever gone out with. Three times maybe. Four would be pushing it. A thought of Mackie slipped in. Okay, he was a good guy too but—somehow, they'd just never seemed right. Kris did not think he would mind her dating his friend. But she should talk to him when she saw him again.

"I like your friend, Jam," he went on. "Or James, isn't it?"

"Yeah. Um, speaking of friends, I didn't know you and Alan were buds. Fellow surfers?"

Will broke up on that one. It took him a little while before he could answer. "You figured it out! Nah, though he has offered to take me out sometime. And I've offered to get him lifting weights. The boy's awful skinny." He glanced toward Alan's back. Ronnie and he were walking side by side, close but not touching, not particularly seeming like a man and woman who were together. They seemed more interested in Joey and Jam's banter. "We like the same kind of books."

That was enough to know for now, Kris decided. She should read more herself. Like her friends.

"It looks like the party is winding down," said Joey, when they reached the Summerlin house. "Or has wound down." Half the lights had already been turned off and Preston Summerlin had deserted his station at the grill.

"We'd better just get out of here," Kris said to Jam. "Tell your folks we enjoyed it. And thanks for the invite." Her friends murmured similar sentiments.

"Let's go down the beach to our cars," said Alan.

That made sense. There was no point in going back up to the street here. "I'll walk with you," said Jam. He seemed in no hurry to be with his family. No one spoke until the pier loomed above, all too tired, too full of the night. They filed up the weathered wooden stairs from the sand, to the equally weathered decking.

"I think I'll leave you here and walk out to the end," said Jam, not very loudly, as they stood there. He turned and went, becoming a part of the dark.

The others went the opposite direction. A couple minutes later they were at their vehicles and Alan was unlocking his. The triumvirate stood together for a moment, watching, not quite ready to say good night to each other.

"I wanted to pump Jam about Lin's writing," confessed Joey. "Maybe I'll get another opportunity." She snickered. "As long as I'm dating him and all." She fell into the back seat of Alan's Rambler. "I'm ready," she announced. "Launch the Wesolowskimobile!"

Ronnie slid into the front and the big wagon pulled away. Kris watched it disappear around the corner. Then, there where the spreading banyan cast a darker shadow on the shadows of night, her lips met Will's for the first time.

Chapter Sixteen

Joey

She could have driven the Corvair and if the weather hadn't been nice she might have. She felt sort of sluggish this morning. Up too late last night, too much heavy food. Yeah, Joey acknowledged, even the little bit of beer she drank might have played a role. Anyway, a brisk bike ride would get all of that out of her system.

The smell of mosquito spray lingered in the air. She'd heard the planes before stepping out of the house, back and forth over Naples, strategic bombers in the war against the mosquito. It wasn't the ideal time to be breathing deeply. She pedaled up Eighth Terrace, around the curve. She remembered the old man who'd lived there. He had an accent, German she thought. That was when she was a little girl. What became of him? Probably what usually became of older people, she told herself. He'd been a nice old guy.

Probably not a Nazi in hiding, but that would make a great story, wouldn't it?

Joey hairpinned around on Eighth Avenue to Tenth Street. It paralleled the Trail, running a block east of it. She could follow it all the way downtown if she wanted. She was inclined to change that up. It was usually busy further down. Not on an early Sunday morning. If she had been headed to the Deerfields' house, she would have gone right across the Trail at Eighth, opposite the old *Beach Club* golf course.

Instead she stuck to Tenth, taking it down to where it was all businesses, offices and light industry. There was a lumber yard. She'd visited it with Wayne a couple times. The train depot, right before reaching the Trail. The highway had taken a left turn at Four Corners, a block west of here, and now ran east—more or less—toward Miami. Across she went. Liquor store over there. Then houses. Old Naples, but the not the part where the rich folks lived.

As property values went up, that was changing. Much further and she'd overshoot the church. She took a right, rode past St. Ann

School, and pulled into the church parking lot. Mostly empty, as usual. She made certain to chain the bike. What would people think if she took it inside and leaned it against the back wall, next to the holy water? Probably best not to find out.

Joey found her usual pew, well back on the left side. She didn't vary it much, maybe a row further forward or back. She just felt comfortable in that spot. Kneel, a quick prayer that held more feelings than words, settle back into the pew and look around. Fewer than twenty, so far. That might be all this summer Sunday morning.

Up front, other side. Tall, even while kneeling. Dark hair, long hair. That was surely James Summerlin. Yes, she saw his face as he sat and glanced her direction. On his own, no family, just like her. Father Rouse had come out, not fully vested yet, just surplice, and went over to say something to him. James nodded, rose, and followed the priest into the back.

A minute later, James emerged to light the candles at the altar. A couple minutes after that, both returned, with James serving as altar boy. Why not? He'd been one when they both went to Saint Ann School. He looked incongruous though, towering over Father Al.

But Jam knew his way around an altar. And he moved so—elegantly, that was the word. If it were theater, she would say he was upstaging the priest. If it were his sister, she would say it was being done on purpose. Not James though; that was just him as he was. The way he always had been.

Instead of leaving immediately at the end of mass, Joey sat and watched James do the usual after-mass altar boy things, like snuffing the candles, removing the cruets, the towel and bowl the priest had used in the washing of his hands. He came out and sat down beside her when he was done and back in his civvies.

"You slowed things down," she informed him. "Father Al wasn't able to hurry through at quite his usual clip. Also, your surplice was too short for you."

"I'm taller than the average altar boy."

"I take it some kid had been scheduled and didn't show up. And Father Rouse recognized your inner altar boy."

"I'd introduced myself to him a few days ago. I, um—well, I'm thinking of becoming a priest."

"Damn, Jam. Oops, I shouldn't say that here."

"Probably not. And I'm still just thinking. I know some guys have a strong sense of a vocation early on." He shook his head. "Not me."

Joey had no idea what to say about that, so she rose. "Time to head home."

"Come over to the house. We'll feed you breakfast."

Why not? "Sure. My folks will probably just think I got hit by a car when I don't show up. They know the hospital will call sooner or later." In truth, they were used to her not hurrying home after church. "Does your mom cook breakfast?" Somehow Joey couldn't see Maria Summerlin flipping pancakes.

Jam snickered. "She might be able to make toast. We've always had a cook, as long as I can remember. And Mom's always complained about how much we pay her. Good help was so much less expensive back in Cuba!"

They headed out into an empty parking lot. "You walked over?"

"It's only a couple blocks or so." He gave her bike a once-over. "I'll have to get a bicycle. I don't even have a car. I didn't see any need for one."

"You can borrow my new car. It's a Sixty-two Corvair."

"Which is why, I assume, you ride a bike."

"Just for that, I'm not going to give you a ride." That would have been impractical anyway, with the big side baskets. Maybe if he sat facing rearward. She ended up pushing the bike as they walked toward the Gulf.

"So, a priest. Really?" She didn't wait for an answer. "Most Sundays, I think God and I are just surprised that I showed up at church again."

"Well, that's good, isn't it? It shouldn't be a routine." There might have been the suggestion of a sigh. "Maybe that's one of the things I'm concerned about. Falling into the routine of ecclesiastic life."

"That's kind of true of any career. Even if you run off and join the circus you still have to shovel elephant poop every day."

"But you don't take a vow to use that shovel the rest of your life." Both silently considered that point for a moment. "That's a good line, by the way. If I remember, I'll jot it down so I can trot it out some-time and take credit for it."

"That's from Ronnie's dad. Mister Deerfield. Where he got it from you'd have to ask him."

"Ronnie didn't say a whole lot last night."

"Ronnie's shy, but she hides it, always acting outgoing even though she isn't. She thinks she's supposed to or something, so she tried to be involved in everything in school."

"That's the sort that has nervous breakdowns," observed James. "Her date seemed entirely willing to embrace his inner introvert. He was her date, wasn't he?"

"You'd have to ask them, and they might give you different answers." They stood at the corner of the Summerlins' lawn, beneath a row of tall, gracefully bowed coconut palms, rosy light and luminous blue shadow playing along their trunks. The faintest of offshore breezes rustled the fronds. All else was still. That wouldn't last; beach-goers flocked to the water on a clear Sunday morning, many of them driving over from the east coast.

"Where should I stow the bike?"

"Drop it anywhere. No one's going to steal it from our lawn." Jam headed for the back, toward the porch. Bits of litter from last night's party still dotted the grass. Like mushrooms, thought Joey. She leaned her bike against one of the tiled tables on the open patio and followed the boy inside.

"Will your family be getting ready for church?" she half-whispered. She did not want to disturb anyone.

"Dad's still officially a Methodist, not that he ever goes. As to my sisters, I wouldn't have high hopes of either making it to church today. Mom, maybe."

"My mom doesn't make it very often either. She doesn't seem to be up yet."

No one seemed to be up, not even the cook Jam had mentioned. Maybe she didn't come this early. Joey was pretty sure the Summer-lins didn't have live-in help. "I've never been in here before."

"Haven't you? Hmm. I think Kris has. It's not much of place, really. None of these old beach houses are all that large. Three bedrooms up the stairs and only one bath for all of them. I tell you, mornings are hell when my sisters are here!"

They had passed through a dining room, with a large kitchen off to the right. Jam peeped into the living room. Despite his claims of being cramped, it was at least twice the size of the one at home. "Library door is closed. That means Dad is in there, reading the paper. We're not likely to see him."

"Tell him to pass out the funny papers. That's all I ever read."

"He won't relinquish it until he's read the whole thing and put it back together properly. Just the way my dad is. Let me fix you that promised breakfast."

The kitchen mixed the old-fashioned and modern. It had certainly been redone from time to time since the house was built. In the Twenties? Joey thought that was likely. Before the Depression. Not by the Salas family, though people still sometimes referred to it as the Salas House. They had bought it in the Forties, despite some family members complaining the nearest professional baseball teams were in Tampa and Havana. Hadn't Ronnie's dad told stories of some of them playing in the amateur games at Cambier Park? That used to be a bigger thing, before people sat home watching television at night.

The only Salas left here was Lin. Maria was a Summerlin now. What had her maiden name been? She wasn't about to ask Jam, who was busy in the big refrigerator. "Whatcha want?" he asked over his shoulder. "Pancakes? Waffles? French Toast? Or a bowl of Frosted Flakes?"

"I can get cold cereal at home," she informed him. "I expect better from you."

"I'm going to fry some eggs for myself."

That actually sounded good to Joey. "I'd go for that. Can you fix grits?"

"Of course. Not as good as Sylvie, but they won't be too lumpy."

Sylvie, she assumed, was the missing cook. Just as well she wasn't here with them underfoot. Joey watched him fuss with pans for a minute or so before walking over to join him at the range. "So you might be going to a seminary come fall?" she asked.

"Yeah. In fact—well, I'm already accepted. That doesn't mean I'm going through with it. Water's about to boil. Get some plates down, will you? Those ones over there."

There were no closed upper cabinets. Everything sat out on shelves. Joey liked that. She'd want to go that way herself if her dishes looked good enough to let people see them. She opened various drawers until she found flatware and placed it besides the plates.

"What does Jelly plan to do?" she asked.

"She's refusing to make plans. She thinks she should have a year off like I did."

"Oh, yeah, you graduated early, didn't you?"

"Yeah. Maybe they just wanted to get me out of there." For a moment, Joey thought that was all he was going to say. "You know after I left Saint Ann, I went to a Catholic prep school. Upstate New York."

"I knew you went *somewhere*. You didn't exactly keep in touch."

"No, I didn't. Are you heading to college somewhere?" He began breaking eggs into a skillet. "Sunny side up or turned over?"

"Turned. I'm just going to Edison in Fort Myers for the next two years. I'm hoping it doesn't take me any more than that!" She sniffed. "Are you frying in olive oil? Dang, just like my mom."

"Dad hates it. Sylvie always uses peanut oil for him." There came a thump from overhead. "Someone in the bathroom. Probably my mom."

"All five of you have to share it?"

"There's one down here too. Right over there." He gestured vaguely. It was somewhere. "I've been sleeping in the library and letting them have the upstairs. My sisters would be constantly fighting if they had to share a bedroom."

"Plus you can come and go."

"That's true." He slid three eggs onto each of their plates. "Grits for you." He spooned it out. "And toast for me. I'm sorry, Dad, I'm just not Southern enough." He had turned his head in the direction of the library but raised his voice only slightly. It was unlikely Preston Summerlin had heard him.

Jam sat down across from her at the sturdy kitchen table. "I should tell you," he said, after a sip of orange juice, "my sisters are deceptive.

Lin seems more together than she is and Angelica's flakiness is some-thing of an act."

"And what about you?"

"That's for you to figure out. I sure can't. Good morning, Mother. You know Joey, I'm sure."

Maria Summerlin stood in the doorway, wrapped in a long powder-blue robe. She took in the scene before saying, "And you did not fix any for me?"

"Coming right up! Say, I'm thinking of getting a bicycle and having races with Joey."

"Ah. Do let him win now and again, won't you?"

Chapter Seventeen
Ronnie

"Your boyfriend came by my office," said Howard Deerfield. Boyfriend? "Alan?"

Ronnie's father only raised an eyebrow at her. "Daryl Sterne. Who's Alan?"

"Never mind him. What did Daryl want?"

"It seems he's decided against engineering and is going to be an architect like your dear old dad. He spoke to me about interning next summer."

"It will be convenient for his father to have someone in-house for that," observed her mother. "He won't have to give you his business." Patty Deerfield then turned to her daughter. "So you and Daryl aren't together anymore?"

"No, Mom. I guess we aren't." She wasn't sure whether her mother was disappointed.

"Can't expect high school romances to last," said her dad.

Patty smiled. "It wasn't really much of a romance from what I could see."

"And now we get the summer romance, eh?" Ronnie was feeling distinctly uncomfortable with the direction this was going.

"With a surfer boy, yet," said her mom. "He is a surfer, right? I saw the surfboard racks on his car."

"Yes, Mom, a surfer. He's a friend of Joey and—and we only went out the once and it wasn't really a date." Ronnie couldn't think of any good way to continue so she stopped abruptly there.

"Of course not, dear," said her mother. "You are working again tomorrow?"

"All the rest of the week. The last week."

"Hate to see a business go, especially a book store—"

"And good people like the Brookses," interjected her mom.

"Yes, to be sure. But that building really was an eyesore. It's one piece of the old Naples I won't miss."

"Maybe someone will hire you to design its replacement," said Ronnie.

"One can only hope."

The next morning, Tuesday, she was back at *Brooks Books and Looks*. The store was beginning to look bare as they consolidated their stock and removed the empty shelves. Forty and fifty per cent signs were taped up here and there.

It was almost as bare of customers. "We'll lower the prices once more tomorrow," said Stuart Brooks. "That will be the last time."

"Everything at one-third," added Suellen.

"We'd better mark it thirty-three per cent. One-third might confuse people."

Thirty-three might confuse the cashier, thought Ronnie. Not that she had great hopes much more merchandise would go out the door.

It was mid-afternoon when Daryl entered the shop. He was dressed in polo shirt and plaid shorts, and carried a bag from *The Record Bar*, over on the other side of Fifth. "I see you're not digging footers today," Ronnie commented, before he could say anything. She had felt it best to speak first.

He let out a self-conscious chuckle. "No, I have the day off. Back at it tomorrow." Then, what he had probably come in to say. "I should have let you know I was out of town this past week. Up in Tallahassee, arranging some things, and it ran into the weekend."

"College?"

"Yeah."

"My dad said you'd changed your major."

"Uh-huh. Not that it matters much at this point. Anyway, sorry I didn't let you know. I should have."

Yes, he probably should. That didn't matter much either. "I don't think we'll be going out anymore, Daryl," she said and hurried to add, "We both knew it was going to happen in a month or two."

"Oh. I suppose so." There wasn't much to read in his expression. "Are you, um—no, that's none of my business."

What was he trying to say? Or not to say? Oh, of course. "Yes, I guess maybe I am seeing someone else." In honesty, she wasn't sure she was at all, nor how Alan might see things. "Alan Wesolowski."

That did bring a reaction. Surprise, maybe it was. Maybe even disbelief. "He's a friend of my brother," she said, though there was no reason, and it was only sort-of true. Why was she explaining herself? She'd resolved not to when this happened.

"I've been in some classes with Alan. He's smart. Really smart, but he doesn't like to let anyone know."

Daryl was smart too. Ronnie had always known that. He'd made it into advanced classes that were beyond her. "He does seem self-contained," she ventured.

"In his own dream world a lot of the time. Reads constantly."

Ronnie started to giggle, unable to keep herself from it. "I think you know more about my new boyfriend than I do!" She immediately sobered, though, on letting the word 'boyfriend' out, and rushed to change the subject.

"James Summerlin invited a bunch of us to watch the Fourth of July fireworks from his house and said we could bring people along so now you're invited too. And you can bring someone if you want."

Daryl frowned. "Summerlin? Like the attorney?"

She hadn't been thinking. Daryl didn't know any of the Summerlins. "Yes, that's the family. Jam, I mean James, is a, uh, friend of Joey."

"I guess you have a lot of friends I don't know about." He gave her an almost accusatory look, but then chuckled. "And I suppose I have just as many you don't. We never really shared much, did we?" She cautiously shook her head.

"Who knows? Maybe I will get there. I'll see you, Ronnie." With that he was out of the door. And without buying anything.

Chapter Eighteen
Kris

There were so many pilings. She didn't have to show all of them, did she? Kris put down her sketchbook and gazed out over the Gulf of Mexico, not at all satisfied with her pencil drawing of the pier. She should have some sort of portfolio ready when she started college. That's what she'd heard but she doubted it mattered much for a freshman.

Shouldn't she be a freshwoman? Yes. She would insist on it. She would tell her friends to, also. The triumvirate would all be fresh-women together.

Together—not really. She didn't like to dwell on the truth, that this summer would be an end of 'together.' It could never be the same again.

Enough with paper and pencil. It was mid-morning and already hot. She would take a quick dip and head home to air conditioning. Kris slipped her pad into her beach bag and was starting to peel of her tee when a loud, close honk made her jump.

"It works," came Joey's voice.

"She'd certainly get out of my way." She turned to see Joey and Jam perched on bicycles. "Hey, Kris. My new bike has a horn! Isn't it grand?"

It didn't look grand. It looked very ordinary, aside from being shiny and new and black. "Just marvelous. When did you get it?"

"Picked it up this morning at the hardware store."

"The *Sunshine*," interjected Joey.

"Yeah, *Sunshine*." He looked at his companion. "Isn't that near where Ronnie works? We could have stopped in and annoyed her on her last day."

"There's still time."

"That's true. Anyway, Joey met me over there and I picked it out and here we are! I looked at the racing bikes with all their gears but riding one of them seemed too ostentatious. So this is what I chose. A civilized three-speed in the British style."

"So your plans for the rest of the summer are to ride your bikes around?"

"You can join us if you can keep up," said Joey, with just a trace of a snicker. "Ronnie, too. We'll all be unemployed as of four this afternoon."

"Maybe I'll look for a job myself. I could probably lifeguard some if I wanted. I'm certified and all."

"Me too," said Jam. "There are worse jobs."

Joey had to be contrary. "Unless someone drowns on your watch."

"Oh, I've never let more than two go under in one day."

"High standards! Three is good enough for me," stated Kris. "I'm going to get in the water myself right now. I guess it wouldn't do any good to ask you to keep an eye on me."

"Better yet, we'll go in too. Darn, I didn't think to buy a chain."

"We'll run mine through both," said Joey, "not that anyone will take it with us right here. You'd better slip your wallet into Kris's bag."

Kris only nodded an agreement to this. It would be a lot more convenient for Jam to swim in front of his own house, a few blocks north. No matter, though. She certainly didn't mind the two of them showing up.

Less than a week ago, she and Will had watched the sunset here. Well, yeah, a block south. There hadn't been much chance to see each other since; he'd taken this week to visit the college that had recruited him. Some place in Alabama, one of those schools they called 'traditional black colleges.' Not Tuskegee, she was pretty sure. Stillman, maybe? She knew he'd mentioned it but wasn't sure if that was the place.

For a guy who planned to be a priest, Jam sure wasn't shy about looking her over in her bathing suit, was he? That wasn't what she meant by keeping an eye on her! He didn't look so bad shirtless himself. Hey, turnabout was fair play and all that, right? They splashed into the water. It was warm, almost bath-like, but still better than the air. That might have crept into the nineties by now. Around eleven in the morning tended to be the hottest time of day, before the rains showed up, almost like clockwork at this time of year.

"You have any plans tonight?" asked Joey, surfacing from a long dive. "Doughnut will be back, won't he?"

"I promised my mom I'd attend a service with her this evening. You know, we start the sabbath at sunset." She hadn't needed to add that, had she? Of course, Jam would know all about things like that. And Joey had been around her long enough she ought to. "Tomorrow, maybe."

"I would hope so. Does Mackie know about you two?"

"Will told him and let me off the hook! He says he actually seemed happy about it."

"He's a good guy," observed Joey.

"They both are."

"Yet you're hanging around with me," said Jam.

"We just like your house," Kris told him.

"And your cooking," added Joey. "Your dad's cooking too, for that matter. Will he barbecue on the Fourth?"

"Nope. You attended his one obligatory summer cookout. Next one is in the fall. Almost fall. Labor Day. Maybe I can light up the grill."

"That's only a week and a half away," sighed Kris. She lay back and floated, staring at the sky. She floated effortlessly, more buoyant than either of her companions. "Summer is moving way too quickly!"

"Then we'll have to hurry to catch up with it. On our bikes!"

"Too hot now. I'd rather lie on the beach," said Jam. "Or under the palms in my yard."

"Until it rains," Joey reminded him. "It always rains."

"Yeah. Good old Florida. Hey, you know you're always welcome to come over to our house. You can even lie in the yard. Your friends, too." He stood up, waist deep, and gave the girls a lopsided smile. "My folks would like to think I have friends."

"Oh, we can come and pretend to be your friends," said Kris.

"Any time. Ronnie too. We could celebrate her unemployment this evening."

Joey shook her head. "Ronnie is going out with Alan. Their first real date, not that they haven't been seeing each other all week."

"I guess we have to consider them a couple," Kris said. "He's certainly a big change from Daryl."

"She had nothing in common with him except being in the same social circles at school. And that's over."

That it was. Kris glanced at Jam. "We gossip about you, too, when you aren't around."

"I'd never doubt it."

Joey smirked at the boy. "He'll hear lots of juicy stuff when he's a parish priest."

"That's not where I'm headed. Probably not. I'm going to be a Jesuit."

"Wow. That's a lot of work."

"The more reason to goof off the rest of the summer."

"Absolutely," said Joey.

Kris could not disagree.

Chapter Nineteen
Ronnie

"Yeah? I play guitar too."

"I just play *at* guitar," admitted Ronnie. "It hasn't been out of the closet in weeks. My father's the real player."

"Ah." He raised an eyebrow and gave her a stern look. "You aren't Martin people, are you? We Gibson players can't be seen with that sort."

"How about cheap Harmony players?" She wasn't about to tell Alan her dad had a Martin guitar tucked away in its case under his bed.

"From the *Sears and Roebuck* catalog?"

"Maybe."

They sat without saying much, working on their milkshakes, in no hurry to go out into the heat and humidity. It was still early, not even sunset, and Alan had picked her up at the Brooks store as they closed. Closed for the last time. Ronnie had to take some time to say goodbye to them. Oddly, she hadn't cried. She'd expected to.

He looked at her for a moment and then asked, "Can I tell you a secret?"

"You're wearing women's underwear?" Where had that come from? She never said things like that.

"Darn. And I wanted it to be a surprise." He became suddenly embarrassed. "That doesn't sound so good. I wasn't actually going to show you my underwear." His voice sort of trailed off and both sat, not knowing quite what to say next, for a few seconds. "Actually, I'm wearing a swimsuit under these jeans. Almost always do, so I'm ready to get into the water."

"But that wasn't the secret, I'd guess."

"No. The secret—I've never been on a date before. Not a real pick-up-a-girl-and-take-her-someplace date like this."

"I've never picked up a girl and taken her on a date either." She hadn't really been surprised by the admission, though it might not have been something she would have guessed.

"You're on a roll this evening. You're not like that when you're with your friends."

She had to laugh. It was quite true. "They come up with things to say quicker than I do!"

He nodded sympathetically. "I know how that goes. Oh, yes, I do."

"We're just both kind of slow, I guess."

Alan gave that a smile but seemed to be in a mood to speak seriously. "If I script my lines first I'm okay. I have to write them in my head."

"But do they ever sound as good when we actually say them?"

"How could they?"

Alan had seemed like a big change from someone like Daryl yet in some ways, not so much. These were the same old familiar trappings of a date, weren't they? They were going to the same kind of places. Still, they were saying things to each other that she and Daryl never would have.

She didn't really know this boy. Could she, in the couple months of summer they had left? Maybe she shouldn't worry about it. Maybe her dad was right and it was just a summer romance. She wouldn't mind having one of those.

Ronnie Deerfield having a fling? Unbelievable!

"Both your parents are vets, right?" she asked.

"They are. And my big sister is in college learning to be one too."

"How about you? Or am I being nosy?"

"Probably but I don't mind. I'm not sure where I'm headed. It just won't have anything to do with animals! I'm thinking maybe anthropology. So, how about you? I can be nosy too."

"I'm as much in a muddle as anyone. I have a deep-rooted fear I'll end up as an English teacher."

"That would give me nightmares," said Alan.

It did give Ronnie nightmares. She thought she didn't want to dwell on it any more. "I sort of know your family, thanks to our brothers. It's almost as eccentric as mine."

"No way. Mine is way more odd."

"Prove it."

"My parents are Buddhists."

"Dad's an atheist. Militant."

"We live in a veterinary clinic. No going home from work."

"My father the architect doesn't want any new buildings in Naples."

"Now, that's hard to top. But—I'm not sure either of us can match up with the Summerlins. I barely knew they existed a week ago."

"You barely knew I existed a week ago."

"A wasted lifetime up to that point!" Alan blushed after saying that but soldiered on. "You knew them, right?"

"Not all that well, and mostly through Kris and Joey. But Jam has taken to the two of us, they tell me, and says we can hang at their house anytime."

"Now?"

"Hmm, maybe not. It's raining anyway."

But their milkshakes were long finished so they stepped out of the drug store, on the corner of Fifth and Eighth. Its entrance faced the intersection, with a faded red tile sidewalk directly in front of the thick glass door. They watched the rain drip from the overhang for the better part of a minute. "We can stay undercover if we go through the arcade," said Alan. "Then we'll have to run for it."

Daryl would have suggested bringing his car around. Alan was unlikely to ever think of things like that. He treated her like—like her friends did. That was it. She wouldn't put it past him to offer to race her to the car, the way Joey might.

Ronnie thought she both liked that and didn't.

The Fifth Avenue entrance to the arcade lay just a little to their right. Ronnie had known it all her life; it might well have been constructed before she was born. There used to be a barber shop down toward the other end, where her dad would go every two weeks. Those were the days when Naples was still a sleepy southern town and lots of businesses closed on Wednesdays or at least Wednesday afternoons.

"I suppose you've had enough of book stores," said Alan, breaking into her reverie. They were standing outside the *Book Nook*.

"Never," she replied. "Do you shop here?"

"Yeah. I pick up a paperback from time to time."

"Me too. This used to be a favorite after-school haunt when I was in junior high."

"I was school-bussing it and couldn't do that."

He seemed undecided about suggesting anything so Ronnie opened the door herself and stepped in. Ah, blessed air conditioning! "This was a bit of a rendezvous point for Joey and me back then. I was over at the junior high and she was at Saint Ann's and this was around halfway between."

"And not Kris? I thought the three of you came as a set."

"She'd go to the park and we'd all meet there." The back entrance to the arcade opened right across the street from Cambier Park.

Alan was looking over surfing magazines but didn't pick one out. Ronnie had already turned from the magazine racks and was perusing novels in the center row. Alan came up beside her. "I didn't know you liked science fiction."

"Not science fiction," she told him. "Fantasy. Like this." She pointed to the paperback of *The Fellowship of the Ring*.

"Tolkien? I read *The Hobbit* this past year. It was okay."

"Oh, you truly should get into *The Lord of the Rings*. In the correct order! I started on the third book, not knowing any better, and got thoroughly lost." She picked up an unfamiliar title and scanned the back cover blurb, before replacing it.

"Burroughs is good," Alan said, nodding toward a large selection of his books. "*A Princess of Mars* was my gateway drug to science fiction at twelve."

"That's practically fantasy," she pointed out.

"I suppose it is. Okay, I'll try Tolkien." He picked up the first book in the trilogy.

"I could lend you mine."

He put it back. "Then I can afford something else. This looks interesting. *The Worm Ouroboros*."

"I've heard it's good. You'll have to lend it to me when you're done." She only hesitated a second before telling him, "I'm not sure you're pronouncing it correctly."

"Neither am I."

The rain had slackened by the time they were at the rear of the arcade, looking out into the parking lot. "It's early yet," he said. "This is around the time I should have been driving up to your house to pick you up."

"It's too soon to eat again. That shake filled me up."

"Movie?" He sounded so unenthusiastic Ronnie had to laugh.

"Anything would be better than that!" All the movies she ever watched with all the boys she'd ever dated merged in her memory into one indistinct, drawn-out night of utter boredom.

"Then how about this?" He bent down to put his lips to hers, lingering only a few seconds.

Yes, that would be better. Much better. She reached up and drew him back down to her. Much longer this time.

They straightened up and looked at each other, nothing more, for what felt like eternity but probably was quite a bit less. At last, Ronnie turned her eyes to the parking lot. "It's stopped raining," she said. "How about going down to the beach?"

"Sounds good."

That it did.

Chapter Twenty
Joey

"He's a surprisingly good kisser," Ronnie reported. "Maybe even an exceptional kisser."

"And you've had a large sample to compare him with?" asked Joey, as they slowly pedaled their bikes, side by side.

"Large enough!"

"Maybe I should borrow him and check your results. But enough talking about guys. We've done way too much of that lately."

Ronnie made no answer. Maybe she did want to talk about guys but Joey wasn't letting any boy get in the way of their last summer together. The three of them came first.

Yet here they were going to a boy's house. Kris had promised to meet them by the Summerlin house. Any day other than Saturday they might have chosen to meet at the pier or maybe Third, but they could avoid the weekend crowds some this way. It would have been just as good to show up at the Greenes' house. It was close to the beach and had always been a good place to leave their bikes. If they even wanted to go onto the beach.

Maybe Kris had other reasons for naming this spot. They stopped at the corner. Joey peered up Gulf Shore, hoping for a glimpse of Kris riding their way. She'd said she would come on her Stingray. "Maybe she's already at the house," she muttered. "Let's see."

They rode toward the beach, along the edge of the Summerlin's lawn. Joey stopped and surveyed the place. No one appeared to be stirring. When she looked back at her companion, Ronnie seemed to have become interested in one the cars parked by the beach access. Just a big Dodge sedan, a couple years old. So what?

Ronnie nodded toward the vehicle. "Dealer plates."

"Huh?"

"Who do we know who might drive a car with dealer plates? Think now, little Joey."

"The Mackerel. And don't smirk at me like that." The car didn't have to be Harold Macklin's ride. His father wasn't the only auto dealer in town, after all.

They rolled their bikes up over the curb and across the lawn toward the patio. Where was that music coming from? Joey stopped to listen.

"Who is playing the guitar?" whispered Ronnie. "They're really good!"

"Over there," said Joey, laying her bike down on the grass. Ronnie did the same and both went in search. "Hiding in the hibiscus." She had a pretty good idea who was playing. Yes, Jelly was sitting cross-legged on the ground, a classical guitar in her lap. Three large young men sat in a semicircle before her, seemingly entranced. Whether by Jelly or her playing was debatable.

Mackie. William. Some guy she'd never seen before. She gave them a little wave and settled down at the end of the row. Ronnie remained standing, her eyes focused on Jelly's hands.

Maybe a minute later, Ronnie put a hand on her shoulder. "Kris is here." Joey nodded and rose. Jelly played on.

Kris was walking toward them, having dropped her bike beside theirs. "So what's up?" asked Ronnie.

"I'm meeting Will here. It's kind of Jam's idea." She looked past them at the group around Jelly. "So Mackie brought him."

"Looks like it," said Joey. "Why meet him here?"

Kris hesitated, which was unusual for her. "I'm just a little leery of having him spend much time at my house. I shouldn't be, I know. I shouldn't be concerned about what people think."

"Your parents?" asked Ronnie, her voice low.

"They wouldn't say anything but I know they would see Will differently. They would act differently, despite themselves." She looked again toward her boyfriend, and sighed. "You understand that?"

"I—" Joey started, but was unsure how to go on. "I hate to admit it but I have—oh, let me start over. Maybe it's just the way I've been brought up but some little piece of me, way inside, feels uncomfortable with it too. And I don't want it to."

"That's a part of all of us, Joey. Even me and I'm the one who's dating him."

Ronnie was slowly nodding, thoughtful. "I bet even William feels something of the sort."

"Just wait until he takes you home to meet his parents," said Joey. It was too good an opportunity not to say it. Enough with this somber mood.

"I'll tell him to do that," said Kris. "Let's go on over and break the trance Jelly has them in."

As it happened, Angelica Summerlin wound up her piece a few seconds later. Joey suspected she just cut it off wherever she wanted. All she knew was it sounded sort of Spanish and sort of classical. And that Jelly was really, really good. She already had been four years ago when last she'd heard her.

The guys rose to their feet. "Hi," said Mackie. "This is my friend Jeff. Jeff Yoder from Dade City. I met him a couple months ago."

"I'm staying with the Macklins for a few weeks," drawled the young man. He was as tall as Mackie but leaner looking, and about as blond as people are allowed to be.

"We're both going to be on the team at Ohio," continued Mackie.

"Oh," said Jelly. "You're going to be a Buckeye?"

"That's Ohio State. I'm going to Ohio University, further south in the state. Athens." Jelly simply smiled and nodded at this. "Loved your music, Miss Summerlin. Thanks for playing for us."

"That's Angelica," she said. "I'd be happy to any time. For either of you."

Joey groaned inwardly but tried not to show anything.

"That would be nice, Angelica," said Jeff. "Ready to go, Howard?"

Howard? Kris silently mouthed to her friends.

"Sure. Good to see you all." With that, the pair were away. Joey was not particularly interested in knowing where they were away to.

Jelly watched them go. "Jeff is cute. Both of them are. And both unattached?"

Will had a look Joey couldn't recognize. Embarrassment? No, something else, maybe. Discomfort. "Um, yes, neither one has a girlfriend right now." He came close to mumbling this information, before he hurried off in the company of Kris.

"Mackie used to be Kris's boyfriend," Joey decided to add when both were gone. She wasn't completely sure why. Perhaps just to see how Jelly would react.

The girl only smiled. "I won't make any snide remarks, Jo-jo."

Joey hated to be called Jo-jo. Jelly had stuck her with the name when they both went to Saint Ann School. Fortunately it had not followed her elsewhere.

"James invited them to come by on the Fourth," Jelly went on. "Maybe we'll see them. He's up in the house by the way." The three started slowly walking that direction, Jelly with guitar in hand. It was hard to say which had initiated it. "You and James?" she asked abruptly.

"We're just hanging out," Joey replied, almost too quickly. "I mean, he's kind of, um, not going to be involved with girls, right? The priest thing."

"We'll see about that. My brother has been off and on about it for years. Both being a priest and being involved with girls!" Kris and Will had settled at one of the tile-topped tables. "Come on in. We'll let those two talk in private. Hmm, he's kind of cute too, isn't he?"

With a laugh, she continued into the house.

Chapter Twenty-one
Kris

"I can get assistance but not a full scholarship," explained Will. "Fact is, when I look at my options it doesn't offer much more than going to A and M and not playing at all."

She didn't even know what Will wanted to major in. Whatever it was, he'd better commit to some college or another or he'd be facing the draft. "But this place is more prestigious, right? Your academics helped get you in."

Will gave no more than a distracted nod to this. "You know," she ventured, "if finances are an issue you could go to Edison. Like Joey."

"Yeah, or Alan. Don't think I haven't considered it." He reached across the tabletop to take her hand. "Let's not worry about it anymore today."

He was the one who had been worrying. Kris was afraid she would too, now. She knew the military was still in the back of her boyfriend's mind. That would solve any financial problems, but at what new cost? Suddenly, unexpectedly, she felt tears come.

"What's the matter?" Will sounded concerned, surprised, baffled, all at once.

"It's all just—just so much. Why do things have to be so hard for you? For everyone?" Yes, her too. She was feeling sorry for herself, she realized, and tried to call up a stern inner voice to tell her to knock it off. She rose from her patio chair. "Let's do something. There's no point in sitting here."

"Sure," he said. Will came around the table to her, put an arm around her shoulders. She turned, wrapped her arms around him, buried her face in his chest. The stifled sobs still managed to break through.

"We have so little time," she whispered. "Then you'll be gone. Everyone will be gone."

"Yeah, Kris, I know. All we can do is make the most of it."

That wouldn't be enough. She knew it wouldn't. But maybe she should pretend it was. "Where'd everyone go?" she asked. Her eyes were dry now. Mostly wiped off on Will's shirt.

"In the house, I think. We could go in—um, are you sure it's okay with the Summerlins for me to be around here?"

"Jam says it is. Ask him yourself, if you want, 'cause here he comes out the door." Followed by Joey and Ronnie.

"Did Jelly abandon you already?" she called to them.

"Oh, she went upstairs to put her guitar away," answered Jam. "She treats it like a baby. Probably better than she would a real baby."

Kris wasn't sure Angelica Summerlin should be issued a baby. "Ronnie can play guitar some," she volunteered. "Her father taught her."

"She might prefer I didn't tell my sister that."

Ronnie shrugged. "It doesn't matter much. Alan plays too, or so he claims."

They began to walk in the direction of the Gulf, without any particular intent. "Where's the other sister?" asked Joey.

"Sleeping in. She's still on New York hours. Maybe she'll rouse herself enough to shop later." He smirked, just slightly. "Probably steal one of the cars, too."

"You could do that," Joey reminded him. "Or don't you have a license?"

"My speedy three-speed is all I need," he replied, avoiding the question.

"How much longer is Lin staying?" asked Kris. "Didn't you say a month vacation?"

"Yep. She rolled in the night I ran into you all on the beach and she'll head back the weekend after the Fourth. The Sixth or Seventh."

"I think we ran into you," said Joey. "You weren't moving fast enough to run into anyone."

"True enough. You know, I haven't smoked weed since that night."

"There's a lot of summer left," Kris reminded him and then remembered she'd just been saying the opposite to Will. It was enough to make her chuckle aloud. Barely aloud, but Ronnie gave her a curious look.

"This looks like as good a spot to sit down as any," Jam said. "Do I hear differing opinions?" He didn't wait for any but sank onto the impeccably mowed lawn. The others followed his example.

Kris gave Will a sidelong glance and then spoke. "William wants to be assured no one minds him being here. So assure him."

Jam looked innocently into the air. "Well, I don't mind. How can I speak for anyone else?"

Joey gave him a shove. "Assure, boy!"

"Okay, okay. Everyone loves Will. Oh, Lin probably doesn't notice him and Angelica doesn't care about much of anyone and Mom is more a snob than a racist. Hey, there's a pretty good view of the Gulf from this spot, isn't there?"

"Yeah. The beach is getting crowded," said Joey. "If we want to swim we'd better do it soon. Is your Alan coming, Ronnie?"

"Hun-uh. He's on kennel duty. And he's not 'mine.'"

"Yeah, sure he isn't. How about your father, Jam?" Kris did want Will to be thoroughly assured.

"My father would go out of his way not to appear racist. I used to think that was hypocrisy but I know better now. Dad makes a real effort to rise above the prejudices of his upbringing." There was the touch of a grimace. "I'm afraid there is no hope for my grandfather, however."

Will's forehead wrinkled into a sort of frown. "Isn't what is inside us what is really important?"

"Spoken like a true Protestant," quipped Joey. "Just believe the right things and you're okay. Or believe you believe them."

"Now, now, be nice, Joey," James admonished, but a brief smile followed. "I think it *is* important to be able to recognize racism in ourselves and in our society. But it's more important not to do racist stuff. Doing the right thing will help turn your mind and your world around. Ha, a sermon! I'm already sounding like a priest."

Joey looked skeptical. "That doesn't sound like anything I've ever heard in church."

"You haven't been around Jesuits."

A brief silence was broken by Ronnie. "I think I like your father," she said. "Maybe I should be a lawyer."

"I've given that some thought myself," came a voice from behind them. "You should talk to our dad."

"It wouldn't hurt," said Jam. "Sheesh, now I'm being agreeable to my sister."

"I'm sure it will pass." Jelly sat down with them, between Ronnie and Kris.

"Donny might be on that path too," Kris told her.

She only nodded, rather disinterestedly. "By James's reckoning, then," Jelly said, "Will is doing our father a favor by being here and letting him practice being not racist. Have I got that right, brother mine?"

"I guess so. Anyway, everyone is glad to have you here, Will."

"Um, okay, I think. You could have just said that to start with."

"Oh, that would be no fun."

"Swimming would be more fun," declared Jelly, rising again to her feet. "Who's with me?"

She doffed her loose white shirt—it looked like a man's dress shirt, down to the little stitched monogram on the pocket—uncovering the skimpiest bikini Kris had ever seen. "You're not," she said, turning to Will. "Remember you're with *me*."

"Yes, ma'am," he replied, but she couldn't miss that his eyes strayed.

Angelica only smiled and headed for the sand.

Chapter Twenty-two
Joey

Linda had always been the girls' idea of sophistication. She had graduated from a prestigious women's college in the north. She had modeled while a student and interned at a fashion magazine. Now she had a prestigious job in New York City.

Seemingly prestigious. "My job title sounds a lot bigger than the job itself," she told Joey. "I'm really just a flunky."

Joey reminded herself that this woman was not much older than she was. Six years. Lin had only left school two years ago. She had lots of life ahead of her, lots of time to keep succeeding.

Lin was succeeding, wasn't she? It was hard to tell from her attitude. She had bouts of being introspective and moody. Jam had told her about that, but drew a clear line when it came to actually gossiping about his sister.

But Joey could tell he worried about her. Some, at least.

"I meant it when I said you could model," Lin went on. "You are the most stylish of your friends."

"But the one least able to afford it! How much further do you want to go?"

"Not much. I'm out of shape!" They were pedaling along Second Street, well south, down where the name changed to Gordon Drive. Lin had commandeered her brother's bike after church and demanded Joey ride with her.

The people they passed could well have taken them for sisters, both tall, both tanned, both dark haired. They even wore similarly short hairstyles. Joey looked more like Linda Salas than her own sister did. Half-sister. Jelly had way more curves than either of them, viewed from any vantage point.

"Ronnie's dad designed that one," she said, waving an arm toward a beachfront mansion. This was where the *really* rich people in Naples lived. Ordinary millionaires built their houses elsewhere. Were the Summerlins millionaires? Preston wouldn't be on his own. He'd be well to do, sure, but the lifestyle, the house, those were from his wife's fortune.

The Salas fortune. Or maybe the Morales fortune. That was Maria Summerlin's maiden name. She'd been curious enough to investigate —mostly by asking Howard Deerfield, who was a trove of such information—and found they were wealthy too. Would that Salas money be going to the only Salas in the family? Would Lin inherit the 'Salas House?'

That was a question for a lawyer and she could be certain Preston Summerlin had everything worked out. "We're close enough to the pass we might as well ride to the end," she said.

"You can't get in to see Gordon Pass, can you?"

"Only if you own property along here or use a boat. Or if you're willing to walk a long way on the beach."

Lin nodded. "Yes. I remember doing that."

"Kris's father has a nice boat. We could probably get him to give us a ride."

"I think we could find someone younger and better looking to give us boat rides." Lin gave her a quick glance and smile. "Don't you?"

"Oh, we'll hang around on the city docks!" enthused Joey. "Hey, sailor!"

That broke Lin up. "You'll make me fall off this bike! I can see why my brother likes you." Joey was okay with that but Lin went on. "You're smart and you're funny. And you write, too?"

"That doesn't mean I write well." She was feeling just a little embarrassed by the way this conversation was going. Uncomfortable. She'd always shunned compliments.

"Dead end," said Lin. No more pavement ahead of them, only an overgrown bit of property. Gordon Pass, the inlet into Naples Bay, lay hidden somewhere beyond. Across the pass, lots of mangrove and islands and not much development. Joey hoped there never would be.

"We have docks right here," said Lin, gazing at the small private marina beside the road. "Should we look for sailors?"

"If we want rich ones, it's a pretty good choice." They stopped, straddling their bikes, looking about. No sailors appeared so they turned around and began peddling back north.

North past Cutlass Cove, north past the Port Royal entrances. Biking around that neighborhood's winding streets could be fun but they were too tired now for Joey to suggest it. On north. "Kris's house is over that way." She pointed right. "The city docks too," she added, attempting an air of innocence.

"Maybe later for them but let's jog over a block and ride up Third."

Through the 'Old Naples' shopping area? Nothing would be open on Sunday morning. Even this late. It looked pretty deserted as they rolled through. Lin brought her bike—Jam's bike—to a stop. "My dad's office is over there," she said, nodding toward the west side of the street. "*Summerlin and Summerlin*. I call him 'Dad,' you know. I barely remember my birth father."

"But you don't use the Summerlin name." Lin didn't answer. It hadn't been a question anyway. "Close enough to walk from your house."

"Yes. Dad does that sometimes. Maybe not as much as he used to. The office has been here since the Forties." She laughed. "And so have most of the clients!"

They pedaled slowly on. The ancient, narrow two-story building that had once housed the *Seminole Market* rose on the right, a small balcony above its entry. Antiques now. Joey had faint memories of her mom buying groceries there sometimes when she was a very small girl. The place looked like it belonged on the set of a western. Beyond it, the *Beach Store* and the theater in its eyesore of a Quonset hut. And across the street—

"Do you remember when the public library was in that old building?"

"Not so long ago. The new one wasn't built yet when I last lived here."

"When I was little, our family doctor had his office back behind it."

"And behind that was the *Naples Hotel*, in all its long-gone glory." The sprawling, rickety place, Naples landmark or not, had been eventually torn down. Lin undoubtedly had stronger memories of it than Joey.

Memories were what Lin had when it came to Naples. It wasn't her home anymore; it hadn't been since she went off to school somewhere as a teen. She was getting more out of this bike ride, this revisiting, than Joey. To her, it was the same-old. Not that she didn't appreciate the beauty of a summer morning along these streets, the clustered blooms of hibiscus and bougainvillea, in reds and whites and corals, rioting through the intense greens on every side, the sky standing serenely clear above.

Would she be willing to trade that for the sort of life Linda Salas had? Or even to go away to a university somewhere as her friends intended? Maybe it was good she couldn't afford to!

They cut back to Gulf Shore on Broad and then right to Lin's home. Nothing much was going on. Jam had disappeared. Everyone had disappeared The two young women sat in the kitchen, guzzling iced tea.

"We'll have to talk more," Lin told her. "And I'd like to see some-thing you've written."

There was no point in pretense or protest, so Joey simply said, "Okay."

She thought about what she should choose all the ride home.

Chapter Twenty-three
Ronnie

"And when I showed up yesterday, Jam told me she met a guy on Sunday night and decided to go to Miami with him for a few days."

"Just like that?"

"Just like that. Jam said to expect that sort of thing from her. That's sort of—well, that's one reason I decided not to hang at the Summerlins for a day or two. I've been there too much anyway. But I don't have a boyfriend to fill my time like you and Kris."

"I can't be with Alan all the time. Unless I want to help him clean up dog vomit."

"So what can *we* do? I know we aren't going to see anything of Kris this morning. Her mom roped her into something at their country club."

"Golf," said Ronnie.

"Really? Golf?"

"You knew she played sometimes. Or used to."

"It's probably just an excuse to use the pool there."

"She should have invited us. We could have made a foursome with her mom." Not that either could play.

Joey made a face at that suggestion. "Or I could have picked up some money as their caddie."

"Oh, I remember you used to do that. Right over here at the *Beach Club* course." Both girls lived practically next door to it. Different doors, though, Joey to the east, Ronnie a few blocks south of the greens. Ronnie had been too shy to try it herself, nor did she have that jaunty, athletic air Joey projected and the golfers seemed to like. "We both could use some money."

"Gee, girl, you've only been unemployed half a week. Enjoy your vacation. Gather hibiscus buds while you may!"

"In your yard I'm more likely to gather sand spurs. Hey, let's walk somewhere."

"Um, you remember you brought your bike, don't you?"

"I don't feel like riding." She wasn't sure why. She just didn't. Or maybe she wanted a slower pace today, a chance to see things the way she used to see them. Who knew if she might ever again?

Joey locked the house behind them, the side door in the cluttered carport. Both her stepdad and mom were at work. The pair strolled up the narrow, curved street. There were kids playing, in the yards, in the street. Little kids with toy soldiers in the white sand, focused on whatever wars they were fighting. Kids playing tag or throwing balls, hiding from each other, pointing cap guns. Kids yelling, kids being kids.

Joey seemed to like them. She was smiling at them anyway. Ronnie wasn't so sure. Maybe a child or two would be okay, someday. They stopped at a corner.

To the right would be Lake Park Elementary, as the street curved around a lake, first east, then more north. Both had attended there, though Joey only through fourth grade. "Want to mess around on the swings or something?" she asked, nodding in the school's direction.

"Not particularly." Joey looked the other direction. "I did walk this way to and from Naples High most days."

Ronnie was certainly aware of that. She did too, sometimes, but had been as likely to ride the bus, and then she had the Simca her senior year. Joey would rarely take her up on a offer to drive her home.

The two stood there a little while. "It's not the same, is it?" asked Ronnie.

"That's not necessarily a bad thing. Come on."

Not to the high school. There would be no point to that. They walked a circuit of the neighborhood, around the lakes that gave it its name. This too was the town where they had grown up, "Naples is more than beaches and big houses," Ronnie mused. "It's places like this. People like this."

"There's an whole other world on this side of the Trail."

"A Naples that looks away from the beach."

Joey snickered. "Into the swamps!"

"The mighty Everglades. Cypress and saw grass! Some of the guys here are probably counting the days till hunting season when they can drive their buggies through the mud." A realization hit her. "Oh, Swamp Buggy Days! I think I'll miss the parade this year. I've never done that before." That suddenly felt like a very big thing, much bigger than Ronnie would ever have thought. "Watch it for me, won't you?"

"Will do. But I won't go to the swamp buggy races." They were back to Joey's street and turned left onto it. "Though that's part of Naples too, isn't it? You can lose sight of all that when you hang around with people named Summerlin."

"Or Greene?" Ronnie asked, as innocently as she was able. She recognized she probably wasn't too convincing.

"Oh, but we trained Kris properly. We got to her early."

"Yeah. Saved her from a lifetime of privilege." Kris. Joey. Damn. "Everyone will be gone, won't they? Kris and me and Will and all the Summerlins and—everyone."

"Alan will still be here. We can get together and gossip about you."

They stood in front of the Varney house again. It was a homely little flat-roofed concrete block place. Not even stuccoed, and painted a pale green. They didn't go inside but sat down in a pair of lawn chairs. The webbing was frayed but they probably wouldn't fall through. She hoped not.

Or was this the Planter house? Joey's mom was married to Wayne Planter now. Joey had been saying something about Lin Salas and the Summerlin house. Maybe it was the same but she doubted it. That was a question for experts. Legal experts. "I've been researching being an attorney," she told Joey. "What courses I should be taking and that sort of thing."

"Pre-law? Isn't that a thing?"

"I think so but it looks like I can pretty much stick with what I already had laid out for me the first couple years. Get my degree in English maybe." Or one of the social sciences. Definitely no education courses. Ruling those out had lifted something of a cloud that had been floating about on Ronnie's horizon and annoying her.

"So you don't have to decide anything right away."

"No. Not until I graduate with my Bachelor's, in theory. Not that I won't be looking past that."

"I'm barely looking beyond my first semester. Maybe I should aim for an English degree." Joey closed her eyes for a moment. Ronnie thought she was just going to sit here in the sun without saying more. "I have been writing. A lot."

"That's good."

"I hope so."

Chapter Twenty-four
Kris

"Did you hear they caught the guy who shot King? In England!"

Jam greeted her news with a lazy nod. "My mom's more interested in the new income tax surcharge. She'll be grumbling about it the rest of the summer."

"And into next summer," added Lin. Obviously, she was back, and soaking up sun in the Summerlins' lawn as if she'd never disappeared. Her bikini was, if possible, even tinier than her sister's. Kris tried not to stare at the long, taut brown body, stretched on a beach towel.

She definitely felt self-conscious about her own short freckled one. But then, why should she? Lin was no more intimidating, physically, than her friend Joey. Not even as good-looking. She'd certainly never minded being around Joey. It was just this woman's air, her attitude, wasn't it?

"No Will this morning?" Jam went on.

"He's promised to wander this way later. He's playing with his friends right now." The guys who'd been his teammates through school, Mackie and all the rest. Will was saying goodbye too, in his way, and that way involved sweating and yelling. To each their own!

Lin sat up, removing her dark glasses. "I was unkind to your friend, running off after talking with her."

"So I've heard." She was *not* going to be intimidated by either Summerlin sister.

Lin's laugh seemed genuine. Maybe it even was. "I can imagine! I may have decided to go on an impulse but I didn't stay with the guy. He'd already bored me by the time we got to Miami. But I decided to spend some time as long as I was there. We have relatives I'd intended to visit anyway." She gave Jam a quick glance. He might not care as much about those relatives. Cuban, Kris assumed. "Then Angelica drove over and picked me up last night. She brought your friend with her."

"Joey?" That seemed unbelievable.

"No, the mousy one. Ron, isn't it?"

"Ronnie," said Jam. "They call her Ronnie."

Lin shrugged. It looked less elegant with her slightly bony shoulders exposed. "Angelica called her Ron. They seem to have hit it off." She practically shuddered then. "They talked a lot about politics."

"Ronnie's let everyone know she plans to go into law now," Jam told her.

"Yes, they talked about that too." Lin picked up a wide-brimmed straw hat but only to retrieve a pack of cigarettes inside it. "Do you smoke?" She held out the pack to Kris, who shook her head. Jam did the same when she offered them to him. Because she was there? wondered Kris.

Lin lit one for herself, and tossed lighter and pack back into her hat. She took a few puffs, holding the cigarette between slim, long fingers, the nails short but perfectly manicured. Clear polish, thought Kris. She hadn't bothered with anything like that since graduation.

Lin's act was polished too, and almost as clear. She was playing her role as New York sophisticate, the girl who partied in Miami. She expected Kris to be awed. But she hadn't been that way with Joey. Her friend had reported how approachable, how *normal*, Lin had seemed when they biked together. Maybe it was a matter of her mood. Maybe she would ask Jam about it sometime.

Kris had no particular plans beyond waiting for Will so she settled onto the grass beside Jam. "Angelica's been making noise about demonstrating at the convention in Miami," he informed her. "Don't let her talk Ronnie into going."

Lin looked up. "Weren't you thinking of going too?"

"Not with my sister. Neither one."

"I'll be back in New York," she said. "You'd do better to come visit for a while."

"Or go to Chicago and do the convention there too. No, sister mine, I intend to take things very easy until the last moment of my freedom slips away."

"It needn't ever slip away," replied Lin. She tossed her cigarette aside and again reclined. After a moment, she turned over. It seemed unlikely Lin Summerlin had any more to say.

Jam gestured toward the house with his head. Kris nodded and both rose and headed for the porch. Jelly was seated there, sipping iced water beneath the slowly rotating ceiling fan. "Sylvie turned me out of the kitchen," she complained. "Said I was distracting her." She giggled. "Well, she didn't use that word. She said I was bothersome."

"I can imagine," said Jam. So could Kris, even though she barely knew the Summerlin's cook. She thought Jelly could be bothersome herself.

And maybe she should go bother Sylvie for some cold water. Later. Kris sat down in one of the rattan chairs by the siblings. "I get the feeling your sister doesn't like me," she said. "Not you, Jelly. I already knew you don't like me."

Jelly only smirked.

Jam seemed to consider this statement for a moment, looking up into the air. She knew this meant a theory was coming. Possibly an outlandish one. "You're the alpha females of your packs. Expect her to bristle at you."

"Me?" She could see that label on Lin but not on herself.

"You don't realize you're the leader in your little group?" He snickered. "The pushy one?"

"Hey!" But she had to laugh too.

"And where you push, they follow."

"What am I then?" asked Jelly.

"The lone wolf," declared her brother.

"Hmm. I guess that's acceptable." With that she threw back her head and howled. Jam and Kris couldn't help falling into hysterical laughter.

Sylvie stuck her head around the corner. "Whatever is going on, children?"

"My sister has discovered her inner wolf."

"Inner bitch," amended Jelly.

"Miss Angelica!"

"Sorry, Sylvie. I'll be good."

The diminutive, middle-aged black woman—she must be shorter than Kris—seemed satisfied with that. "Do you need some cold drinks out here?"

"Sure do," said Jelly, jumping up. "I'll come in and help get 'em." For the first time in her life, Kris felt she might like Jelly a little.

But she hardly knew her, really. Much of what she did know had been seen through Joey's eyes. "Lin *was* being sort of, um, standoffish just now. She'll get that way," said Jam.

"Oh. Like—no, I'd better not say that."

"She reminds you of someone else you know?"

Kris nodded. "Lin is shy, isn't she? That's why she puts up a front sometimes." Like Ronnie. "It must be difficult in her line of work."

"I think it is," Jam agreed. Nothing more.

Jelly emerged from the house with a tray of tumblers.

"Still on the subject of our sister?" she asked, handing out the iced teas. Kris was happy to find them unsweetened. One never knew in the south.

"Kris thinks she's an introvert."

"I didn't say that. I said shy. That's different."

Jelly nodded. "Social anxiety. I'd buy that."

Everyone seemed satisfied with the diagnosis so they sipped their tea in silence for a while. I should try to sketch one of these two, Kris told herself, peeking at one or the other over the lip of her glass from time to time. Maybe both. Not at the same time. Or—she turned around to look at Lin, still lying prone on her towel. She'd moved her arms up to pillow her head now. Too far away to draw from here?

At the moment she felt shy herself. She always did when trying to sketch around Ronnie or Joey, too conscious of their presence. But these two? They were like an audience that might applaud or boo, but would leave the theater at the end of the show. She slid her sketch book and box of pencils out of her commodious bag. Kris had seemed to be toting that everywhere lately.

She tried to ignore her companions and within a few seconds they truly did disappear from her consciousness. There was just the scene, the one when she lifted her eyes, the one when she looked at her paper. The same scene and not the same scene. It was good that she was backed off from her subject and couldn't make out details. Even though she had slipped on her glasses! That was her usual mistake, wasn't it? Getting too involved with the details, missing that proverbial big picture.

Was that any good? She looked up, she looked down. That's enough. Don't overwork it. The palms weren't bad. It wasn't a picture of Lin at all. She'd become just another shape in the landscape. Kris turned herself back around, started to return the sketchbook to her bag. Darn, all the ice had melted in her tea.

"Hold up," ordered Jelly.

"We want more than a glimpse over your shoulder," said her brother. Both stood up and came over to look at her scribble. The audience wasn't supposed to do that!

"Pretty decent," Jam went on. "And through the screen yet."

That had disappeared as she drew, also.

"The negative space could be handled better," Jelly commented.

"Yeah. It could be handled worse too. Okay, the art critics are done, Kris. You can put it away."

"But we're going to expect you to come and draw all the time now."

"Paint too."

"Only if you play your guitar. And you—" She scrutinized Jam. "Do you have any actual talent?"

"No," said Jelly immediately. "He's just a pretty face. And speaking of pretty faces, there's a cute and very sweaty boy coming our way."

"It's about time," called Kris, as Will Booth made his way across the lawn. "Let's get right into the water."

She raced him to it but let him win.

Chapter Twenty-five
Joey

"What a scrawl! It looks upside down!"

"Maybe because she's left-handed," said Joey, folding Lin's note and slipping it into a pocket. She could read it more thoroughly later.

"I never noticed," Kris admitted. "She just asked me to give it to you."

"Alan is left-handed," Ronnie dropped into the conversation. "Not that it has anything to do with what we're talking about."

"And not that you need an excuse to talk about Alan. Alan this and Alan that and, oh, did you hear about Alan?"

Joey laughed but thought maybe Kris was being just a little too mean. "So tell us about your Miami adventure."

"We went in Missus Summerlin's station wagon. It's bigger than Alan's."

Kris made a noise at the repeat of Alan's name. "What is supposed to be her wagon. Angelica says she prefers the convertible and lets her dad drive the Electra a lot of the time."

"How did she come to invite you, anyway?"

"She just did. I happened to be there with you-know-who, and she asked if I'd like to go. That was Thursday afternoon. If I'd known how late we'd get back I might have said no!"

"I assume you let your parents know," said Kris.

"Of course. I couldn't let them think I'd run off with, um, some guy I just might know and be dating."

"Maybe," said Joey, "she should have invited said guy too. I would have felt better if I'd known Alan was with you. If I'd known you'd gone, of course, which I didn't."

Ronnie shrugged. "She didn't so she didn't. Nothing went wrong anyway, except that Lin wanted to take us clubbing before we left. Angelica put the ol' kibosh on that."

"So no fun at all."

"The ride was fun. Seeing Miami was fun. Coconut Grove. That's where we picked her up at one of their relatives' home. Talking with Angelica was fun. In fact," she nonchalantly informed them, "I'm seriously considering dropping you guys and making her my brand-new very best friend."

Kris turned to Joey. "I think I'd actually rather hear about Alan than Angelica."

"I think I agree. Hey, what were you and Alan doing at the Summerlins anyway?"

"Looking for you. You kind of went missing after I saw you on Tuesday."

"Oh. I guess I did." She had needed some alone time. "I was riding and writing."

"Simultaneously?" asked Ronnie.

"And at the same time?" piped up Kris.

"Sure. Sort of. I think of lots of things when I'm on the bike and try to remember them, or stop and jot them down in a notebook." Her notebook had become her constant companion lately. "Speaking of said Summerlins, are they on anyone's agenda today? Chances are I'll see Jam tomorrow morning."

"He's not taking you out on a Saturday night?" asked Kris. "Hey, we need to find a guy for Jelly so we could all go out together. A quadruple date."

"Why not one for Lin while we're at it?" She suddenly started to giggle despite herself. "At the docks."

Her friends weren't in on the joke. That was okay; they could just go ahead and look at her oddly. No one seemed to be planning to go anywhere, did they? They were an unenthusiastic bunch this morning. Getting to be late morning. "You got your guitar out," she commented.

"Even tuned it," said Ronnie. "Both Angelica *and* Alan told me I should."

"The two-for-one," mumbled Kris.

"Next thing we know you'll be telling us you played it too."

"Some. And I've played Alan's too. It's way nicer than mine. But," she confided, "not as nice as Dad's. Don't let him know that."

"Isn't his a classical, like Jelly's?"

"It is, but it's a Martin. Hers is from Spain. Dad doesn't play classical style, anyway. He just does his Burl Ives impersonation."

They all knew Howard Deerfield was a musician of the folk persuasion. He was not one to hide that sort of thing. Joey thought of asking what sort of music Alan played—Ronnie certainly would know—but decided maybe it would be just as well not to start down that road.

And it didn't look like she would pick up her own guitar, despite the hint. Joey looked over a stack of books by Ronnie's bed. "The Worm Something-or-other?" she asked, picking up the top paperback.

"Borrowed from Alan. He thinks it's great. I'm not so sure. We can't agree how to pronounce it, either."

"I wonder what language it is. Maybe made up, like Tolkien?"

"I don't think so. Hey, if it's Latin or Greek or something, Jam would know, wouldn't he?"

"Then bring it over tomorrow. I'll tell him to expect you. Bring the guitar too."

"Let's all descend on him," suggested Kris.

"Good enough. But now, what the heck are we going to do with the rest of this day?"

"Naps are good. And, um, Alan is picking me up later."

"That's a hint to get out," Kris confided to Joey. Confided loudly.

"You think? No, Ronnie wants us to stay and make her boyfriend comfortable. Hey, we'll tell him all about the time she peed her pants in first grade."

"I spilled my drink," she protested.

Kris nodded. "Sure you did."

Joey got up. "I ought to get home anyway. I promised to help Wayne with some chores."

"Okay then," said Kris, rising also. "I'll see you all tomorrow." All three walked outside. Kris's Bug was parked there but Joey had come on her bike, as usual. It was hardly worth riding it here, as she could take short cuts on foot and arrive nearly as quickly.

There was the stink of melaleuca blooms in the air. Cajeputs, she'd always heard them called as a kid, or sometimes punk trees by old-timers. They used to be a popular planting but, like the equally popular Australian Pines, had become a nuisance. Part of Florida, the

Florida she had grown up in, but a part no longer welcome.

It looked like rain. Those chores might be postponed to some other weekend. There would be plenty of them free.

Chapter Twenty-six
Ronnie

"He took me to a surf movie. I didn't know much about what was going on but it looked like a lot of fun."

"I'll bet the audience was like ninety per cent guys," said Kris. "Grubby dragged me to a surf film once."

"At least. And really enthusiastic." As soon as she paused for dramatic effect Ronnie knew she shouldn't have. She continued to her punchline anyway. "And from the smell, mostly stoned."

"Not that I would partake, of course," Alan stated. He said this with a completely straight face but anyone could tell he wasn't being very serious. Did he smoke pot? Ronnie had no idea. There was so much they still didn't know about each other.

And so much they did know. "It's time you get that out," she said, nodding toward the boy's guitar case. "They've heard so much about it but have yet to see it." They had just arrived, having ridden over in her Simca with both their instruments in the back seat. Ronnie had pulled her car in along the street, beside the Summerlin property. There had still been parking open at the beach end of the street. That would be gone soon, as beach goers filled all available spaces there on a Sunday morning, and lined the street too, all the way down to Gulf Shore. Neither the Summerlins nor their neighbors on the other side of the pavement nor most of the other homeowners along the beach here had any complaints about these weekend crowds; things had always been that way.

The newer Neapolitans, the ones who'd moved down with all their money and northern ways, didn't always understand this. Some would close off the beach altogether if they could get away with it. Ronnie could help fight against that sort of thing if she were an attorney, couldn't she? Her thoughts about her new career choice hadn't progressed much beyond that. It wasn't a bad place to start though, was it?

"It's a Gibson," announced Alan, laying the case on a table and beginning to undo the clasps. "A Hummingbird."

"And here I was expecting a vintage Southern Jumbo," came Jam's lazy voice from where he reclined in a lawn chair. He hadn't even bothered to change out of church clothes yet. Ronnie assumed those were church clothes. She'd never been to church in her life though she'd gone into Saint Ann's a couple times with Joey when there weren't any services going on.

"Ha, I wish!" Alan said and then chuckled. "'Cause then I'd sell it and buy a Dove."

"Heathen," said Jam. "The Jumbo was Woody Guthrie's guitar. Hank Williams, too! I'll bet you play bluegrass on that thing."

"I might. But Keith Richards claims this is the perfect acoustic for rock."

"Oh, well, if Keith says so I guess it's okay. Just ignore me."

"We already do," Joey told him. "Go back to sleep."

"Didn't you use to play?" asked Kris. "I remember you playing."

"I could never hope to match my sister so I kind of let it go."

"Like you could never match my height so you stopped growing," Joey told her.

"Ooh. That's harsh," said Jam.

"Just what I expect from her." She plopped down in a chair beside him. "She's jealous on *so* many levels. Not the least of them my handsome and athletic boyfriend."

"I don't see any boyfriend," Joey said, looking about. "I think he must be imaginary."

"He's at church, like most good boys are on Sunday morning. I—don't know if he'll come by later or not."

"Joey and I took care of that early again. Six-thirty mass. Fortunately, I didn't get roped into serving this morning."

Ronnie wasn't sure what 'serving' meant. Not like a waiter, she was sure! The Catholic mass was yet another mystery to her. She suspected, however, it meant the two of them got to sit together today. "Oh." She went over to her own guitar case, a cardboard affair partially held together with tape, and pulled out a paperback. "We need to ask James if he knows how to pronounce this."

"Okay." Alan followed her over as she handed the book to Jam.

He gave it a glance. "That looks interesting. Lend it to me when you're done, will you? I do know the word Ouroboros. The snake that swallows its tale, a symbol of eternity or something along those lines. Anyway, the strongest accent is on the third syllable."

"Told you so," said Ronnie.

"Yeah, but you were pronouncing the first syllable wrong," Alan shot back.

"Well now you both know and won't embarrass yourselves if you're ever asked on national television." He gave the pair a bit of a wicked grin. "Assuming you believe me."

"They might," said Joey. "They don't know you as well as me."

"Get another opinion," Kris advised.

Ronnie was getting tired of this endless banter. Yes, it was her friends and yes, they had been this way since they were tykes together. On another morning it might not annoy her as much. She went back to her guitar and lifted it from its case. An experimental strum. Already out of tune. It didn't hold it very well to begin with but riding in the back seat on a hot morning didn't help either. She'd turn tuning keys later. Alan's instrument looked so much nicer. That finish was called a cherry sunburst, right? The hummingbird picture on the pick guard was a bit gaudy, though. A bit much.

Alan was still talking with the others about something. She walked toward the Gulf. Maybe it would be nice to swim right now. She'd been shown—by Angelica—that there was a place she could shower off the salt water around on the south side of the house. She hated to go about sticky-prickly all day after a swim, with dried salt on her skin.

Much less sand! The yard rose just a little as it approached its rear edge, where a fringe of sea grape bushes divided it from the beach. Maybe a natural dune, now covered with lawn. Beyond lay tall grass, sea oats—maybe with a few sand spurs sprinkled in—and beyond that, sand, the famous sugar-white sand of the Naples beaches. People here liked to think it famous anyway. There was a concrete bench back here, in the shade of the towering coconut palms. Ronnie sat and gazed out at the Gulf. More green than blue and almost dead calm. Alan probably hated that. He liked to drive to the beach just on the chance of unexpected waves.

She wouldn't cut through here and trample on the fragile natural growth. That would be poor payback for how this family had treated them these past weeks. Oh, she wouldn't have done it anyway, even if she happened to hate the Summerlins. Some beach goers didn't care. They'd push through instead of going around. There were people on blankets. Kids running, splashing. Radios turned to conflicting stations. Some of them Latin. Lots of Miami Cubans would drive over here on Sundays. Maybe Lin's relatives!

She preferred quieter weekdays. And she liked it just as well when it was cold and windy and big gray slabs of wave rolled in. Ronnie turned back around, toward her friends. Lin and Angelica had joined them. And Mister Summerlin, wasn't it? For some reason, she felt shy about going back and saying hello. Not just to Preston Summerlin. All of them. They were too much at times. She'd like to be at home.

Here came Alan. Smile and be nice. Smile and be friendly. "What's up?" he asked. "Are you okay?"

"I guess so." She amended that. "Yes. Yes, I'm all right. I want to swim." She suddenly half-sobbed and half-giggled. "And swim and swim, all the way to Mexico!"

"Oh. Feeling like you need to bust out?"

Ronnie turned to him, surprised. "You know about that? Do you want to do that sometimes?"

"It's my life, Miss Deerfield. I think it's why I surf. And at this time of the year—" He nodded toward the flat Gulf. "I get particularly antsy. I'd had high hopes last weekend with that tropical storm churning over by Texas, but it didn't deliver."

She wrapped her arms around him. "Maybe this will help both of us."

"It can't hurt," he said, before his lips met hers. Then neither said anything.

For a while, neither said anything. "You do have to take me surfing someday," she told him.

"But this should do until then. Let's make them all jealous again."

Ronnie thought it a pretty good idea. "Now let's go play our guitars," she said sometime later.

"Not swim?"

"Maybe in a while."

Chapter Twenty-seven
Kris

"Who would like to cruise around town?" asked Lin Salas.

"On our bikes?" asked her brother. "Unfortunately, Joey didn't drive the Corvair over."

"But there is the Simca. Don't forget the Simca. Ronnie wouldn't even notice if we stole it." The three guitar players were ensconced under a towering hibiscus, and oblivious to the rest of them.

Lin sighed. "I was thinking more along the lines of a classy convertible."

"But I didn't bring the Bug, either," Kris informed her.

"And it is definitely a convertible," said Jam. "I wouldn't guarantee the classy part."

"Classier than what any of the rest of you drive."

"I'd agree with that. But it's not what I had in mind either." Lin wore a bit of a smug smile.

"So Dad's gonna let you drive his baby, is he?" asked Jam.

"Well, I've always been his favorite, you know." She wrinkled her nose at him.

"Yeah, he looks at me and shakes his head. Another mistake!"

Now Lin shot a look of disapproval at her little brother but followed it with a shrug and a smile. "He can blame someone else for me. Anyway, he did give me the keys to the Caddy." She held them up and jingled them. "He'd probably let you drive it if you had a license."

"Too much bother. Tests and stuff and I'm not going to be living in Florida anyway."

"Whatever you say. Follow me. And make sure you don't have anything nasty stuck to your persons before boarding Preston Summerlin's Magic Carpet."

"Maybe we should have candy to throw to people as we pass by," suggested Joey. "Like a parade float!"

The Summerlins' two car garage fronted on Gulf Shore, away from the house. The frame structure seemed to have nothing to with the stuccoed residence it sat beside, with a screen of hibiscus and tamarinds separating one from the other. It was like they didn't want to acknowledge its existence until they needed their cars. Those two cars, the Cadillac convertible and the Buick station wagon, sat gleaming side by side when Jam and Lin swung wide the old-fashioned hinged wooden garage doors.

"Wow," said Joey on beholding the Cadillac. "I want one too."

"I don't blame you at all," said Lin. "I'm glad the top's already down. Just pull the cover off. There we go. You may all just gaze upon its splendor for a while first, if you'd like. Dad looked at a new el Dorado and claimed it didn't have as much space, but I think he's just too much in love with this car ever to part with it. It's a Sixty-two de Ville. It had red upholstery originally but he had it redone in white so it would be cooler in the sun."

"Shotgun!" called Kris.

"And I'll ride in the back. like the queen," said Joey, giving her best Queen Elizabeth wave. "You can be my consort, Mister Summerlin. Just remember to walk a few paces behind me if we get out anywhere."

He gave her a bow. "Your highness."

"That's not cutting it. You should have already been holding the door for me. Oh, never mind." She vaulted into the rear seat. "You're way too slow."

Jam opened the right-hand door and slid into the back beside her. Kris followed him, dropping into the front seat. It was a big seat and, boy, was that a big door! The massive piece of metal was easy to pull shut, though.

Lin settled beside her, behind the wheel. "I'm always nervous about pulling out here," she admitted. "It's a little hard to see if anyone's coming until your nose is almost in the street. And this car has an especially long nose."

"Kris could perch on the hood and be a lookout," suggested Joey.

"A hood ornament," added Jam.

"Must we take those two?" Kris asked. "They're not sophisticated enough to ride in a car like this."

Joey only made a rude noise at that. She did, however, shut up. She was being a bit over the top today, wasn't she? Maybe that was because of Lin. Joey might feel a little awkward around her after this past week. Or not. How would she know? Lin cranked the big vee-eight and it started at once. Kris only knew it had a big vee-eight by rumor but was willing to believe it. What else should a Cadillac have?

Lin eased it onto Gulf Shore without mishap, turning left. "We need to go where people can see and admire us," she announced.

"Then just keep going along the beach," Kris told her. "At least as far as the *Beach Club*." That was the *Beach Hotel and Golf Club*, officially, but people had called it the *Beach Club* pretty much from the time it was built.

"They'll recognize the car there. Dad golfs there sometimes," Jam informed them. "Hey," he said, turning to Joey, "didn't you caddy for him once or twice?"

Kris didn't hear an answer. Maybe her friend had nodded her head. "Doesn't Dad golf at the country club?" Lin asked, over her shoulder. They cruised past Fifth Avenue.

"*Beach Club* is convenient, especially when he plays with his old cronies."

She wished Will could be riding beside her but he hadn't shown up. He'd said he might not. Or he could be waiting when they got back, couldn't he? It was still morning. Clouds were beginning to pile up out to the east, white and nonthreatening at the moment. It didn't look like it wasn't going to rain right away.

It would spoil at least half their fun if they had to put the top up. "We should have music!"

"Let's see what my father listens to," said Lin, switching on the radio.

"Just as likely to be Mom's choice," Jam told her. It turned out to be the local station, WNOG, 'Wonderful Naples on the Gulf.' Either one could have tuned that in. And none of the four currently in the Cadillac wanted it.

There were, however, buttons to push and what station any one of them might pull in was a mystery. Kris doubted any were tuned to WQAM or any other source of rock music. Someone talking. She pushed another. Latin music filled the air.

"We can guess who's been listening to that," said Jam. "Leave it there."

"And turn it up," Joey added.

She did so, saying, "It seems to suit this car."

Lin nodded. "Doesn't it, though? I wonder if my mother drives about with it blasting like that."

"I wouldn't doubt it," Jam said.

"Crowded at the *Beach Club*. It would be a good place to turn."

"Right, I assume." That didn't require an answer. The area around the rambling hotel and golf course was packed, every parking space full, including the street before it. The street before that, too. Further north was uninteresting, at least to Kris.

The tree-lined street onto which they turned, rather unimaginatively named Golf Drive, wound beside the course. There were plenty of golfers, most on foot. It might be nice to have it like that at the club to which the Greenes belonged. For Kris, the best part of golf was being able to walk about. Riding in a cart ruined that. Even having other people in carts zipping about spoiled things some. It hurried the game up too much.

"Ronnie lives right over there," Joey announced, waving an arm to their right.

"And Joey right on the other side of the Trail," Kris had to add. "Might be best to turn back south there."

"I think we want to see Joey's home," said Jam.

"No, you don't," was all Joey had to say about that.

"Oh, but wouldn't it be cool to cruise by?" Kris asked

"I don't need to show anyone up."

Maybe Joey had a point. Jam was sitting right behind her but from the corner of her eye Kris could see him nod his head in agreement. They turned right on reaching the four lanes of Forty-one, the Tamiami Trail, and cruised south, slowly, radio blasting. Kris felt silly but she also felt good. This was what she had wanted from her summer, her friends and the sun and forgetting everything but having fun.

Oh, of course it wouldn't, couldn't, last but a few minutes. Joey and Jam were going on about something in the back seat. They'd been jabbering since the ride began.

But Lin—she looked amused, maybe, but not really happy. Had she seemed happy anytime Kris had seen her these past couple weeks? That thought didn't stay with her long. There was too much to see today, too many people to wave to. Some of them she even knew and that was a bonus!

Lin kept going straight ahead when they reached Four Corners. "Hey, Joey, it's time to visit the city docks!"

"We'll have to make Jam get out so we can fit in sailors for each of us!" came the reply.

Kris had no idea what they were going on about but at least the two appeared to be friends again. There were lots of cars parked at the docks but not many people moving about. No sailors for her friends! Most boaters would already be on the water, and not ready to come back yet. They turned right at the intersection, where a tall mast stood, its flags furling and unfurling in the modest onshore breeze. That mast had come down in Hurricane Donna, in Sixty. Kris remembered riding her bike down here and looking at it, the steel shaft lying crumpled on the pavement.

Toward the beach again. Oh, and Lin was taking them right by her house. Whatever Joey might prefer, Kris didn't mind showing off to her family at all. "Wave, everyone!" she ordered. Aw, no one outside. She stood up and waved anyway, one hand on the top of the windshield.

A right on Third. Maybe cruise the Old Naples area? Not much going on there. Lin took a left onto wide, palm-lined Broad Avenue and then left again to Twelfth, the pier street. Parking was crowded along it too, and the sidewalks were busy.

"What the heck is that?" asked Jam, of a sudden. "It looks like a Jeep impregnated a golf cart at some time."

Lin took a look and slowed down. "Oh, a Mini Moke. I haven't seen one since I visited Bermuda."

"Grubby Rhein drives it," Kris said, taking care to sound casual about it.

"Grubby?"

"Ex-boyfriend," explained Joey. "The sort she'd just as soon humiliate."

"Nah, just show him up a bit."

"I understand. I have too many exes of that sort myself." She pulled alongside the little open vehicle, stopping in the street. Two boys were sitting in the car, drinking sodas. Grubby and the younger guy who seemed to follow him everywhere. His disciple.

Grubby gave them a lazy looking over. "Hi, Kris. Hey, that's one nice ride."

Lin leaned forward and grinned. "Wanna race?"

He laughed easily. "I'd have a better chance if I ran. Hey, Jam-man. Jambalaya!"

"My friends call me Jam," he called back, "but you may address me as Mister Summerlin."

Grubby shook his head. "Can't you find anyone better to ride around with, Kris?"

"The other two are okay," she told him.

Grubby's companion leaned forward, looked around him. "Yeah, where's the nigger you've been dating?

In one move, without one seeming moment of hesitation, Grubby turned and punched his buddy in the middle of his chest. Hard. "Don't you ever talk like that around Kris," he growled. Kris didn't remember ever seeing Grubby angry. He was always the laid-back guy. "Or me."

The boy looked like he might say something. Instead he got out of the Moke and walked off, his shoulders shaking. Anger? Humiliation? Or maybe just having trouble catching his breath after taking a body shot.

Jam stood up and applauded. A moment later, Joey joined him. Grubby only laughed as they pulled away. "See you on the Fourth," Jam called back to him.

Well, that wasn't how she'd expected her encounter with Grubby Rhein to go. But it was a fitting conclusion to this day. The last day of June. One month closer to the end of this summer in the sun.

JULY

Chapter Twenty-eight
Ronnie

"Joey is much better looking than I am. I would kill for such cheekbones." Lin's sigh might have been just a little too dramatic. "I look like our mother."

There was some truth to that. It was unlikely Maria Summerlin had ever been particularly attractive, as far as her face went. Age had not helped her cause. She must be in her mid-forties now. Late-forties, maybe? But she was tall. All the family was tall.

That made up for much. "She still has a good figure," ventured Ronnie. She probably did look quite a lot like Lin when young, though Maria's features were a little heavier. Some might even say masculine.

"True, but Mom is, well, plain. When I'm her age they're likely to say the same of me." She gave them a bit of a comical grimace. "If they're not already!"

"Never!" claimed Jam.

"Almost never," chimed in Jelly.

Ronnie would never say it of her face, even if she thought it. It was a face almost rectangular, a little too much jaw, maybe, and not much to notice otherwise. It might be a plain face but Lin was not a plain person.

"I'm going to swim before it gets any hotter," announced Lin, and headed for the beach.

"That seems backward," commented Jam. "I'd want to jump into the water when it got hot."

"Have you been in the Gulf lately? It feels like a bath. Our sister will hole up in the air conditioning when it gets too hot for her. I think she's writing."

Lin had seemed to be just filling time, keeping busy at doing nothing, until she would be flying back to New York. "Writing?" asked Ronnie. "Stories?"

"Sketches, I think. Right?" Jam asked his sister. "We're probably good material for her."

"Uh-huh. The sort of thing that goes over with her editors, or she thinks does. Editors in general, I suppose."

"The ones in the world she lives in now. It seems kind of a small world to me."

"Maybe not from where she's standing. It might look like it's everything to her." Angelica turned her eyes toward the beach but her sister was no longer visible from their vantage. "The way school can until you get away from it."

"Run away from it, you mean?"

"I had sense enough to do that."

James made no reply to that but looked as if he at least half-agreed with his twin.

"But it's a good job, isn't it?" asked Ronnie, after a few empty seconds. "I mean, um, the world she lives in?"

James shrugged. "It's the track she wanted to be on. The sort of career Lin always talked about."

"She may have slept her way into her job," added Angelica. "I guess she's good enough to hold onto it."

Again, James had no reply. Whether he agreed at all now, Ronnie was unable to discern.

"She doesn't seem very happy," she said. "Not really."

"I think she's trying to forget she isn't happy," replied Jam.

Jelly nodded. "Has she ever been?"

The awkward silence was longer this time. "You should have brought your guitar," said Angelica.

"Not on my bike." Ronnie had pedaled her old bike over this morning, the one she had inherited from her brother. It remained the dark green it had been when Richard rode it but she had added a white wicker basket to the front. The plastic daisy that had come affixed to that basket had gone into the trash. "Kris's Bug was in front of her house when I biked by on the way here. They must have got back last night."

"We'll probably see them later, then," felt James. "Let's wait in the air conditioned comfort of the palatial Summerlin home."

"Lin would say it's the Salas home," his sister reminded him. "I might too." That last came a bit—what? Pensive? Maybe the girl didn't see this old house as quite being her home.

They passed through the porch and into the house, not through the French doors that opened into the dining room but the door by the kitchen, and past the staircase to the second floor Ronnie had never seen. She hadn't seen much of this floor. "Are your parents here?"

"No one's here," responded James. "Not even Sylvie."

"Oh, then you'll have to cook. Joey tells me you cook."

"Maybe later." Ronnie somehow doubted that. They had entered the large, dim living room, the couches and chairs all upholstered in greens and whites, echoed in the bamboo patterned curtains. A pair of fans slowly rotated below the high ceiling. They most likely predated the air conditioning.

"We could settle in the library and drink Dad's liquor," suggested Angelica. She turned to Ronnie. "That's where he keeps the good stuff."

"Which he wisely keeps locked up. Not because of us," he hastened to add, "but lots of guests are in and out of here."

"So I've noticed," said Ronnie. She was a little surprised she said it. She wasn't the one to try to be witty.

That was witty, wasn't it? Jam did smile. James. She should call him, think of him as James. He drew back the one of the pocket doors to the library, Preston Summerlin's private sanctum. Oh, but James was sleeping there, she remembered.

You couldn't tell. The space had no resemblance to anyone's bedroom. Angelica strolled over to one of the tall bookcases, reached behind a set of dark, leather-bound volumes, and produced a key. "This is where Dad keeps the key to the liquor cabinet, just in case you ever need it," she announced, and returned it to its hiding place. "I suspect the secret is safe with Ron."

"But not with me?" asked her brother.

"Oh, you can always go over to the church and get a nip of the communion wine."

James only shook his head. It was a theatrical gesture. They seemed common in this family. "I would guess the rest of your triumvirate is sleeping in," he said, turning to Ronnie.

Two guesses as to who had used that name around him. "It's a long drive to Miami and back," she said, in their defense.

"UM, right?" asked Angelica, settling into the most comfortable looking of the chairs and putting her feet up on the coffee table. "Maybe I should go there. They have a good music department."

"Right. Kris wanted to drive over to the campus and Joey rode with her."

But not her. Her friends had sprung the idea on her late Sunday, after they had decided to go. But then, Ronnie had been wrapped up with Alan and Angelica and not paying much attention to them. She hadn't even realized they had gone off somewhere with James and Lin.

Just maybe she had resented not being asked to go on that ride. She couldn't sort all that out. All Ronnie knew was she hadn't liked being asked to make a sudden decision.

"Well, I expect all three of you to help me set up for our party. My sisters won't be any use. They think it's enough to sit around and be ornamental."

"That could be seen as a put-down, brother mine," said Angelica. "Ron and her friends are capable of being ornamental too."

James chuckled. "True. Just bring your boyfriends and I'll put them to work."

"You will have to bring your guitars on the Fourth too," Angelica added. "No excuses allowed."

"Okay," agreed Ronnie, looking about the room. Books lined the walls. There was a small, cluttered desk, a couple of arm chairs, a couch, all in subdued colors. Lawyer colors, she told herself and smiled a little at the idea. Dark leather, mahogany, all the cliches.

Maybe she could have a library like it one day.

Chapter Twenty-nine
Joey

"I only intended for a few friends to come and watch the fireworks," said James Summerlin, "but it grew into a party."

"You have only yourself to blame," his sister told him. His other sister nodded agreement.

"And you are on your own," said that other sister. "I've been invited to watch elsewhere."

"You won't get a better view than right here," James protested.

Angelica snickered. "But better company."

Lin only smiled. "I'm going to be on a boat. There's no better view than that."

"You found a sailor?" Joey asked. "And didn't get one for me?"

"It's just my dad," Kris told her. "He's taking their parents out too." She nodded in the direction of the Summerlin siblings. "And Donny, so he won't be showing up here."

"He might be the sort of chaperon we need, with the parents gone," opined James. "I'm not sure why they trust us."

"They don't realize you've invited half the riffraff in Naples to trash their house. Oh, it looks like we're ready to go." The Summerlins had stepped out onto the patio.

"Have a good time, kids," called Preston, as Lin joined them. He looked like he might have thought to say more but decided against it. All three headed toward the garage.

James waved and turned back to his friends. "I *am* going to lock up the house. There's no point in tempting people to get into trouble."

"And you'll have to go down to the beach to pee," said Angelica.

"Do you realize how crowded the beach will be?" Kris asked her. "Wall to wall."

"Walls? When did they put up walls on the beach? They'll get in the way of our walks! Hey, here's Ronnie. Um, or I guess it's Ronnie unless she's broken up with Alan." Joey waved at the big station wagon, being backed around so it could pull in facing east alongside the Summerlin property.

"Early enough to have a place to park," remarked Kris. "I still think we were smart to ride our bikes."

Joey was in agreement with that. "But you'll have to depend on Doughnut finding his way to you."

"Oh, Mackie's bringing him. His friend What's-his-name too."

Angelica provided the name. "Jeff. He's cute."

James shared a quick, enigmatic glance with Alan, who had just walked up with a guitar case in each hand. Maybe nobody but Joey had noticed it.

"Just the man," said James. "You can help me at the grill."

"Um, yes." Alan looked a little uncomfortable. More so than usual. "Maybe no one has noticed it, but I don't eat meat."

"Oh, the Buddhist thing?"

"Sort of."

"Ronnie has mentioned your parents were Buddhists. By the way, hi, Ronnie. Maybe you can assist the chef."

Ronnie looked decidedly uncertain about that. "You need to get the fire going," stated Joey. "I'm the person for that." She looked toward the sky. "In an hour or two. Don't be in a rush, Jam."

The boy looked a bit sheepish. "I'm sure you know better than me, Joey. I don't even have a good idea of how many guests are likely to show up."

"Oh, everyone will tell a friend and they'll tell another friend and they'll—" began Kris.

"More likely the other way around," Alan felt. "They'll all want to keep their ideal fireworks spot secret. I would, anyway."

"Hmmph. We'll see. There's someone pulling up now."

Probably just someone come to stake out a spot on the beach, thought Joey, turning to see a dark blue Falcon parking across the street. "Daryl," was all Ronnie said.

With a girl. There was nothing wrong with that, really, but it was—well, a bit gauche. "I guess that's one of the friends telling a friend things," remarked Kris. "You invited him, Ronnie?"

She nodded. "And I told him to bring a date if he wanted." The girl was avoiding looking at the couple crossing the street.

"I don't think I know her," said Joey.

Kris supplied a name. "Sandy Penn. Russel's sister."

"She'll be a senior this year," added Alan. Then he added something more. "I hope she didn't invite her brother."

Joey managed to stifle her laugh. It wasn't easy. "You know Russel pretty well, don't you?"

"He'd probably say he is my friend. We've always been around each other a lot at school, in the same classes. He's a science fiction guy, too."

"But no connection beyond that, huh?" asked Jam.

"I've managed to avoid one. He wants to be a part of everything. To be—useful, I guess."

"Heaven save us from useful people." He raised a welcoming hand to the approaching pair. "Come make yourselves comfortable. No need for introductions—your friends have already given me all the sordid details."

Daryl looked slightly bewildered. Sandy laughed aloud. She was a small, angular girl, blond like her older brother but not resembling him much otherwise.

"Hey, Jam," said Kris, "you should get together with Sandy's brother. Russel plans to be a minister. He's not coming, is he?" she asked the girl.

"Oh, Russel's over at the pier, being helpful."

Kris went on. "You should meet Sandy's mom too. She has a convertible to rival your father's."

"And a bouffant hairdo no one can rival," said Sandy.

Alan had gone to the patio, placing the guitar cases on one of the tables. Jelly's case was already there, open, but she hadn't taken her instrument out yet.

"I play a little guitar sometimes," murmured Daryl. Joey wondered if Ronnie had ever known that. She was too far away to hear her former boyfriend now, and busy tuning.

If the two had never shared that sort of thing it was just as well they broke up, wasn't it? She took a seat in one of the lawn chairs when the players settled onto the grass. No need to light Jam's fire yet. Ha, that sounded odd put that way. Good thing she hadn't said it out loud.

"So your parents are Buddhists?" asked Jelly, idly picking at her strings.

"They claim to be Buddhist. I've come to recognize that's more an attitude than a religion for them. We didn't grow up with Buddhist scriptures lying around the house or anything."

"But you're Catholic, right?" said Ronnie.

"So they tell me. In fact—" The Summerlin girl started playing a tune that seemed no more than vaguely familiar to Joey. She was pretty sure her friends wouldn't know what it was.

"Franck, right?" said Alan. "Some Latin name."

Jelly looked up without missing a note. "I'm impressed. It's his 'Panis Angelicus.'"

"A lot of classical music gets played in my home." There was a self-conscious chuckle. "My folks claims it soothes the animals."

"Leave it to my sister to know more Catholic music than I do," said James. "Not that she's heard much of it inside a church."

Jelly stopped playing. "And you've neglected your own musical talent."

"I stuck with choir," he protested.

"My brother has a great voice," she told them all. "And a considerable range. He should do more with it than sing a mass now and then."

"That's not a bad use for it," said Joey. She wasn't quite sure why, nor why she would defend Jam.

"Oh, I know, he's the good Catholic boy and some days he's all into it. The next day I'm not sure but what he's an atheist.

"Neither am I," admitted James Summerlin.

Chapter Thirty

Kris

"I think that's the last of it," said Will.

"That doesn't mean we have to get up."

"No, I suppose not."

They had watched rocket after rocket launch from the end of the pier, to explode in bursts of light and color, reflecting across the still Gulf. Far out over the water, nature had provided fireworks of its own, lightning playing against distant clouds. Fortunately, none of them and their attendant rain had found their way to land. The crowds on the beach were now moving toward their cars or homes, some at a considerable distance. People would walk quite a way for the best seats in town.

Kris was willing to sit here on the Summerlin's grass, with Will's arm around her. They had become serious, hadn't they? But no sex. No fireworks! Not yet. It was going to happen before this summer was over, wasn't it?

She thought she was ready for it. Ready in every way. Of course, Kris's mom had made sure she was on the pill quite some time ago. Her lips rose to Will's, her hand slipped under his tee, to slide across his firm midsection. He was probably aroused but it was not the time nor place for anything more than this.

Not that she would mind his hands exploring a bit too. Yes, like that. "Mmmm."

Then, "Mackie's taking you home, isn't he?" she whispered. "We should probably find him before he finds us."

"Yeah." Will breathed in and out, deeply. "Good idea. I think he and Jeff were watching over there." He rose and gestured toward the dark southwest corner of the lawn, made darker by the shadows of the tall hibiscus hedge between the Summerlins and their neighbors. They walked, hand in hand, not speaking.

Ah, there they were—among the shadows, two more shadows. One shadow put its arm around the other, lips met. Kris and Will backed away quickly.

"Do you think they—they knew we were there? That we saw them?" she whispered a few seconds later. For some reason, she did not feel very shocked. More embarrassed, really.

"Dunno." Will sighed. "I kinda knew about Mack," he admitted. "I mean, he never said anything and neither did I but—"

Yeah, that 'but.' It found its way into so many uncomfortable conversations. "And you never, ever said anything to me, even when I dated him for months."

"That was up to him, wasn't it? Besides, someone as sexy as you might have turned him straight. I could always hope." A smile might have come and gone quickly; it was hard to tell in the dark. "I mean, he was dating you so I thought maybe he liked girls some."

"'Some' wasn't enough, I guess. Hey, I'm not mad at you about it." She wasn't. Not at all. Mackie was—high school, and high school had ended. "And I'm certainly not mad at Mackie. Let him know that, will you?"

"Sure. You might want to yourself."

Kris wasn't quite *that* comfortable with all this. She and Mackie would probably never mention it. "I really, really want to let Jelly in on this and disillusion her about Jeff. But I guess I should do like you and keep my mouth shut." That did not mean Ronnie and Joey weren't going to hear about it.

"She thinks he is cute, doesn't she?"

"I think she feels that way about men in general. And they do about her. You think she's sexy, don't you? C'mon, admit it. I won't hit you. Probably not."

"You're just as sexy as Angelica. Only in a smaller package."

"Well, that's a pretty good answer. I'll let you get by with it."

"It may be a little awkward riding home with them now," said Will. "If they saw us, um, see them."

"I doubt they would say anything."

"Guess not. Is James gonna do any more burgers?"

They were in the open, near the house now. The moon, a week from full, added its illumination to that of the lights on the porch. "Not much of anyone left," she said. "But then not much of anyone came. Alan was right about everyone keeping it secret. Oh, there's Grubby." She waved toward him. He was sitting on one of the tables, in his usual white tee and shorts, talking to the guitarists. Their cases were all closed and fastened.

His young follower had not come tonight. Maybe he wasn't following Grubby anymore. A few others had drifted in and out. Whether anyone had actually invited them, she wasn't sure. Kris looked around. Daryl and Sandy were gone. Somehow she doubted she would see the two in each other's company again.

Joey and Jam huddled by the grill. Coals still glowed in its recesses, casting their own dim orange-red light on the couple. She started in their direction; Will followed.

"Will is hungry," she announced. "Maybe I am too."

"And here I was just about to put all this away. I really brought out more than was needed." James waved a hand toward the uncooked burgers and hot dogs. "The tomatoes are a bit limp now and Alan's used up all the onions. He doesn't eat meat but he has nothing against onion sandwiches."

"Poor Ronnie," Joey added to this.

"I'm going to throw everything that's left on the grill," James decided. "It's safer, isn't it? I mean to cook it thoroughly instead of putting the leftovers away raw."

"Kris could always take them home to her dog," offered Joey.

"That's my mom's dog and she would have fits if I fed her that sort of thing."

"Well then, Alan could. I'm sure the dogs in his house aren't vegetarians."

"And neither are the cats nor the ferrets," said Alan. He and Ronnie had ambled up. Both looked sleepy. Kris suspected she looked sleepy herself. "We're going to go now. Thanks for having us, Jam."

"Thank Angelica too." James looked around. "Where'd she go?"

"Inside," said Ronnie.

"And, uh, Grubby went with her." Alan looked as if he wasn't sure he should have added that. There was a quick sidelong glance at his companion but her expression didn't change.

"Knew I shouldn't have let her have a key," mumbled James. "Take care getting home." He began laying burgers and dogs on the grill.

A couple minutes later, the AMC station wagon disappeared into the night. "Ronnie's going to college in Gainesville, right?" asked James as he flipped burgers. Joey nodded so he went on. "And Kris in Miami and Joey in Fort Myers. You girls have your plans for fall all set and I'm still not sure what I'm going to do. How about you, Will? Decided to go with Stillman?"

There was a definite pause before Will answered. "Between the draft and, well, money questions, I'm not sure where I'm heading. Have to decide soon." That last sort of trailed off, almost as if he were saying it only to himself.

"We should talk about this some day when we have more time. We could give each other bad advice. These are ready. Get buns if you want 'em. Ketchup and mustard over there, and mushy tomatoes."

Kris informed him, "Joey doesn't like ketchup."

"At least you've learned something about me over the last twelve years. My mom and I put spaghetti sauce on our burgers. Mom puts it in meat loaf too. We like it better."

"I'll have to suggest that to Sylvie, not that she would think of serving us meat loaf. Now who's going to help finish off the leftover beer?"

"Not me or Joey. We need to ride our bikes home."

"Oh, maybe just one," said Joey.

"Yeah, one would be okay. We can't let it spoil!"

"Hey, isn't Macklin taking you home, Will?" asked James. "He didn't leave already, did he?"

"Nope. I suspect he and Jeff will remember me eventually." Will took the proffered beer and chugged half of it down.

"Yes. I suspect they will," agreed James.

Chapter Thirty-one

Joey

"I think Alan and Jam knew. Or suspected." She remembered the look they had given each other.

"And none of us saw it," said Kris, and then she giggled. "Until I *saw* it."

Joey wrinkled up her nose. "It's good that's all you saw."

"Oh, I don't know. It might have been interesting." Both her friends made appropriate noises of disapproval and distaste. "Oh, you know you're curious, when it comes down to it."

"I'll just stick to my imagination," Ronnie stated.

"As long as you don't imagine Will," warned Kris, who then had another fit of giggles. "But feel free to imagine Mackie!"

"You seem to take the whole thing awfully well."

"There's no reason it should bother me, is there? And it sort of lets me off the hook for any lingering feelings I might have had." She sobered, at least some. "I did like him, you know. I still do."

"Yeah," agreed Joey. "Mackie's a good guy." Though he shouldn't have led her friend along like that. Oh, maybe he didn't know, himself. Maybe not for sure. How could she know?

One thing was true: she hadn't been that surprised herself when Kris told them about it. Maybe somewhere inside, she and Ronnie had also felt something of the truth. "You do know," she went on, "we're both going to imagine Doughnut now you've put the thought into our minds."

"Well then, I'll imagine Jam."

"Who wouldn't?" Ronnie asked, and immediately blushed.

Joey debated making some answer to that but Kris jumped into the pause. "I'm finished with Grubby, of course. You both are free to let him into your dreams."

"I'm pretty sure Jelly did more than imagine Grubby last night," said Joey.

"Ooh, no. Poor innocent Grubby!"

"We could ride over and see if she's still holding him captive," suggested Ronnie.

"Too hot. We'll just hang out in your air conditioned room and bug you."

"Yep," agreed Kris. "You're not getting rid of us easily."

"I—don't want to." Ronnie suddenly sobbed. "I wish we never had to—to split up the triumvirate. Like—" A tearful smile appeared as she picked up one of the paperbacks by her bed. "Like that snake Ouroboros we could just make time go round and round, live summer over and over."

"Give me that," ordered Joey, holding out her hand. Ronnie passed it over. "I'm going to have to read this, the way you and Alan have been going on about it. Eddison? Never heard of him."

"He wrote this one too." Ronnie held up another book. "*Mistress of Mistresses*. I like it better."

"Don't start a book club, you two," warned Kris.

"It's not such a bad way to stay connected," Joey shot back. "Even if we're not together we can have something to share."

"Since you don't want to share your boyfriend," Ronnie appended to this.

"But we'll dream about him anyway."

Kris only sighed. "Isn't Lin leaving this weekend? We should see her before she goes."

"Flying out tomorrow," said Joey. "Jam told me last night. He can have a bedroom again."

"Oh, we should go over later then."

Joey shook her head. "They're all going out to eat. A farewell dinner. Tomorrow morning's the time, before her mom drives her to Miami."

"Let's all meet there then," said Ronnie. "Early." Her friends nodded agreement. "I wish we could have got to know her a little better."

Kris didn't look like she particularly agreed. "She did look at some of my writing," Joey told them. "And, um, she told me I could send some to her. If I wanted."

"Well, that's good of her, I guess," admitted Kris.

"Though she may toss my stuff in the wastebasket, unread. I don't have many illusions about Linda Salas."

"The whole family sometimes seems like an illusion."

"Oh, I like that. I may steal it and put it in a story."

Ronnie laughed. "Feel free. I have a suspicion you're writing about Kris and me, anyway."

"I wouldn't doubt it," Kris remarked.

"What will she do when we aren't around?"

"I like Sandy. I may have to adopt her when you two leave town."

"Remember her brother comes attached."

"Ah, but he'll head off to college too."

"Oh, that's right," said Ronnie. "Russel was telling everyone he was accepted at Stetson." She winked at Joey. "That's almost as costly as Miami."

"But less fun," Kris pointed out. "Much less fun."

"More fun than we can afford." Ronnie seemed pensive for a moment. "Maybe I should ask Preston Summerlin for a job."

Joey had ideas. "Mowing his lawn? Cleaning his grill?"

"No, climbing his trees for coconuts," suggested Kris.

"But not babysitting his kids. I've already taken that one."

"This is the sort of thing I should have expected." Ronnie's exasperated tone was nearly as theatrical as any Joey had heard from the Summerlin kids. She'd never do it as well, though. "I meant something lawyer-y."

"You might have better luck with my dad. He might find something for you to do around *Donalson, Greene, and Hein*."

"His name isn't first?" asked Joey. She was pretty sure Tom Greene had started the firm.

"They decided putting the token Gentile first was better for business. Yeah, it's a dumb joke but Dad always trots it out. You're really thinking seriously about the lawyer thing?"

"I am." She sounded completely serous now. "It's a lot to tackle. Lots of school. Lots of money."

"Yes," agreed Joey, "it is."

Chapter Thirty-two
Ronnie

"The ice plant used to be down here, before Naples had refrigerators. Two kinds of ice, one aerated for human consumption and one not, for packing fish." Ronnie was tour guide this morning. She could pull it off. She had heard enough of her dad's lectures on the history of Naples.

"I remember my dad stopping here to buy ice when I was very little," said Joey. "My real dad, not Wayne."

"Way back, the generators that powered the city were here too." They were pedaling along Tenth Avenue South, between Fifth and Sixth Streets. Ronnie, Joey, Kris and James—the rest of the Summerlins were in their Buick wagon, headed for Miami International.

The goodbye to Lin had been brief and not at all emotional. That's not to say Ronnie wouldn't miss her. She was sure her friends felt the same and James even more. He seemed to connect more with Lin than anyone else in his family. Maybe the reverse was also true.

"Where now? Down to the city docks?" They were close.

"We're not looking for sailors anymore," Joey sang out.

"And they'll be crowded on a Saturday morning," Kris added to this. "The rec center would be too." They were only two blocks over from it, and from Saint Ann School, where Joey and James had both attended. A block from the back of the school, and the church too, for that matter. Ronnie was sure they had seen enough of both.

They were building a new, bigger church beside the old one, much grander than the small, simple rectangular place that had been in use since the Fifties. It might be fun to watch that go up. Her father would enjoy it, anyway, all the while grumbling about another change to the old Naples.

"Let's just go around to my house," continued Kris. "We can get a drink and take things from there."

No one raised an objection. The Greenes' residence lay close too. A right at the next corner. There was still some of the really old Naples down here, shanty-like houses from the Twenties or earlier, little businesses that had been grandfathered in. Ronnie had no illusions that these would last forever. Progress and bulldozers would come here sooner or later. There might be some attempt to preserve an artificial quaintness for the sake of tourists.

Right again and headed back in the direction of the beach and Kris's home to the left. Another nondescript ranch on a street of ranches, but that street was in a choice part of town. They left their bikes lying on the front lawn.

"It's about time we hung out at someone else's house," said James. "I may just rotate among staying with each of you for the rest of the summer."

"Why not with Alan, too?" asked Joey. "He could use help with the animals."

To this, Kris added, "I'm sure Will's family would like you as a house guest."

"I would suspect they'd treat me better than you three do. Is your family home, Kris? I don't want to intrude."

Kris looked slightly guilty. "Mom and Donny went to temple. Dad may be somewhere around. His car is here." She nodded toward the dark Chrysler.

"No lawyering on the Sabbath?"

"Or on Saturday mornings."

"Where is his office anyway?" asked Ronnie. She'd never thought about it before. She was pretty certain it wasn't in any part of the old downtown.

"Out the East Trail, close to the courthouse. Further than I'd want to ride my bike, that's for sure!"

Me neither, thought Ronnie, following her into the house. Nor even drive. She didn't think she'd bring up anything about a job with Mister Greene. Probably not with anyone, with half the summer gone.

And she'd be sitting in class in Gainesville in two months. It seemed further away than any map would indicate; she would be as unlikely to get home from college there as if she were attending on the other side of the country. Ronnie had given thought to jettisoning her University of Florida plans and attending Edison College with

Joey. This wasn't something she would tell her friends and it wasn't something she was actually likely to do. But it had been a thought she wasn't willing to completely dismiss.

No one greeted them. "Dad's ignoring us, I think," said Kris. "He doesn't know we snuck a boy into the house."

"And a Summerlin, to boot," added James.

"Shh. If he hears that he'll want to argue politics with you."

"I'm not my dad. And you know, our fathers are really pretty close to each other in their politics. One is a moderate democrat and the other is a moderate republican."

"And our parties have left both of us behind, it seems." David Thomas Greene, attorney at law, was standing in the kitchen doorway in a ragged tee and cut-off jeans. "More importantly, do you know anything about lawnmowers?"

"Only that they're noisy, sir."

"Not when they won't run. Oh, well." He returned to the kitchen.

Ronnie leaned in to whisper to Joey, "I'll bet you could fix it."

"Maybe. Let's get something to drink and then go someplace."

She and Kris followed Mister Greene into the kitchen. To Ronnie, James murmured, "Joey seems sort of—low, this morning."

"She gets that way sometimes." She hesitated before adding, "Always has."

James only nodded, offering no immediate, off the top of his head advice, none of the opinions she had come to expect from him.

"I have sisters, you know," he said after a while. Ronnie could only nod in return. Maybe they could talk about all that later. No, she was unlikely to bring it up. James was not quite someone she felt comfortable confiding in.

Kris returned with glasses of lemonade. "Joey took some out to my dad. Maybe she'll help him get the mower started after all."

A couple minutes later, they heard the raucous notes of a small engine outside. "Either Dad is mowing or we're being invaded by a gang on motor scooters," said Kris.

"Angelica has made some noise about getting a scooter," said James, settled on the arm of an overstuffed chair and sipping his iced drink. "I think she's jealous of my bike and wants to one-up me."

Kris's smile was brief. "I can believe that. I can believe just about anything when it comes to Jelly."

Ronnie could too. For the most part. Angelica could be so, well, likable one moment and so obnoxious the next. And it seemed like a game, like she was completely aware of what she was doing. Not like her sister, whose moods felt very real and very much a part of her.

Joey returned, with her own glass of lemonade. "I moved your bikes so Mister Greene can mow," she informed them. She didn't sit but leaned against the frame of the doorway.

"He should just hire someone like we do," James said. "Like my mother does, I should say."

"He could hire Ronnie. She does want to work for a lawyer."

James gave Ronnie a rather long look. "Really? I could say something to Dad."

Now she was on the spot. "It's too late this summer, isn't it? Besides, the Triumvirate is pledged to only play until—until we say goodbye."

"There's always next summer. You'll be here then, right?" He looked to Kris and then to Joey. "All of you?"

Kris nodded. "I'm not even leaving," said Joey. "And I truly will need some sort of job come fall."

"Small engine repair?" asked Kris.

"You could dig footers for Mister Sterne when Daryl's gone," offered Ronnie. "I can put in a good word for you."

"And I'd be good at it," Joey asserted. "Hey Kris, you should show Jam your artwork while he's here."

"Yes," Ronnie agreed. "Her bedroom walls are plastered with sketches." No sooner had she said it than she thought maybe she shouldn't put her friend on the spot. Of course, she might *want* James to see the pictures.

"What? Your parents haven't taped them to the refrigerator?" he asked, his smile innocent. Then, "I'd love to see a portfolio of your best sometime but I wouldn't think of barging into your inner sanctum."

"A gentleman at last!"

"It's too bad," said Joey, "that none of us are ladies." She drained her glass. "Let's get out of here."

Chapter Thirty-three
Kris

"Ronnie and Alan got awfully serious, awfully quick, didn't they?"

Joey was in agreement. "Those two have hooked up with a vengeance."

And where might they be headed? "I'm pretty sure Ronnie is a virgin."

"For that matter, Alan may be too." said Joey. She seemed reluctant to say more but then let it out. "You know, um, strictly speaking, so am I."

Kris wasn't all that surprised, but the way her friend had put it was odd and maybe a little funny. She rolled over so she could see Joey's face. It was time she got some sun on her back anyway. "Strictly? Isn't that an either-or thing?"

"I guess it is. Let's say I've left guys standing on third base, looking toward home."

Leave it to Joey to use a metaphor like that. "You mean oral sex."

"Yeah. And some hands where they shouldn't be." Her friend looked like she might giggle but stifled it. "Theirs and mine."

Kris knew all about this, or thought she did. Her own sexual experiences, aside from Grubby, had been in the same vein. "I'm not sure why guys are so big on blowjobs," she said. "I would think hands do a better job."

"It's, uh, usually some of both anyway, isn't it? Not that I have that much—" Joey did start to giggle this time. "Hands-on experience."

If Joey didn't have such a deep tan, she was sure she would able to see her blushing. But it was true. Neither of them had much experience, really. A little experimentation, that's all it was. "Ronnie doesn't have any experience at all. We should give her the 'talk.'"

"Oh, yeah, I can see us doing that." There was the sarcastic Joey she knew and loved.

"I can see you doing it. You've always shared more with her than I have."

Joey didn't reply at once. "I'm not so sure of that. But—you know, we have both always shared more with Ronnie than with each other."

"Ronnie is our glue, isn't she?"

"Maybe so."

Yeah, maybe so. It wasn't like they all hadn't talked about sex before but Joey had never been so forthcoming about it. She and Ronnie knew about Grubby Rhein. That wasn't something Kris would have kept from her closest friends. Her confidantes.

Maybe she should undo the back of her bikini top. No, not this close to the pier, where school friends still hung out. Boys, that was. No point in tempting them to make rude remarks, even if they meant nothing by them. She would if she sunbathed in the Summerlins' yard. She could probably find enough seclusion there to sunbathe topless, if she wanted.

What would Will think of that? "I guess Will and I will happen one of these days."

"I didn't think you had yet. Is it a good idea?"

"I'll find out when it happens! Do you want to swim?"

Joey raised her head just an inch or two to gaze at the Gulf. "Nah. I feel too lazy to move. Oh, I'm going to bring our surfboard over and leave it at the Summerlin house. Jam thinks it's a good idea."

For a brief moment, Kris wondered if Joey and Jam were likely to 'happen.' That relationship was way too complicated for her to figure out. "We're not likely to see any waves soon."

"But we could paddle it around."

"When you don't feel too lazy to move."

"Right. Hey, what's that?" Joey got onto her elbows and turned up the volume on Kris's little radio. "I like it, I think."

"Never heard it before." And might never again. One could never tell.

"Suzie Q, baby I love you? Hmm." She waited till the end of the song. "Damn, the deejay didn't tell us what it was. Or who." Joey lowered the volume and reclined again.

"Maybe you should get a job on radio and do things right." Kris snickered. "Like Russel's mom."

"Don't think I couldn't," sniffed Joey. "The Penns live somewhere near the junior high, don't they? Or middle school, I mean. They call it middle school now." The name had changed a year or two after they had left, and what grades attended where was switched around, with ninth graders suddenly appearing at Naples High.

"Yeah, a bit closer to the Gulf and a bit further north. Not so far from Ronnie's house." She tried to keep a straight face as she asked, "Planning to dump Jam for Russel?"

"What idiot would do that? Not that I'm with Jam. He's like the brother I never had!"

"That sounds convincing."

"Doesn't it? And I'm the sister he wishes he had."

"Now that may be more accurate than he'd admit."

"Yeah. That's not what we were talking about, is it? The Penns. Jam has extended the freedom of the Summerlin realm to Sandy. Or maybe Jelly did. I couldn't quite figure that out."

"With Jam and Jelly, that's not unusual," commented Kris.

Both lay there a couple minutes without talking.

"Have you thought about what classes you'll take in the fall?" Joey mumbled. She sounded half-asleep.

"I'm likely to just let my counselor tell me where I should be."

"Yeah. But you know what you want to do with your life. Famous artist!"

Kris smiled to herself. "I'm more interested in design," she said. Kris had no delusions about being a great artist nor did she even have ambitions in that direction. Not really, though one did dream. She *could* see herself at the head of a design firm

"I've looked over what I can take. I'm going to try to get the required stuff out of the way as soon as I can. Stuff that's like a continuation of high school."

"I'll have that too. If I went for a BFA I could dodge some of the academics but the parents insist I get the BA." She could see Joey attempt a lazy but sympathetic nod. "And they're paying for it, so I guess they should get their money's worth." She was going to stop with that but then thought to add, "That doesn't mean I won't follow it up with an MFA."

"Oh, that's way too far to look ahead."

"I don't want to look any farther than tomorrow right now."

"I'd settle for this afternoon."

Chapter Thirty-four
Ronnie

"Preston Summerlin has dabbled in politics for a long time," said Howard Deerfield, "mostly as a perennial loser. Between the traditional southern Democrats sliding over to the Republican party, and the influx of conservative northerners and country club Republicans, an old-school moderate liberal like Summerlin doesn't have much of a base anymore. Not that he ever did in this town."

"That's quite a little speech," his wife told him. "Have you been practicing it?"

"Of course I have, my dear. Haven't you heard me rehearsing in the bathroom?"

"I think I will bring up working for him next summer. Interning, sort of. Or maybe Kris's father if Mister Summerlin turns me down," Ronnie told them.

"I'm sure Tom Greene does more business than Summerlin," said Patty Deerfield.

"That's not necessarily a good thing," her father countered. "You know, you could work for me if you wanted."

This was something he had mentioned before and, as before, Ronnie thought it a very bad idea. "I'm not interested in architecture, Dad," she replied. "Nor journalism," she said to her mother, "though Joey is."

Patty laughed. "I don't think I need much help writing my weekly column. Other than your father's suggestions, of course."

"She always knows to write just the opposite. But if Joey needs a part-time job, tell her to see me. She could run plans to my clients on her bike!"

Maybe she would say something to Joey. Her dad liked her. He liked Kris too. Mom had always been a little more cool to her friends. To her best friends. But then, she had liked Daryl. She'd probably love Russel Penn. Didn't she know his mom?

Ronnie did not think she would bring any Summerlins by to meet her. It was enough for now that she was okay with Alan.

"I'm going to lock myself in the closet for a while," her father announced, and left without further explanation. None was needed; Howard Deerfield had an office but he sometimes drafted in a little room here at their home.

"Is that what you're wearing on your date?" asked her mother. "You used to wear dresses."

"It's summertime, Mom." Shorts and a blouse were certainly enough.

"And the living is easy?"

"Something like that."

"Be sure to dress up a little if you talk to Mister Summerlin. He's a bit old-fashioned about things like that, I think."

Hmm, yes. "I've never seen him in shorts, I'll admit. Unlike Mister Greene." If she went to talk to Kris's dad, she'd wear slacks, she decided. That would work well. It would make her look serious and grown up, even though he had known her since she was a little girl. "But Preston Summerlin has seen me in all sorts of clothes this summer." Including her bathing suit. No need to add that.

Ronnie got up from the table. "Alan should be along soon. I'd better finish getting ready."

Not that there was much to do. She wasn't even bothering with lipstick when she went anywhere with Alan. Maybe some earrings, she told herself, sitting down at her little vanity. Those big clunky bright ones she'd never brought herself to wear in public before. They'd work with this pastel blouse.

Was going out with Alan becoming just something to do on a Friday night? She liked him better than any boy she'd ever dated. Better than any boy she'd ever known. Maybe she was even in love. It didn't feel like the sort of love she'd read about in novels or seen in movies. Ronnie wasn't completely sure that even existed.

And if it did, if she was in love, would it last? She and Alan would be going their separate ways at the end of summer. Things would change between them. That was inevitable. Again, the idea of attending Edison passed through her mind. They could stay together then. That wouldn't be a good career choice, would it? She should focus on her education now.

A nagging doubt arose to nag her again. Was she really good enough, smart enough, for a law career? Would she end up teaching school or something of that sort?

"Here's your surfer," called her mom. "You two start your evenings awful early, don't you?"

"Why waste the sunshine?" Ronnie replied, going to the door. She had it open before Alan could ring the bell. He wasn't dressed up either.

But then, Alan's idea of formal wear was probably an aloha shirt. "Where are we going?" she asked as she got into his wagon. He did open the door for her this time. Alan didn't always remember that sort of thing. "Not another surf movie?" She hoped he could tell she was joking. She hadn't minded the one he's taken her to. Maybe she even like it.

"No, I won't inflict that on you. At least not tonight." He settled behind the steering wheel before going on. "I was thinking of taking a little surf trip to the east coast. Two or three days." There was a short pause, a gathering of himself, before his question rushed out. "Would you like to come?"

"Overnight?" Don't panic! "Where do you stay? A motel?" Separate rooms. That might be okay.

"Oh, I camp. There's a nice campground near Sebastian Inlet, or maybe up at Canaveral Jetty. Russ and I have stayed at both of them."

In a tent with Alan. Her parents would not like that idea. She wasn't big on it herself. "Couldn't we just do a one-day trip sometime? Try it out first."

Alan briefly frowned but there might have been relief in the expression that followed. "Yeah, that's a better idea, isn't it?" He backed out into the street. "If you don't mind a really early start."

"Like Four or Five?" Her father had sometimes rousted the family for trips that early.

"Like Two or Three. It's a pretty long drive."

"Oh. I haven't set my alarm clock since school ended." Maybe she should suggest someone else come along. That wasn't something to bring up right now.

"I like to be in the waves at dawn," said Alan. A laugh followed on the heels of his statement. "I sound full of myself when I say things like that, don't I? The dedicated surfer! There is no guarantee of waves at this time of year."

"It would be cool to watch the sun rise over the Atlantic. I've never done that."

"I'd be lying if I said it looked a whole lot different from the sun setting over the Gulf."

"Except in reverse. Hey, if you drove fast enough you could see both in one day!"

"Wouldn't have to be very fast. There should be time enough to stop and have lunch on the way. But how about dinner, now? Do you like seafood?"

Was Alan suggesting a real dinner-date? This was a first for them. "Sure. Isn't that off-bounds for a vegetarian boy?"

"Shrimp are okay. Or scallops or even oysters, though I don't much like those. I avoid anything with a spine." He pulled the wagon out onto the Trail, driving south. She went through a list of seafood places in her head. He could be headed for any of them.

"As long as you don't consider me spineless," she quipped, a little too late maybe but it had sounded witty to her. In her head, it had.

Rain spattered on the windshield. "Never," he answered switching on the wipers. A moment later, he decided to do the same with the headlights. "You and your friends are a spiny bunch."

Ronnie had to laugh aloud at that bit of absurdity. She was still chuckling when they crossed the bay and pulled in at the *Fish House*. A mingled aroma of fried fish and Naples Bay greeted her as she stepped out of the car, in front of the low, wooden building. This really was the old Naples her dad went on about. This place was about as old as any restaurant in town, and commercial fishermen had brought their catch to the docks behind it even longer.

And she just had to kiss this boy, her boyfriend, before they went inside.

Chapter Thirty-five
Joey

She was not going to sit up front with James Summerlin. She never felt comfortable there. Besides, Father Al believed James was going to become a priest. It might disillusion him if he had a girl at his side.

And the priest already knew she wasn't one of his sisters. If Jam wanted to come back and sit next to her, that was up to him. There he was. She'd beat him to church this morning. Jelly was with him. Now that was a surprise. Or even a shock! Joey hadn't thought she ever attended mass. Nor even got up this early.

Father Al pounced on Jam immediately. He must need a server again. That answered the seating question for another Sunday, as Jelly settled into a pew on the other side of the nave.

Joey felt her mind wandering as mass began. Pay attention! For a minute or two, she managed it. Then came memories of the beach and the sun and her conversation with Kris. Sex and all those things that were less than actually having sex. Those were ways to sidetrack overly insistent boys. She hadn't been about to lose her virginity to any of the guys she dated. Lose? That was altogether the wrong word. You didn't lose your virginity any more than you lost a gift you gave someone. Joey intended to be very careful to whom she gave this gift.

She shouldn't be thinking about that in church. Her attention turned back to the altar. Jam sat upright, eyes straight ahead, in one of the chairs flanking the altar, as Father Al prepared to deliver his sermon. It would probably be brief. Oral sex wouldn't break a priest's vow of celibacy, would it? Not strictly speaking. A vow of chastity would be another matter. Celibacy was an either-or thing but chastity was something of a moving target. She had definitely missed that target a few times.

No matter. Joey wasn't about to see any of it as much of a sin. He was done talking already? The service moved on into the offertory. She couldn't be blamed if her mind drifted again as she sat there. At least she didn't fall asleep; this early, people sometimes did.

Joey had devoured *The Worm Ouroboros* and then borrowed *Mistress of Mistresses*. She was inclined to agree with Ronnie that it was the better book. Such gorgeous language! And most of it so superfluous. She would rather write like Hemingway. Or maybe Katherine Mansfield. Did her attempts at writing sound imitative? Lin hadn't said anything like that. She really hadn't said much of anything at all.

She wasn't sure Lin even knew much about literature. At the end of mass, she thought she would just sit there and wait for Jam. But Jelly nodded toward the door as she passed by in the main aisle, so she followed her and everyone else outside. "What do you think?" asked the girl, with a grandiose sweep of her arm toward a shiny motor scooter.

"It's red," said Joey.

"Oh, you noticed!" The scooter was chained to one of the benches beneath the ficus trees. They'd gotten large, hadn't they? She remembered climbing in them when she was little. They'd seemed big to her then, too. "It's a Vespa," announced Jelly. "Here comes my errant brother. Ready to ride home?"

"I"m going to walk, if Joey is willing to come over for breakfast with me."

"You'll have to fix me some too, this time!" Jelly opened up the throttle and rode across the lawn and into the street. The grass would recover from being torn up just a bit, Joey felt.

"Let me get my bike," she told Jam. Herself she told, no way am I pushing it all the way to his house this time. I'll just ride slow. Or ride circles around him if he dawdles. "You should have brought your own bike."

"I didn't want to disappoint Angelica the first time she offered me a ride. There will be opportunities for that later."

There might not be more offers. "She should wear a helmet."

"Maybe you should too. I've seen bicyclists in helmets."

Joey hadn't. It did sound sort of sensible, not that she would give up having the wind and sun in her hair. A few minutes later they were in the Summerlin kitchen.

"Pan perdu, garcon," ordered Jelly, already waiting at the table.

Joey was baffled. "What's that?"

"French toast. That's what we sophisty-kates call it."

"Oh, I want to be a sophisty-kate! Gimme some pan-pertooty, too. That's French, right?" she asked Angelica, taking a seat. "I don't know any French. We did have a pretty good Spanish teacher at Naples High." Which was no guarantee she could communicate with a native Spanish speaker.

"I speak Spanish and French. Better than my brother, too."

"Ah, but you can't speak Latin," Jam countered. "Much less Greek." He busied himself with eggs and milk and butter and thick slices of French bread. Joey considered getting up and helping but decided against it.

"Would anyone like to go on a surfing trip?" she asked. "Alan invited Ronnie but she wants moral support, even if it is just a one day thing. She asked me to go along."

"Does Alan know that?" wondered Jelly.

"Maybe not. We could surprise him."

"I might be up for it," said Jam.

Jelly glanced up at her brother. "And for Miami?"

Joey felt left out of the conversation again. Maybe this was something else sophisty-kates knew about. "Miami?"

"The Republican convention. I'm still thinking of going over and helping to raise a ruckus."

"So am I," said Jelly. "Our parents would be more likely to let Jam go."

"Not that we aren't both—aren't *all*—" he asserted, giving Joey a nod. "Old enough to decide on our own."

"I prefer to choose my battles and that one isn't worth fighting," was what Jelly had to say about it. "That's not to say I wouldn't go too, if Mom and Dad don't object."

Joey could not see herself going to Miami and demonstrating in the streets. She could see herself going and writing about it though, couldn't she?

"Okay, make yourself useful, you two," ordered Jam. "Joey, plates and forks. Jell, find us some drinks. The first of these will be ready shortly."

They already smelled great. Too bad, thought Joey, as she set the table, he's going to be a priest. He'd make some girl a great husband. And she'd never have to cook.

Chapter Thirty-six
Kris

"I was just walking along the beach—from the pier, you know—and saw you here and remembered you said I could visit and here I am!"

She wasn't surprised to see Sandy Penn. She *was* glad the girl was alone. Jam or Jelly would have told her she could bring her brother or probably anyone else she wanted. Was it selfish not to want to share the Summerlins?

"No Daryl today?" asked Kris.

"Oh, no." The girl didn't exactly screw up her face in disgust but one got a definite feeling she was not eager to be in the vicinity of Daryl Sterne. "He's a buddy of my brother, you know. That's kind of how I ended up with him on the Fourth." She sent a radiant smile in James Summerlin's direction. "And how I ended up here!"

"So that's the direction the wind blows," Joey whispered in her ear. Kris nodded; it wasn't hard to see. She somehow doubted the girl had just chanced to come by.

"It's still early," called Jelly, lounging at one of the tables behind Jam, doing something with her guitar. Tuning probably. Kris didn't think she'd been paying any attention. "Hang around all day if you want."

"Thanks! I have to go to the airport later. I'm a cadet with the Civil Air Patrol and I get to ride with the sunset patrol on Sundays!"

"That," observed Jam, "seems both like fun and an inconvenience."

"Oh, I love it, you know? I'm going to be a pilot!" She gave the boy a disconcertingly direct look. Kris might have been willing to call it a stare. "Is it true you're going to be a priest? A Catholic priest? My brother plans to be a minister."

"It's possible. They seem to be expecting me at the seminary." He shook his shoulder-length locks. "I might even have to cut my hair."

"Ooh. Doesn't the bible say men shouldn't have long hair?"

"Ah, but how long is long?"

Sandy giggled. "Three inches!"

"That's a good answer to the old 'how long is a piece of string' question," commented Joey. Kris didn't know that question but let it pass. Joey simply said things she didn't understand sometimes and sometimes she could get Ronnie to explain them.

"Ronnie and Alan have arrived," announced Jelly, looking past them. Everyone was here now but Will. He'd promised to make it after church.

"Hey, Alan," called Joey, waving. "You've got to teach us to surf. We got the board out." After spending the last few days in the Summerlin's garage, the long surfboard now lay on the lawn, the big blue fin pressing down into the grass. It looked kind of battered, thought Kris. The foam under that fiberglass would have been whiter when it was new.

"I didn't notice any waves," came Alan's answering shout. He and Ronnie were retrieving their guitar cases from the back of the wagon.

"It's safer that way!"

Alan came over to give the board a disinterested look. "Any of you ever surfed?"

Kris didn't think Joey had ever been on a board. Nor Ronnie. She had tried it out a few times. Boys had always been willing to give her a lesson. Usually a hands-on one. "I have," she admitted. "Just playing around at it."

"I've skied," volunteered Jelly, standing and slipping her guitar back into its case. "I did that a lot in Switzerland."

Jam shook his head. Was he truly annoyed by her bit of pretentiousness? It was frequently hard to tell when he meant something or was just indulging in theatricality. "We both ski. And water ski."

"Me too," said Kris. "Water ski, I mean." Not that she was any good at it.

"I used to ride this board, sort of inherited it when Russ went to a shorter one. Mine is shorter now, too." Alan went off without further words to join Ronnie at one of the tables.

"So who's going to carry this beast down to the beach?" asked Joey.

"Not me," Jam informed her. "It belongs to you young ladies so you have to tote it around."

"I'll help!" blurted Sandy. "Um, I mean, can I come too?"

Joey jumped on that at once. "Let's vote on it."

"You're already part of the club, Sandy," Jelly assured the girl. "And watch your step, Miss Varney, or we'll vote you out of it!"

"Oh, you mean I can't be a sophisty-kate anymore?" Then, a little more seriously, "I kind of dislike the Varney name. I was thinking of using my mother's maiden name when I write. Or maybe Italianizing my own to something like Varese."

"It's been used before," Jam had to point out. "What's the other name? Your mom's."

"Montini. I don't like it that well either." Kris didn't think she had ever heard it before. Maybe Ronnie had. In fact, it was likely.

Ronnie and Alan had returned to the group bunched up around the surfboard. "It's not all that heavy," said Alan. "A bit over twenty pounds."

"But unwieldy," added Ronnie. "We found that out when we loaded it on top the car. I'll take one end," she said, and tucked the board's nose under her arm. Sandy took the tail before anyone else thought to move, and they marched toward the Gulf. The rest followed, even Jelly.

Kris ran ahead of them, to stand splashing the water around her ankles. "Everyone into the pool!" she called out. It was like a pool today. Or a bath, considering how warm the water felt.

"I'm still in my church clothes," protested Joey.

"I can lend you something to swim in," Jelly said. "We're close enough in size." The girl might have smirked a little. "Except in the chest. I need to change too."

Everyone else had bathing suits on or had worn them under their clothes. Even Jam. Shirts and shorts were doffed in a pile on the white sand and the group waded in. Kris lay down on the board and attempted to paddle it. Slippery. Didn't the surfers put some kind of wax on them to make the tops sticky? She tipped over on the next stroke.

Maybe hand over hand wasn't the best idea. It threw her off balance. But she'd seen guys paddle that way. Alan had retrieved the board and was up on his knees on its deck.

"Paddling from a kneeling position isn't so easy with the new smaller boards," he told them, "but it works well on one this long." Which he demonstrated, paddling in a circle around them. "The important thing is to find the ideal spot to be in balance. Not too far back or you'll bog down. And not too far forward—that straight bottom up front on this board makes it better for nose riding but it also makes it easier to pearl."

"Pearl?" asked Sandy.

"That means the front end goes under the water and you slide off ungracefully," Kris informed her. She knew from experience.

Alan came to his feet for just a second and dove off. It was all one movement and probably a lot harder to do than it looked. The board did spin away from him and Sandy went to retrieve it. She enthusiastically tried to climb on, succeeding in turning herself over.

The girl came up laughing and then waved toward the shore. Kris turned to look. Joey, returned in shorts and a tee. They did fit her well enough.

She and Jelly had Will in tow. "Come on in," she called to him. "Alan's finally going to be able to give you those surfing lessons."

He tossed his tee aside and waded in, wearing cut-off jeans. Ooh, she liked the way they clung to his muscular thighs. Kris made an effort not to stare.

Will gave her hand a little squeeze but nothing more. He was still reticent about public displays of affection—they both were—and Naples beach on a Sunday was about as public as one could get. "I never heard of any black surfers," he said.

"Go to the Caribbean and you'll see plenty," came Alan's reply. "Though I have run into a couple over in the Cocoa area. We'll probably get there." His eyes went to Ronnie. "Whoever happens to be going with me."

"He knows about us?" asked Joey, who had followed Will into the water. Jelly still stood on the beach, gazing south toward the pier.

Ronnie nodded. "I sprung the idea on him as we were driving over here."

"So she did," said Alan. "I'm okay with it, as long as I don't have to pack too many of you into the wagon."

"Just Jam and me, I think." She turned to the Summerlin boy, who was steadying the surfboard as Sandy attempted to mount it again. "Your sister wasn't interested, was she?"

"She'd just as soon not hang around with me. She's also likely to be riding her new toy all over town. Oh, you two haven't seen it yet," he said to Alan.

"He means her motor scooter," Joey put in. She turned to Kris. "Maybe she'll give you a ride if you're sure you don't want to come."

"I"d rather stay here with Will. If he takes up surfing, I'll go with him." She couldn't help giggling at a sudden silly thought. "We'll be on surfari to stay."

She was rightly ignored by the others. "Tough crowd," she whispered to Will.

"There is a chance of waves toward the middle of the week. Not a big one and maybe no surf at all. I've been looking at the weather maps."

"Oh, I love weather maps!" enthused Sandy, splashing with her arms as she attempted to propel the board toward them. "If I wasn't going to be a pilot, I'd be a meteorologist!"

"And you could let Alan know whenever waves were coming," said Jam. "So, Wednesday, maybe?"

Alan nodded. "That's what I was thinking. I've cleared it with my folks so, well, I'm going no matter who decides to ride along."

Sandy had deserted them and gone to talk with Jelly. Or talk at her; the older girl mostly just smiled as she carried on. "We're going to go walk on the pier," Jelly called.

Ronnie had taken possession of the board and was on her knees, attempting to emulate her boyfriend. "Ow, that hurts," she complained.

"That's where surf knots come from," said Alan. "Another reason I'm not that big on knee paddling these days." He lifted one leg out of the water to display a bump just below the knee. "This used to be bigger. I suspect it will disappear in another year."

Will scrutinized it. "Calcium deposit?"

"Yep. Also know as housemaid's knee."

"Surf knot sounds a lot better," felt Jam.

"But I bet they both hurt just the same," said Ronnie, slipping off the board and back-stroking away.

Chapter Thirty-seven
Ronnie

"So we'll sleep at the Summerlin house tonight," finished off Joey, "and Alan will pick us up there way too early."

All three of the girls had slept over at each other's houses on occasion, since they were little. Ronnie's parents would not have an objection to a sleepover with Angelica, even if they didn't know her well. Nor should there be much concern over a one day trip. She was eighteen, after all, and an adult.

Never mind that she didn't feel like one right now, seeking her parents' approval. "I assume your surfer is not going to be at the Summerlin's tonight," said her mother.

"Alan is being sensible and getting his sleep," Ronnie replied.

"He has to drive," added Joey. "We can go back to sleep once we hit the road."

Ronnie's mom nodded. "Alan seems trustworthy."

"I'm not inclined to believe that boy would ever misbehave," said Howard Deerfield.

"Unless encouraged," replied his wife. "Boys can always be encouraged."

"Not by me," claimed Joey. "And I'll keep an eye on your daughter. Between the two of us, we can make Alan behave."

"We'd better head over there," said Ronnie. "You sure that's all you need? We could swing by your place." Joey had walked over from her home with a small bag, barely large enough to hold a change of clothes.

"It'll do. After all, we intend to frolic nude on the beaches once we get over there. Bye Mister and Missus Deerfield," she said, heading out the door.

"Be sure to put on lotion first," Ronnie's father called after her. "Have fun." Ronnie gave them a wave goodbye and followed her friend.

"We didn't say a word about James," she said, as she settled behind the wheel of the Simca.

"Which is probably just as well."

Yes, it probably was but Ronnie did feel guilty about not mentioning him. And what if her parents heard he came along? She would have to lie and say he decided to join them at the last moment. Oh, stop worrying, she told herself. You're going to have fun tomorrow.

A couple minutes later, they pulled up alongside the Summerlin property. It should be safe to leave her car parked here. Still, she didn't completely like the idea. Maybe they should have come over on their bikes. The sun was low but not yet set and the sky was clearing after the afternoon rains.

Stop worrying about things, Ronnie told herself. Again. You're just nervous about this trip. Even with moral support, it was a step forward in her relationship with Alan. A small step yet a step she had never taken with anyone before.

"They actually did set Alan's tent up," noted Joey. "I didn't know whether to believe it."

A fairly roomy-looking wall tent stood near the rear of the yard, just this way from where the lawn rose gently to the fringe of sea grape bushes. Blue? It was a dark silhouette against the setting sun.

James came from the house, raising a hand in greeting. "Alan and Angelica pitched it. I supervised."

And Alan was gone. "It might have been nice to talk to him before he went home."

"We'll see him soon enough," said Joey. "He'll come to wake a couple Sleeping Beauties in the middle of the night. And James."

"And Kris and Will are coming by, right?" asked James. "A camping party. All we need is a campfire."

"It was all Ronnie's idea." Not that her friends didn't fall in with it right away.

"No Sandy this evening?" she asked. A mosquito buzzed by. Maybe camping out wasn't such a great idea in the summer.

"No Sandy, but she has been by both this morning and yesterday. Hmm." James didn't look quite sure of saying what he said next—but he said it anyway. "Grubby came by too. I suppose he wanted to see Angelica but she was out scootering."

Joey nodded knowingly. Maybe too knowingly. "I would guess she isn't really interested in him."

"So would I. He's not the sort to hold her interest."

Headlights in the darkening street. Yes, Kris's Beetle. It pulled in behind Ronnie's own car. Was Doughnut—Will, that is, riding with her? The top was up so she couldn't see.

There he was. She wondered if she had picked him up at his own home. Anyway, she'd have to take him away again, so Kris wouldn't be staying the night with them. One less camper. Maybe Angelica would want to join them. Ronnie wasn't sure how she'd feel about that.

Will followed Kris into the yard, carrying a small, dark object. The way he held it suggested it was heavier than one might expect from its size. A tiny cast-iron hibachi. "This will be our camp fire," Kris announced. Will set it down by the tables.

"We could roast marshmallows over that," noted James, "though there's only room for one at a time."

"You'll have to provide them. The charcoal too. I know there's plenty of that around for your dad's grill." She surveyed the tent, hands on hips. "It's a little warm for sleeping out. Humid too."

"With all that warm Gulf water right next to you, it won't cool off much overnight," James added. "Remember you can come in. Lin's room is at your disposal. My room now, but I'm sleeping downstairs tonight so I won't bother anyone when Alan shows up at some ungodly hour."

"Have you heard from Lin?" asked Joey. She was trying to sound not overly interested in the answer. That's how it seemed to Ronnie.

"Called when she got to New York. Nothing since."

"Called collect," said Angelica, emerging from the porch.

"Which is better than not at all. She'll write sooner or later. She might even write you, but probably at this address." His eyes went to Ronnie. "You didn't bring your guitar?"

She could only shake her head. No point in telling him she hadn't intended to take it on the trip tomorrow and didn't want to leave it here. Leaving her car was bad enough.

"Let's go back to the tent and get you settled in," suggested Angelica. "Bring your stuff."

Closer up, one could see lots of screened openings, door and window. That would be good both for letting in cooler air and keeping out bugs. Unless it rained in the night and they had to shut them. Ronnie thought she might make a run toward the Summerlin's comfortable house if that happened. At least as far as the porch.

"Surfer Boy left those," Angelica said, gesturing toward a pair of sleeping bags rolled up by the back wall. "I didn't think you'd want to sleep in them so I brought some cushions and sheets back."

Joey dumped her little bag. "Thanks. We might unroll them as sleeping pads," she said and stepped back out of the space.

Maybe, thought Ronnie. Had Alan and Russ used them on their own camping trips? She hoped someone had aired them out! She put her own bag down and followed her friend outside.

James had taken a seat on the grass, hunched over a guitar. It was small, smaller than hers or Alan's or even Angelica's. Over-sized white pick-guards lay on either side of the sound hole. "You got yourself a guitar," Ronnie said. What a dopey thing to say, she told herself at once. Of course it's a guitar.

"Already had it but it's been sitting unused the last couple years." He briefly held it up for inspection. "An F-25, Gibson's almost-a-classical guitar."

Ronnie could see it had nylon strings, like Angelica's, but it differed in more than a few other ways. "A folk guitar, right?"

"So it was advertised. Alan wasn't too impressed when I showed it to him, despite it being a Gibson, but he had to admit it's a sweet-sounding guitar." He picked a few random notes. Yes, it did sound nice. Sweet was a good description.

Angelica didn't seem interested in getting her instrument out. She spent more time gazing beyond them toward the darkening Gulf. Stars were beginning to emerge from the sky. The waning moon would be making an appearance tonight, still bright but probably not enough to bother their sleep.

James ran through some chords before putting the Gibson aside. "Let me get that charcoal. A little campfire *would* be nice."

"Don't forget the marshmallows," Kris called after him.

"And sharpened sticks for them," Joey added. "Holding them in our fingers while they toast isn't a good idea."

He only lifted an arm in acknowledgment as he ambled toward the house.

Angelica came out of her reverie. "Let's go down on the beach while my brother fusses with starting a fire."

It seemed as good an idea as any. They drifted to the street and then down onto the sand. "The water is glowing," said Angelica.

So it was. Each tiny wave that lapped at the shore shone with a pale green phosphorescence as it broke. That was common in the hot midsummer. "If there was something more than these ripples we'd get a real light show," said Kris. "Or we could jump in and make our own."

No one proved eager to splash in the dark water. "If there were waves we wouldn't need to go to the east coast," Ronnie said. Not that Alan seemed optimistic about there actually being any surf over there.

"I don't think they get this sort of thing in the Atlantic, do they?" No one was certain one way or the other.

They dawdled at the water's edge for a few minutes before heading back. Angelica was last to follow, turning at last from gazing out over the black water and joining them. James had a fire going in the hibachi and was strumming his guitar, singing softly. He did have a good baritone voice. His sister hadn't lied about that—when? She'd mentioned something about him being in a choir.

It wasn't important. The heat from the little charcoal fire certainly was unnecessary this evening but she liked its ruddy glow. Such a contrast to the cold light of those breaking waves, made by millions of tiny living creatures. Living and growing while fire only destroyed. Their light should be the more attractive of the two.

James was lighting up a smoke. "Want some?" he asked his sister. She nodded and took it, inhaling deeply, and offering to return it. "Keep it. I'll light another."

Angelica passed it to Kris who also took a long pull, before holding it out to her boyfriend.

"I'd better not. I have my scholarship to be concerned about." William frowned. "If I decide to use it. I have to decide soon."

"You do," Kris almost whispered, taking another hit and handing the joint back to Angelica.

James offered his joint to Ronnie. Pot. She'd never tried it before. Her head told her there was nothing wrong with it but her heart was pounding. She took the proffered cigarette, gave it a tentative puff— not inhaling—and passed it along to Joey. That wasn't so bad.

From the corner of her eye, she noted Joey did not inhale deeply either, only taking the smoke into her mouth and holding it before allowing it to slowly escape. Ronnie decided to do the same. After all, marijuana might be as bad for the lungs as tobacco. Another quick pull on the joint when it was handed back and she passed it to James.

Was he laughing at her? Not aloud but he certainly looked amused. "Where are the marshmallows?"

He reached behind himself and tossed her an unopened bag. "I brought toasting forks too. Where—oh, there they are." James handed them over. Telescoping metal, four of them. Ronnie took one and passed the others to Joey. A few seconds later, she had the first marshmallow browning over the coals.

"Thanks," she said, absentmindedly, as another joint was handed to her. She didn't know whether it was James's or Angelica's. Jam's or Jelly's. She took a deeper pull this time and passed it along.

"I haven't decided yet where to go come fall either," James was saying. To Doughnut, she assumed. "The seminary is waiting for me. Well—not exactly a seminary. Better to call it a religious college."

"As if there's a difference," commented Jelly.

"On the one hand, it does keep me out of the draft. On the other, there's the whole celibacy thing to look forward to. I am rather fond of girls." He stopped short and nodded in the general direction of Ronnie and Joey. "Make that women."

"There is always regular college, like the rest of us," Kris pointed out

"Or running off to Canada, for that matter. Or maybe go visit my mom's relatives in Cuba."

"Or you could do your service," William said.

"I don't believe the government has any right to demand that," blurted Ronnie. "It isn't—isn't—" She searched for a word. "It isn't God." It wasn't the word she wanted, she was sure. She didn't know anything about God anyway.

But James agreed. "Nationalism is a form of idolatry," he stated.

Angelica let out a dramatic gasp. "Oh, don't get started on theology."

"Okay. No golden calves this evening. But are you really considering the military, Will?"

"It has its attractions. I'd be making money and wouldn't be any sort of burden on my family. And it would pay for my college when I get out."

"Assuming you get out alive," came Kris's voice, almost too low to hear. "Don't go off and get killed on me, William Booth." Ronnie could make out a tear, just one, glistening in the dim light of the small charcoal fire.

That would be unfair. Unfair to Kris and to everyone who had cared for Doughnut. Even more unfair to him! Ronnie took a joint someone held out to her. That was a new one, wasn't it? It looked bigger.

Life was unfair. So people told her all her life. Why should it be? She'd do something about it. Yes, she would.

"You plan to keep that?" asked Joey. She handed it on to her.

"It's time we get going," said Will, rising. "Better let me drive," he told Kris.

"Okay. Have fun tomorrow!" With that the two of them wandered off into the night. Probably to Kris's Beetle.

Ronnie popped another toasted marshmallow into her mouth. Had they used up the whole bag?

"Time we wind down too," announced James, picking up his guitar. He should have played some more, felt Ronnie. She'd like to hear his voice again too.

"I'm hungry," she said. Why she told everyone this, she wasn't sure.

"We can fix that," said Angelica. "Wait here." She slapped at something. "Or in the tent."

Ronnie and Joey slipped in quickly and zipped the screen door behind them. She flipped on the little electric lantern Alan had left. A minute later Jelly came back and was admitted. She had a large bag of potato chips in each hand. "We'll have to send someone back for sodas," Joey told them but no one volunteered and they forgot about it in a minute or two.

The girls didn't say much as they shared and what they did say was not very important. Ronnie felt herself growing sleepy. She had almost nodded off when Jelly stood up. Almost up—she had to crouch a little inside the tent. Maybe Kris could stand up straight in here.

"I'm going to go sleep in comfort," she informed them. "See you, um, tomorrow night I guess." She unzipped the screen and slipped out.

Joey grunted something in return, and switched off the lantern. Ronnie was not sure she said anything at all.

Chapter Thirty-eight
Joey

"Should we bang some pots together?"

"The neighbors might complain."

"We're awake, guys," Joey called out. Tried to call. She was a little hoarse on awakening. Dry throat. She shook Ronnie. "It's time to go."

"Already? I'm not sure I ever fell asleep."

"I don't know who was snoring then." Her friend had surely slept better than she had. Joey and insomnia were old acquaintances.

"Let us pee and we'll be with you," she told the boys, on emerging. And splash some water on their faces as long as they were inside. She did hope Alan had thought to bring some breakfast. Even if it was vegetarian.

The boys were huddled by the wagon when they came out. A single surfboard was in the rooftop rack. She couldn't make out any details about it. "Ready?" asked Alan. "If you want I can flatten the rear seat and you could sack out a little longer."

"Don't bother for me," Joey responded. "Shotgun!"

She suspected Jam and Ronnie were just as willing to let her sit up front. They all settled in and Alan eased his car away from the curb and out into the night. Plenty of streetlights here. It would be dark out in the empty country between here and Florida's other coast. Dark—

Joey jolted awake. "Where are we?"

"Immokalee." This came low, almost a whisper.

She looked out the window. Still dark but there were dim-lit store fronts alongside the road. "So we are." Joey had been in Immokalee before but never at three in the morning. It had a reputation for being a rough place any time.

"We have a bunch of options from here and my brother and I have explored them all at one time or another. I'm not taking the shortest route but it might be the quickest. Up through La Belle and across to Fort Pierce."

Joey turned to peer into the rear seat. Both passengers asleep. They'd best stick to whispers.

"Coffee?" asked Alan, holding up a thermos.

Coffee! "Sure." She took it from him as he eased to a stop.

"Always make sure you stop completely in a strange town in the middle of the night," he stated. "The cops need something to break their boredom and a car with surfboards on top is a favorite choice. There are paper cups right there." He pointed as he slowly accelerated.

This guy is a lot more knowledgeable of the world than he lets on, thought Joey. She carefully poured out half a cup. "Want some?"

"Hmm, not until we're closer to a rest room. By the way, I put a fair amount of milk in there, the way I like it."

"Okay with me." Joey rarely drank coffee at all. "You could always pull over. I'll close my eyes."

She sipped the coffee as they emerged into open country. Again, not that she had seen the empty fields and swamp land between Naples and the little farming town. Joey put down her empty cup and fell back into sleep.

"What *is* that stench?" someone was asking.

She took a deep whiff. "Orange juice factory."

"That was quick," said Alan. "I thought you were asleep."

"Was. We must be near Lake Okeechobee, right?"

"Not too far."

James leaned forward to talk to them. "Smells like they're burning the oranges. And letting them rot first."

"Maybe they are," Alan answered. "Never been in one but driven by a bunch of times." He glanced into the rear view mirror. "Waking up, Ronnie?"

"Ummumm," she answered. "Do I have to?"

"Not for at least another hour. But if you are awake, there are snacks in that box behind you."

She turned around, kneeling on the seat, and dug into the cardboard box. "Granola? Who snacks on granola? Ah, fruit. I don't think I could eat an orange with that smell."

"We could always stop in Okeechobee. Hmm, no, probably nothing much open yet. We passed through La Belle while you all were asleep."

"Who wants an apple?"

"Send one up here," said Joey. "Where do you stop?" she asked.

"Fort Pierce, most often. At least for the public restrooms in one park or another."

"Ooh, candy bars! That makes up for the granola. Want one, James?"

"Hand it over. And you can send some of that coffee back here, Joey."

On into the darkness Alan steered the big station wagon. Shortly, he took a right, heading east toward the Atlantic at last, and cruised through the town of Okeechobee. There might have been the slightest suggestion of light along the horizon before them when they pulled into Fort Pierce. "I've surfed here on occasion," said Alan, as they crossed a high bridge across the bay. It lay gray and motionless below them, a few lights shining across the water. Fishermen were parked along the causeway leading to it; shadows moved in the mists of morning. "Usually further north but there can be decent waves at the inlet down that way." He waved an arm toward the south.

"Are there ever good waves in Florida?" asked James. "I haven't seen much sign of them."

"Naples doesn't get much in the way of waves in the summer. Florida doesn't, really, but there's a better chance on the east coast. Up north, like Cocoa. Not Miami. The Bahamas get in the way of any summer swells there."

"So Cocoa is where we're going?" This from Ronnie.

"We'll see."

"He sounds like my dad," she said.

"One of us has to be the responsible adult," Joey told her. "I'm not volunteering!"

"And not that my dad is a responsible adult."

"Here's A-1-A," announced Alan. "That means we're officially on the coast, even if we haven't seen the water yet. We can follow this road north all the way to Canaveral." He turned left. A short distance up the road, he pulled into a little park on the left hand, illuminated by a single overhead light. "Restroom break."

That seemed an excellent idea to all. James went to look at the small embossed metal sign. "Pepper Park. Oh, named for Claude Pepper."

"Red Pepper?" chimed in Ronnie. "I've read about him."

Joey only knew the man was someone important in Florida history. That would have been enough for her not very long ago. Now she felt she should be more knowledgeable about things like that.

But *right* now she felt a need to visit the restroom. When she returned, the others seemed to be in some sort of earnest discussion. "Oh, Joey," said Ronnie. "I was telling Alan about what we talked about last night. The draft and all. He agrees with James." She turned to the boy. "I think."

Alan smiled. "I'm certainly as eager to avoid the draft. And—yeah, I get a bit miffed at the whole idea of the government having the right to ship my body off wherever it wants."

"Oh, that's looking at it from a slightly different angle," said James. "More libertarian, maybe? I'm not sure I understand patriotism, honestly. We have a duty to our country or we're supposed to love it? Why? I never heard a good answer to that. I certainly don't see morality having anything to do with it."

Ronnie cocked her head at him. "Don't you feel you have an obligation to anything?"

"Only to do what is morally right. And to people. They're real. A country is just an idea."

"Like the *logos* made real?" asked Joey. She had to laugh at his expression. "I haven't forgotten everything Catholic I learned."

"You have a point. The concept is something like that except, again, it isn't God." He grinned at Ronnie. "As our friend told us last night."

Joey sighed. "If we're going to talk about this kind of thing I need to get stoned again."

Alan raised an eyebrow at this. He had no idea what they'd been up to in his absence. He chose not to pursue the subject. "Let's hit the road again."

It grew lighter as they drove northward. Clouds were banked to their right, out over the ocean, but the skies were clear above.

Through some town. No one bothered to ask the name and Alan didn't volunteer one. Then a high bridge rose ahead of them. "Sebastian Inlet," their driver announced. "The perfect place to watch the sun rise."

He pulled onto a dirt road and brought the car to a stop in the shadows beneath the span. "It's actually illegal to surf here. Close to the jetty, that is, but that's where the waves are good." There might have been a trace of an uncharacteristic cockiness in his smile. "I've admittedly broken that law."

A pretty unlikely outlaw, thought Joey. You think you know people but they sometimes insist on surprising you.

All four strode toward the water. "It's kind of primitive, isn't it?" asked James.

"That's supposedly going to change. Whether for the better or worse, I couldn't say."

Ronnie leaned in and whispered to Joey. "Now he sounds even more like my father."

A long jetty of massive gray rocks and concrete extended into the Atlantic, beside the wide inlet, where the water flowed fast and rough with the tide. "There are loads of sharks in there," said Alan. "And out further." He nodded toward the ocean. "Yet guys persist in surfing way out there when big swells break. Most other places become unridable."

"Have you?" asked James.

"No way." He surveyed the beach. "More surf than I expected, to be honest. But this isn't the place to ride today."

Fishermen holding heavy poles at varied angles lined the jetty, black cutouts against the light of dawn. My dad would have loved this place, thought Joey. Who knows? Maybe he has fished here. She didn't know much of what he had done after the divorce. Joe Varney had pretty much disappeared altogether when her mom remarried.

"And here it comes," whispered Ronnie, as the red orb peeked over the horizon.

Chapter Thirty-nine
Ronnie

"Zinc oxide," claimed Alan, "is good both for diaper rash and blocking the sun." He was streaking a liberal amount of it on his nose and cheekbones.

He had called this place along the beach Patrick Pier. It lay across the highway from the runways at Patrick Air Force Base and, yes, there was a pier but it was long since anyone had been able to walk on it. Only a few broken pilings jutted from the water now. "These waves are barely large enough," he continued. "I'll probably get frustrated. Maybe it will improve a little as the tide changes. Or get worse."

"They look pretty big from down here on the beach," said Joey.

"I would consider them good-sized waves in Naples," he replied. "The bottom is different there. Finer sand that packs down harder, more of a gentle slope. These ones—" He nodded toward the water. "Are mushy and mostly breaking right on the shore. You getting that filled, Jam?"

James was inflating an air mattress with nothing but lung power. One of us should spell him, thought Ronnie. She didn't volunteer. "Is it safe to swim?"

"Should be but be careful. And don't get too near the old pier. There are pilings underwater that can scrape you pretty badly." He knelt and began rubbing wax on the top of his surfboard.

"That's a pretty board," said Joey. Ronnie had seen it before but was entirely willing to agree. A bit like a spear, with a floral logo on its deck.

"It's a Gordon and Smith, like the one Russ sold you. What they call their Hot Curl model. I like it. Way more than Russ's first short board, which was one of the vee-bottoms popular—well, just half a year or so ago. Boards have been changing a lot, very quickly."

"The whole world has been," Ronnie said. Changing far, far too quickly.

Maybe they all felt that way but none added anything. Alan carried his board down to the water and launched, stroking out in a prone position, hand over hand.

Joey went over to supervise James. "You'd think one of us would have the sense to bring a bicycle pump."

A red-faced James nodded in response and blew some more. "Give me that," she said and took over the process of inflation. Ronnie didn't think she was interested in trying to paddle a mat around, much less attempt to surf on it, even if Alan said people did.

She waded into the water. It did drop off quickly, didn't it? This far from the shore in Naples she would be in to her shins. Here the water came to her waist. A wave foamed and broke around her, without a great deal of force. Further out, Alan was paddling about, looking for a wave large enough to break in the deeper water. Mostly they just rose up and then backed off, maybe feathering a little. There must be a sandbar out there. Or maybe rocks.

There he caught one. Only for a moment. It flattened out too soon. Alan, undaunted—at least so far—turned around and paddled out again. There was a handful of other guys out, attempting pretty much the same thing. No girls? More girls should surf.

One of them was riding. Actually riding. When the wave flattened out—there was a deeper channel there, she decided—he pumped it back and forth with his legs and managed to get through to where it broke close to the shore. Ronnie wasn't sure it had been worth the effort.

And over the next hour more waves were ridden. Maybe they were getting better as the tide changed. Maybe they were even getting bigger. Alan rode, and rode again. Joey and James launched on their air mattress and wallowed about in the broken waves near the beach. Ronnie mostly waded, occasionally swimming along a little, not straying far out. It was nice going someplace different.

No, it was *good* going someplace different, doing something different. Cocoa Beach—was this Cocoa Beach or was that further north? Didn't matter. Cocoa Beach was good to visit but it wasn't Naples. She would always love Naples. A place. A real physical thing, as James had said one should love. The concept of Naples? That was changeable from day to day. Maybe her father loved it, his idealized 'old Naples,' but that wasn't something Ronnie really cared about. She would love the colors, the scents, the feel of the place. It existed. That was enough.

She floated on her back, watching the cars pass on the highway, well above them. She could just see them from this angle, above the high dunes. Now and again, a plane took off and passed over them, its jets thundering. All the surfers put their hands over their ears when it happened. They must be used to it.

Alan rode a wave close to the shore and paddled the rest of the way in, allowing the beach break to carry him onto the sand. "I need a rest," he declared. "And a drink."

Joey and James followed him in. "You're surfing backwards from the other guys out there," noted James.

"That's because I'm left-handed. A goofy-foot, as surfers insist on calling it." He sounded a bit like the wise and tolerant elder speaking of the rabble. "I do turn around and surf like a right-hander some-times."

"You play guitar like a right-handed person too."

"Just the way I learned. More convenient too. Most guitars are made for righties."

"You know," observed Joey, "you're just a little too competent for your own good, Mister Wesolowski. We all liked you better when you were that hesitant, bashful guy we knew in school."

He only laughed. "But you didn't know me, did you?"

James chose to disagree. "They knew some of you. Now they know more of you. See you from a different angle."

"Ah, it's all relative to the observer's position."

"Now I really need to get stoned," stated Joey.

"I'd rather eat. Something from the car, or rinse off and go to a fast food place?"

"Fast food for vegetarians?" asked Ronnie.

"Milk shake, most of the time."

"Let's hang here a while," said Joey. "We can clean up later."

Ronnie nodded her agreement. "It's a plan then," said James. The sun was still less than halfway up the sky and it was a glorious morning. They should make the most of it.

"Good enough." Alan turned and looked out over the water. "It is getting better. I'm entirely likely to leave you three to entertain yourselves while I surf some more."

"And we are not at all surprised," Joey told him. "But we do expect you to teach us how to surf someday."

Chapter Forty

Kris

"Hi!"

"Someone's waving at us," said Kris. She should probably slip on her glasses.

"Sandy." Will waved back to the girl.

"Bugging Jelly, no doubt. Shall we go to the rescue?"

"I don't think we can pretend we didn't see her. Ronnie's car is still here," he noted.

"Didn't expect them back before dark. Hey, Jelly."

Angelica, ensconced in a lawn chair, languidly raised a hand in greeting. "Didn't you drive?"

"Walked over from my place. It's not far."

"And not raining." Will looked to the cloudy sky. "For now."

Sandy gazed upward too. "It might be clearing. I'd better get on my way home."

Angelica gave the girl a mildly interested glance. "Walking too?"

She nodded. That was a good distance further than Kris and Will had come. A dozen blocks or more.

"I'll ride you over on the scooter." Angelica rose and stretched. "Maybe meet this brother of yours I've been warned against!" Sandy giggled at that. "You guys make yourselves at home. The parents have gone off to some sort of party somewhere."

The two headed toward the garage. "I saw you give Jelly the once over when she got up. You know you're only supposed to have eyes for me."

"She intended for me to look." Will pondered something for a moment. "But maybe not consciously?"

To be sure, Angelica had been a bit blatant. But maybe no more than usually! "Are you a psychologist now?"

"There are worse career choices."

Kris didn't really know what Will intended to study, did she? He'd never spoken about it and she hadn't pried. "Do you know what you want to do with your life, Will?" she asked.

"Honestly, no. That's another reason I've been—hesitating."

Hesitating. They'd both been hesitating. It was time that ended. All they had for certain was this summer; let come what may in September, that would remain.

The sound of the scooter revving reached them. "There they go," she said. "Shall we go in and raid the kitchen while everyone's away?"

"Missus Cooper is likely to still be here."

"Missus Cooper?" Kris had no idea whom he meant.

"Sylvie. Not that she wouldn't feed us if we asked but, ah, I don't think she approves of us."

"But Sylvie always seems so understanding. She puts up with Jam and Jelly!"

"She works for their parents. I know she wouldn't say anything to us, not here, but I would also know she was judging me."

Well, she wasn't going to make Will uncomfortable. "Let's go down to the beach."

The sand was relatively empty, the afternoon storms having sent most beach-goers home. Some would venture out now, the sunset walkers. Night would send them back to their houses, too, to lights and dinner and beds. To families, most. Who knew about some of those lonely walkers, solitary surf-casters, the ones who lingered into the darkness? Did they have anything, anyone, to go home to? Maybe that was why they stayed long.

Will and she went only as far as the pier and turned back. After all, they'd already had a walk this afternoon. They would need to walk back to her home again later, where Will's truck sat. No hurry on that. No hurry at all.

And they did not hurry back to the Summerlin house, dawdling along the way. "We timed that right," said Will as they came up from the beach. Jelly was riding up the avenue from the other direction.

She circled and throttled back, to putt along beside them. "I left Weather Girl in front of her house. No sign of the alleged nerd brother."

"Nerd? I don't think I've ever heard that word before."

"I have," spoke up Will. "That's people like Ronnie. Alan too, I reckon. Bookish."

"Sort of," agreed Jelly. "Or artistic, sometimes. Socially inept, as a rule, and sometimes oblivious of it. Kris is the anti-nerd."

"Um, I guess I should take that as a compliment?" A bit backhanded, as was typical between Jelly and her.

"You're annoyingly well-adjusted," Will told her.

Angelica burst into laughter. "I could never have put it better! I'll get this back in the garage now." She gunned the scooter and sped away, to turn a few seconds later onto the little gravel drive behind the garage, hidden by the tamarinds and the hibiscus hedge.

"Angelica sounded a lot like her brother when she explained the word," he said.

"Even I wouldn't tell her that to her face." It was true though. She was every bit the intellectual Jam was, even if she didn't let people see it. She might well be smarter than her brother. Why shouldn't she be?

That didn't count for much if one didn't use the gifts they were given. "So I'm boring and normal?" she asked.

"That's why I love you," Will said, leaning down for a kiss.

Had he ever said he loved her before? Not that she didn't know! She might be willing to give him a pass on the rest.

An older car was backing out where the scooter had just pulled in. "Sylvie," said Will. "She was probably waiting for Angelica to get back." The girl emerged from the back of the house a couple minutes later. They had already taken seats at one of the tables in the yard.

"You look like you're ready to order," said Angelica. "Am I supposed to be your waitress?"

"Let us in and we'll find something of our own," Kris replied.

"Come on then. Don't expect me to cook like my brother."

"I can. Hey, is that too ordinary? Will thinks I'm boring!"

"That I don't believe." She gave the young man a sly look. "He sometimes seems pretty, ah, excited when he's close to you."

You couldn't tell if Will was blushing, but Kris guessed he was. She might be burning a little herself. Angelica always seemed able to do things like to her.

"All right, Miss Summerlin. But really, am I too, well, conventional?" She asked this of both or maybe of neither. Of herself, mostly.

Will pretended to give the question deep consideration. "You do come from a pretty conventional family. Complete with a stay at home mom."

"You mean a stay at country club mom."

"We both have one," Angelica pointed out. "The same country club, too."

"I don't think they're friends when our dads aren't around."

Jelly seemed almost pensive for a moment. "I hate to say this, but my mom carries a lot of baggage from her upbringing in Cuba. Prejudices."

"Against Jews?" wondered Will.

"Uh-huh. She's not so big on your people, either. She'll confide that you were much better behaved when she was growing up." Kris wasn't quite sure how to take that. It was dreadful but also just a little humorous. "But Daddy makes up for it."

"That's true," admitted Kris. Will nodded agreement. They trooped into the spotless kitchen.

"Sylvie won't like it if we mess the place up," she said.

"Oh, James messes it up every morning before she arrives. He's the only one who eats early, most of the time." Angelica turned to her. "You don't really want to cook, do you?"

"Nah. Something in a bag with too much salt would be fine. And something sugary to rinse it down."

"She does not eat well at all," asserted Will.

"There are cokes in the fridge. Or pop or sodas or whatever you prefer to call them."

"You hear them all in Naples. People come from all over."

"The same in the schools I was stuck in." Angelica perused the contents of the refrigerator. "Beers too. Oh." She shut the door and opened the freezer compartment. "Ice cream. I want ice cream."

"Floats! We'll make floats!"

Angelica set out two cartons of Sealtest ice cream, chocolate and vanilla. Kris was already searching through the cabinets for proper spoons and bowls. "Get some soft drinks, Will. Root beer if there is any."

He searched through the fridge. "Just Cokes. Oh, and RCs. I'll bet your father drinks those, Angelica."

"Yep. Bring the Cokes."

Half an hour later, they lounged on the porch, thoroughly sated. Angelica's guitar was in her arms. "I'm just going to sit here and prac-tice my scales," she told them. "Go get in trouble somewhere."

The two wandered out into the darkened yard, hand in hand. "We could walk back to your house now," suggested Will.

A lethargic nod. "Yeah. I kinda wanted to wait for our surfers to come." She wasn't about to admit it but Kris was just a little worried about them. She'd feel better knowing they were home safe.

"No hurry. I guess it can wait. But this can't."

He took her in his arms. Lips met hers and then brushed down her neck, found where her tee shirt hung loosely off one shoulder. Her hands slipped inside his own tee and up his back, sliding across its broad sinewy expanse. She felt him shiver in response to her touch, her fingertips gliding back down to his narrow waist.

His left hand cupped one breast while the other arm encircled her, his mouth still exploring her skin. She stepped back and pulled her shirt off over her head. As she often did, she had worn her bathing suit under her tee and shorts. They might yet swim tonight passed through her head for some reason, before they again embraced.

His lips found the valley of her breasts. Her head arched back in sudden pleasure. "Your shirt too," she managed to whisper. Off it came and her mouth, her tongue, found the muscular chest, toyed with one nipple and then the other. Her hands now slipped down the back of shorts, felt the tight muscles of his buttocks, and worked their way around to discover the fully engorged manhood. One lingering stroke only she gave it as she withdrew her hands, causing Will to gasp in ecstasy.

She felt his fingers busy with the strings of her bikini top. "Not here," she whispered. "The mosquitoes would eat us up!"

"I'll eat you up," he half-growled in response. He turned his head toward Alan's tent. "In there."

"Yes." A few seconds later they were kneeling inside, ready to at last fully share themselves. In the distance, Angelica's guitar sang in the night.

Later, as they held each other, the moonlight filtering in on their naked bodies, they heard voices, doors slamming. "They're back," whispered Kris.

Will whispered back, "They don't have to know we're here."

"Yes, that's best. Let me take a peep." She knelt and peered out through the screen. "There go Ronnie and Joey in the Simca. And Alan's following them."

"Damn, you look good in that light, girl," said Will. "Come here."

"Again?"

"One for the road?"

She giggled and returned to her lover. But they had to leave sometime. It certainly wasn't yet midnight when they crept from the tent. The house looked dark. It was likely Preston and Maria Summerlin had returned and were in bed. As they crossed the lawn, hand in hand, a figure rose from one of the lawn chairs. Jam.

"Angelica told me you were here." His voice was even, expressing no emotion one way or another.

Will nodded mutely. He might have been uncomfortable. "And now it's time we go," said Kris. To her house and Will's truck. It wasn't that late. Her parents would think nothing of it.

"I'll walk with you," James offered. "For appearance sake."

It was a good idea. Darkness swallowed the three figures as they strolled into the soft summer night.

Chapter Forty-one
Joey

"And you were right there in the tent? Both of you?"

"Well, yeah. It takes two, you know."

"Not necessarily!" Her joke didn't get the response she might have hoped. Ronnie might even have blushed. It wasn't like they all didn't do it! Did Ronnie fantasize about Alan? Or someone else maybe.

"It's as well we didn't know," opined Ronnie

"And we won't ask for details." That didn't mean she wouldn't have liked to hear them. Some of them. "So where from here?"

Kris didn't quite sigh. "I wish I knew." It was followed by almost a giggle. "I'll tell Alan to leave the tent pitched the rest of the summer!"

"I don't think the Summerlins would approve," Ronnie said, pretending to take the idea seriously. "He already took it down this morning, anyway."

"Maybe the two of you can share it the next time," said Joey. She definitely blushed now.

Kris only smiled slightly. "Enough about tents. Will and I will figure things out." She might not be as sure of that as she was trying to sound. "So tell me about your day."

Thunder rumbled outside, rattling the windows. Those were very old Florida style, jalousies. Was this house as old as the Deerfields'? Both might have been built in the early Fifties. Maybe even the late Forties. That kind of thing could be looked up. There would be records somewhere.

She let Ronnie tell most of their story. Alan was her boyfriend, after all, and had invited her. Not Joey and Jam. He'd only tolerated their presence. Alan was a tolerant guy.

"When we were done playing in the water," Ronnie was saying, "we showered off outdoors at another spot just up the highway. It was late morning by then."

"Ten-thirty," Joey interjected. "If we'd stayed out longer we'd be even more sunburned."

"No place to change clothes but Alan did it in a towel. None of the rest of could bring ourselves to do that."

"Didn't matter much. Our suits dried pretty quickly."

"And then he drove us around and pointed out stuff. Points of interest. Like that big surf shop."

"Ron-Jon's."

"Yeah. We went in there. Nice to be in the air conditioning. And we went by the pier and all the way up to Port Canaveral and watched the big ships coming and going."

"Sounds like a lot to do in one day," commented Kris.

Joey collapsed back onto the couch. "Yeah, we're exhausted." There was some truth to that.

"But best of all was when he drove us along the island that runs down the middle of the bay when we started back. Merritt Island. It's almost as beautiful as Naples!"

Maybe it was. And it had that relaxed feel Naples seemed to be losing. It would probably disappear there too.

"So, seriously," said Kris, "are you going to go on a longer trip with Alan one of these days?"

"I—I don't know." Ronnie looked uncomfortable with being put on the spot. "I don't know about Alan at all. He can be—distant, sometimes."

Joey nodded. "Self-contained. It's like he doesn't really need anyone and is just putting up with us."

"Exactly. Or forgetting we were there! I could see that better yesterday, when he was, um, what? On his home turf, maybe. Something like that."

"His home surf, you mean." Ronnie had it right. But he was really the same Alan and Joey thought he was a pretty good guy. Ronnie had lucked out with him.

"Is your mom going to be home soon?" Kris asked.

"Working an evening shift. I'll have to fix something for Wayne to eat when he gets home. That'll be a couple hours yet."

"No point in trying to go anywhere then. Raining too hard anyway."

That it was. "Mom's been hinting I'd better look for a job myself. Not right now, but in the fall." Fall—she didn't want to think about it yet. "It would have to fit my class schedule."

Ronnie's mind might have been wandering but that brought her back. "My dad said he might have a job for you. I'd forgotten all about that!"

Deerfield's office wasn't too far from her home. It might be worthwhile to go over there and see if he was serious about it. Not for a while.

"So, who is up for the beach in the morning?"

Chapter Forty-two
Kris

She wondered idly what Mackie was up to. It had been weeks since she'd seen him, hadn't it? On the Fourth. Okay, two weeks. His boyfriend might have gone home by now.

Boyfriend. Wow. That still seemed so strange, so outside her experience. Kris had known, intellectually, about homosexuality. Shoot, one of the teachers at Naples High had been scooped up in a raid at some bar in Miami and had never returned to his job. But it had not touched her personally before Mackie.

She pedaled her Stingray around the corner and up the avenue by the Summerlin house. They always met here now when they went to the beach, didn't they? Almost always. Not the pier or Third. Wasn't that Grubby's Mini Moke there at the beach parking?

She rode up to it. He was seated behind the wheel, gazing out at the Gulf. A friendly nod as she came alongside. A distracted nod, maybe.

"I would guess you came to see Jelly."

"Why would I want to do that when the cutest girl on the beach is right here?"

She snorted at that. Damn, I sound like Joey, she thought. "I'll be considered cute for a few more years. Then they'll probably call me dumpy."

That was rewarded with no more than a slight smile. "Yeah, I thought maybe I'd run into her. No luck."

Kris gave him a long appraisal. "You had sex with her, didn't you?"

"Well, not exactly. She didn't want to go all the way."

No? Kris considered this. "So she blew you." She was just a little surprised to find herself speaking so frankly to the boy. But then, they'd been through some stuff.

"Yeah. And was kind of, um, feeling herself while she did. I think she got all she wanted out of it."

"I suspect she's got all she wants out of you." It was harsh but she thought it was true.

He only gave a slow nod to this. "Where are you going to college?" she asked. A change of subject could only help.

"South Florida."

"Photography still?"

"That's the plan." He reached over into the front passenger seat and lifted out a camera. 35 mm, she would guess. "I should get you to pose for me."

"With Angelica?"

"Don't put thoughts like that in my head! I can imagine it a little too well."

She had no doubt of it. "Maybe with my friends, though. Here they come." Joey and Ronnie were biking their direction. "Hey guys, wanta be in a photo shoot?"

"I have twenty-four exposures waiting to be exposed," Grubby added to this.

"And we're supposed to expose ourselves?" asked Joey, sliding to a halt beside her. Ronnie came up on the other side of the Moke.

"Within reason. It's a great morning for some beach pictures."

"In glorious color!" said Kris.

"I'm shooting black and white. Yeah, I know it was stupid to load it on a day like this but so it is."

"He was hoping for boudoir photos of Jelly," Kris told her friends.

"Ha, I could wish. I just intended to wander around and photograph palm trees and houses and whatever." He surveyed the Summerlin's yard. "Wouldn't mind shooting some in there, if no one minds."

"I doubt anyone would." Kris snickered. "Except Jelly. Let's get our bikes put away."

No one came out into the yard as they left them on the lawn near the tables. Maybe everyone was gone. It didn't matter. They had come to swim and lie on the beach. Or maybe here on the grass.

Ah, she would like to lie here on the grass with Will. She wanted to see him more, every day. All day! The trio grabbed their towels and returned to the beach.

"You're wearing swim suits under those shorts and shirts, aren't you?" asked Grubby, giving them the once over. He leaned against his little car's fender, fussing with a light meter.

"The tiniest of bikinis," promised Joey. "We'll probably all get arrested."

"I'll document it."

"Would you prefer to shoot by the pier?" Ronnie asked.

Grubby looked down the beach and shook his head. "Distracting. I want the focus to be you girls. Nothing but sand and water and you."

For some reason, Kris felt a little self-conscious stripping down to her reasonably modest suit, a suit she'd worn dozens of times on the beach without thinking about it. It was the presence of the camera. Ronnie felt it too, she was sure. Joey? Hard to tell. Joey might be just a bit of an exhibitionist. At least when the mood took her.

"Water behind you. Hmm, too much glare at that angle." Grubby moved about, attempting to find the best vantage. "Yes, that'll do. You recline over there Kris. Yeah, up on one elbow is great. Joey, stand behind. Hmm, where you're sitting is fine, Ronnie." His Minolta clicked once, twice. "Could you raise your arms, Joey? No. Ah, that's it." More clicks.

"Now one with you making out. Ha, just kidding. Got you to smile!" Click. Click.

"You have a motor drive in that thing?" asked Joey.

"Sure do. I don't want to waste time winding by hand. Single pictures? No?" He lowered the camera. He might have been thinking of snapping a candid shot or two but seemed to decide against it. Grubby was trying to be on good behavior.

"If you want to shoot at the house, I'll walk up with you so no one thinks you're a trespasser," volunteered Kris. "See you in a few minutes," she told her friends.

"The house itself is pretty interesting," said Grubby, viewing it through his camera but not taking a shot. "Not in this light, maybe. This side is all in shadow." Kris walked a short way into the yard before realizing Grubby was no longer with her. Had something caught his attention? She turned to see him point the camera at her.

"Had to get one," he said, lowering it with a grin. "Maybe Doughnut would like a copy."

Grubby spent a couple minutes photographing palm tree shadows and hibiscus bushes. He didn't seem particularly enthusiastic about any of it. Maybe just finishing off the roll of film. Maybe hoping Angelica would come out.

She didn't. "That's enough." They headed back to his Mini Moke and a minute later he had driven off. Kris returned to her friends, sprawling on their towels, Ronnie supine, Joey prone.

"Been in the water? I think I'm going to swim."

"We had enough of that a couple days ago," answered Joey. But Ronnie was already on her feet. "Oh, why not?"

Why not indeed? The opportunities for it dwindled, day by day. They splashed, they swam, they went up on the beach again to lie in the sun.

A shadow fell across her. Kris looked up to see Jam crouching on the sand. "Didn't see you at the house," she mumbled.

"I've been doing some reading and my sister is out somewhere doing something. Oh, Joey, my other sister sent you a letter. Here, as predicted."

Joey got up on her elbows. "I had my doubts she would write at all. Now I suppose I'll have to write back."

"Don't rush to do it." He rose. "See you later."

"We should go get rinsed off in a while," said Joey. She lay down again, the summer sun shining on her tanned back

"In a while," agreed Ronnie.

Chapter Forty-three
Ronnie

"So you're really planning to go to the convention?"

"As part of a group. An acquaintance of your father is going as a sort of chaperon, Kris. Robert Mills."

Kris wrinkled her nose. "Bob? He wouldn't be protesting. He's a Young Republican!"

"Just wants to hold a sign outside the convention center supporting his candidate. I didn't ask which one." James looked around the circle. "Does anyone else want to come?"

Joey spoke up. "I'm not interested in waving a sign but it could be interesting to write about. Hey, Grubby could come and take pictures."

Angelica made a face at this. Ronnie knew why. Of course, Kris had filled her friends in on what she had learned. That was the sort of thing they did, share, but maybe she shouldn't have this time. All three had pretty much agreed that Angelica's encounter with Grubby was probably a matter of impulse on her part.

"I think I'd like to go," she said.

James nodded. "How about Alan? We could use his wagon!"

"I don't know." She doubted he would be willing.

"Not for me," stated Kris. "And not for Will."

"Okay. Where are your boyfriends today?"

"Will's going to some dinner with his family. Church stuff," Kris answered.

Ronnie said only, "Working." Kennel duty this afternoon and evening. Someone had to do it and the two of them had gone out last night, after all.

"I'm still thinking about it," Angelica said. She glanced toward Ronnie for some reason. Then her eyes went to Sandy Penn. "I doubt they would let you go."

"I'll bet my brother would want to! He's all into activism and service and, you know, that kind of thing."

"You are yourself, aren't you?" asked Ronnie. They'd been in some of the same clubs in school.

"Uh-huh. It's important to be, don't you think?"

"I suppose. Maybe that's why I'm planning to be a lawyer." She had to smile a bit sheepishly and add, "Or thinking about it. Hey, don't you have some official duty to attend to this afternoon?"

"Oh, sure. Flying! Russel should come by and pick me up any minute now." A horn honked. "And there he is! No time for him to come visit. Bye!"

Sandy ran to the nondescript gray sedan—Ronnie had no idea of the make—and climbed in. She waved all the way to Gulf Shore.

"So I miss the mysterious Russel once again," murmured Angelica, standing at her elbow. Then, "Would you like to come by my father's office with me? You could talk to him about being a lawyer or just soak up some of the atmosphere."

Why not? "When?"

"Tuesday morning?" Ronnie nodded so the Summerlin girl went on. "Come by the house and I'll go over with you. Wear something, mm, a little dressier than we usually do. Daddy expects to see me in shorts but maybe you should aim higher!"

What in the world would be suitable? Hey, it's a couple days yet, she told herself. Don't panic. Not yet. "He's already seen me in a bikini," she said. What a stupid thing to blurt!

But Angelica laughed aloud. "I'm sure he has no complaints about you and your friends hanging around the place in your bathing suits. But that wouldn't quite be appropriate for the office!"

Ronnie had to giggle herself at the thought.

"Hey, you two," James called. "Get your guitars out."

"My brother has been secretly practicing," Angelica whispered to her. "Don't believe him when he tells you he's reading or studying."

"James lie? That's no way for a future priest to act."

"I still don't believe he'll end up in a Roman collar." More seriously, she added, "He really is having one of those religious crises, I suspect. A struggle with belief. Or with identity, maybe."

Ronnie nodded. "Life's confusing." She gave the young woman a sidelong look. "Are you religious, Angelica?"

"I haven't decided yet."

Rain began to sprinkle. Large drops were pelting them by the time they gathered their things and took refuge in the screened porch.

Ronnie looked out at the thick dark clouds. "I wouldn't want to be up in an airplane in this weather."

"I don't think I'd want to be in an airplane with Sandy in any weather," quipped Joey.

"Don't be unkind," spoke Angelica, low and evenly. "The girl is harmless and I think she has something of a crush on someone."

James, of course. They'd all figured that out. Ronnie took her cheap little guitar from its case. Maybe she could talk her dad into lending her his some day. "We've both been practicing more, I understand," she said to James.

"Maybe we should practice together," came his reply. "Work up some songs."

She definitely liked that idea when she heard it. Then she caught herself. Did she like it because of James? Shouldn't she want to play guitar with Alan? They did sometimes, after all. She gave a little tenta- tive nod, and felt guilty.

That fell away when they sat down and started playing. Not that she could keep up in any way with the Summerlin siblings. James might not be nearly as good as his sister but he was far beyond her. They were natural musicians. They could play by ear where Ronnie needed to learn from a piece of paper.

But that was true of Alan too, and he was pretty good. He'd once told her he had never understood music till he saw it written out as notes. Then it made sense to him. He'd confided something of the same sort about language itself, that he'd not spoken much as a child until he learned to read and truly *know* words.

Alan was an odd sort. There was no denying that. She sometimes suspected people said the same about her. Then again, probably not. She kept herself too well in rein for that, did what was expected of her. Maybe she was just a female Russel Penn. My, what a dreadful thought!

"What are you smiling about?" asked Kris.

"Just a strange thought I had." What were they playing now? She

188 One Summer in the Sun

was lost. Ronnie put her guitar aside and listened a little while.

"Good place to take a break," said James. Angelica nodded an agreement. "You guys hungry?"

"Not that we're inviting you to Sunday dinner," said his sister.

Joey stood up. "Maybe we should get out of the way."

"Agreed," said Kris. "I could probably still catch dinner at my house." Thunder rattled the metal roof. "Good thing we all drove!"

Ronnie tried not to sigh. She might have liked to hang around longer. But Joey had ridden with her from her house so if her friend was ready to go home, then she'd better be too. And maybe they were imposing.

"Say, Kris," spoke Jam as they gathered their belongings, "did Lin have much to say?"

"Not a whole lot. She asked about my writing."

"Are you writing?" asked Angelica.

"Yeah. A lot, really." She didn't seem eager to add to that.

They sprinted through the rain to their cars.

Chapter Forty-four
Joey

The electric clock was noisy. Joey had noticed this before when she lay awake in the middle of the night. She turned her head to look at its lighted dial. One AM. Monday, now.

She had managed an hour or two of fitful sleep since turning in. Maybe too early, only nine, but she'd felt tired. She had insisted Ronnie drop her off at her home after leaving the Summerlins. Sure, she would always be welcome in the Deerfields' house but she had felt too restless to sit with them, share their Sunday dinner, hang out in the living room or Ronnie's bedroom.

No reason to lie here. She was half-inclined to go get on her bike and ride around the darkened streets. Definitely unsafe. Walking would be better. It had stopped raining sometime. She reached out to turn on the little bedside lamp and retrieved a folded letter from her nightstand.

Joey had spoken truly. There wasn't much in Lin's letter. But she had written. She had taken the time to remember the girl she'd briefly known before returning to the big city, to her important job. Important in Joey's eyes, no matter how much Lin protested, claimed to be no more than a flunky.

She had written a little about that job. Mostly a few small complaints, a dig or two at her fellow employees and their bosses. Not a word about her own writing. Joey wondered if she had shown anyone what she had written while in Naples. She hadn't even shown any of it to Joey.

But she had read some of Joey's literary attempts. Literary—that was a good snooty sort of word. Lin used it. She'd make sure she did herself from time to time!

She would keep up her own writing. Send any of it to Lin? Joey was less certain of that. She would take Jam's advice and not reply too quickly. Lin was busy, she was sure, and didn't need the annoyance of frequent letters. But she would write. Maybe she should start a letter right now. Or maybe just write.

As she'd told her friends, she'd been writing a lot. Friends? Jelly had been the one who asked about it. They had known each other a long time but that didn't mean they were actually friends. Jam, yes, and more so than in the past. This summer had changed things. Jel and Kris actually seemed to have become friends, though their long-time rivalry remained obvious. Maybe that was more show than real, now. Parts the two enjoyed playing.

Ronnie too. The Summerlin kids had practically adopted her. That might even be a good thing. They would all have new friends, new *lives*, soon. College and then careers. Husbands! Or at least lovers. She replaced the pad she had picked up, the pencil. She didn't have anything in her worth setting down right now. Only this restless feeling, this weariness she could not resolve into sleep.

Relax. She needed to relax, to relieve the tension that filled her body. Don't feel guilty about it, she told herself, as she slipped one hand inside her pajama pants. Um, yes. Images flitted through her head. Boys. Men. Grubby? The thought of him and Angelica. No details, just a blur. She did know the surfer was well-endowed. Kris hadn't held that bit of information back. Joey didn't have a lot to compare him with and couldn't quite envision him. Her left hand played with an erect nipple. Oh! That's it. James? Grubby had morphed to Jam. But not with Angelica! Gross. That thought was banished. It had aroused her more than she was comfortable with.

No images now, just the dim ceiling above her and the sensations of her own body. Let it build, let it build. Yes. Did she say that out loud? Mustn't wake Mom and Wayne. She gasped with pleasure, with the rush, the thrill, the climax.

A deep breath. Her body slowly relaxed. Did gratification come too easy for her? She heard about women having difficulty reaching it. Read about it. What would it be like when she finally did have sex with a man? Real sex. The whole nine yards. Or however much. Would it actually be different?

Twenty after One the clock read. She'd better slip into the bathroom and clean up a little. She needed to pee anyway.

Then maybe she could sleep.

Chapter Forty-five
Ronnie

She was glad she wore trousers. A dress would not have worked nearly so well perched on the back of the little red scooter, zipping down the street with her arms wrapped around Angelica, and holding on for dear life.

They could have walked. It was only something like half a dozen blocks.

Angelica had put on pants too when she spied Ronnie's. Bell bottoms, as she wore the night she had first visited the Summerlin home, the night of the barbecue. Long ago it seemed already though it had only been at the beginning of summer. A month ago.

Down Third Street Angelica steered her scooter, past the theater and the *Beach Store*, past the new prestigious shops springing up along this way, once the heart of old Naples. She pulled up onto the side-walk with no acknowledgment of the illegality and chained the machine to the metal handrail by a low flight of concrete steps leading up from the street level. "*Summerlin and Summerlin* is at the rear of this little courtyard," she informed Ronnie. "First floor. Daddy's clients are all too old to be climbing stairs."

"Is your grandfather likely to be there?" Ronnie asked.

"Almost never and certainly not this early. When he started the firm this building wasn't even here. He had his office in an old wooden building over that way." She waved her right hand.

Torn down now. Ronnie knew about this. It was likely she knew more of Naples history than Angelica. Angelica pulled the oak door, marked only with a small brass placard, open. Ronnie followed her into the cool, dim interior.

"Good morning, Miss Summerlin. Your father is expecting you. Go right on in." The secretary gave Ronnie a bit of a curious look but made no comments.

Preston Summerlin rose as the girls entered his sanctum. Ronnie could glimpse what was probably a library and conference room through an open door before taking a seat beside her guide. The chairs were surprisingly comfortable, covered in a plush dark green fabric. No leather here.

His deep voice, his southern accent, were as attractive and as soothing as ever. "Welcome to *Summerlin and Summerlin*, Ron. Angelica told me she was going to bring you by—and that you are planning to enter the law profession."

Ron? He'd got that from Angelica. No one else called her that. "Thank you, sir. I hadn't expected to come by scooter!" Did that sound too artificial? Ronnie always worried about coming off that way at times like this. Of sounding somehow fake.

"Ah, the scooter. That was a reward for settling down and finishing school." A slight, fond smile. "And maybe a bribe to get my daughter to decide on her future."

"I should take a year off, like James," claimed the daughter.

"I think you already did, just in pieces rather than all at once."

Ronnie was unsure how to react to that, attempted to keep a straight face, until Angelica laughed. Then she allowed herself to smile.

"I still have hopes you'll study law. You're my only hope for a third generation of Summerlins in this office." Ronnie was pretty certain Preston was not being serious with that statement. Not completely.

Angelica shrugged. "It might actually happen, Daddy. But there's always the music."

Mister Summerlin nodded gravely. "Angelica is quite talented," he told Ronnie. "I've no doubt you are aware of that. Some of her teachers have felt she should apply to Julliard."

Angelica did not appear to favor that idea. She chose not to respond to it.

"So," he said, "you'll be taking what they call pre-law these days? We didn't specialize that early when I started out. Just a straightforward liberal arts education."

"That's pretty much what I'll do, sir. A degree in—well, whatever my advisor thinks is best."

"Political science," suggested Angelica.

"Or history," said her father. "That's what I went with. At the

University of Florida, I might add. That's where you'll be attending, isn't it?"

"Yes, sir." Ronnie had already mulled over these choices, more than once, and knew none of it mattered that much and even less when she was a freshman. She could stick with the English degree she'd chosen for her application.

"Let me show you around," the lawyer said, rising from his high-backed chair. "And if you are still interested in pursuing law next summer, we can discuss things then." His eyes went to his daughter. "That goes for both of you."

As they stepped out of the office, fifteen or twenty minutes later, Angelica confided, "Honestly, I could see myself as a small town lawyer. Joining a big firm in a big city sounds like far too much work."

This was something Ronnie had not even thought about. "If we both passed our bar exams," Angelica went on, "we could be Summerlin and Deerfield. Hmm, no, Summerlin, Summerlin, and Deerfield. We'd have to keep Daddy on as a figurehead."

If the eldest Summerlin, Conrad, were still around it would have to be Summerlin, Summerlin, Summerlin, and Deerfield. She didn't think she'd bring that up. Becoming partners was just some fancy of Angelica's anyway. She'd have a different one next week.

The scooter had them home shortly. Angelica chose not to put it away in the garage but rode it across the lawn, up to the porch door.

"Come on upstairs," she invited. "I need to get back into summer clothes. Did you bring a change with you?" Ronnie nodded. "Sensible," was Angelica's only comment.

It might have held more meaning than that one word. Ronnie was always the sensible one, the one who looked ahead. She knew this about herself and maybe Angelica recognized it too. The Summerlin girl gave a little wave to someone as they went past the kitchen entry, Sylvie maybe, or even her mother, before they climbed the staircase. Ronnie had never been upstairs before.

She followed Angelica into her room. It didn't look very personal-ized, more like the guest room it had been all the years Angelica had attended one boarding school or another. It lay on the west end of the house, with a view of the long green lawn and the Gulf beyond. What a wonderful place to live! She would love to wake up to that vista.

"Is James around somewhere?" Maybe in the room at the other end of the hall. Its door was shut. And those doors across the hall must be Maria and Preston's suite.

"He took off early on his bike. No one here but us girls. I wouldn't be all that surprised if Sandy happened by." Angelica rummaged in one of her dresser drawers. "What do you think of Sandy? You and your friends."

"We all think Sandy might have a crush on your brother."

Angelica straightened up, took a step toward her. "Then you're all misreading. Sandy has a crush on me."

On Angelica? She immediately sensed the truth of it. In fact, it was kind of obvious.

"I know," continued Angelica. "I've seen enough of it at the all-girl schools I've been stuck in. And it usually doesn't mean anything. Usually." An enigmatic little smile came and went. "I certainly wouldn't take advantage of Sandy," she murmured. "On the other hand—"

She pulled Ronnie close and pressed her lips to hers.

"I'm not a lesbian." Ronnie backed away.

"Neither am I. That's no reason we can't have some fun."

"No." Then more decisively, "No."

Anger? Something more? Ronnie couldn't read Angelica's emotions, what lay behind those lowered brows, that twist of the mouth. "I'll bet you'd put out for my brother," the girl spat out. "Your little virgin twat is probably throbbing for him right now."

Ronnie could feel her face burning. She attempted to hold back tears.

Angelica's shoulders sagged, almost as if she were deflating. "Oh. You really do like him, don't you?" She shook her head. "Sorry, I go over the top sometimes. Doctor Jelly and Miss Hyde. Forget me coming on, okay? I'm just frustrated and horny and, oh, stuff. Just get out of here." She sat down on the bed and began sobbing.

Ronnie hesitated but knew there was no good way to try to comfort her. She slipped out of the room.

Chapter Forty-six
Kris

"I wish I could go," said Donny.

"No way," replied his father. "Not even if you carried a Rockefeller sign." He turned to Kris. "I'm glad you decided against it."

"I wouldn't even know which side to be on." That was a fib. She very much intended to support the Democrat candidate come fall, whoever he might be. Chances were Dad knew that.

"But your friends are going," said her mother.

"So they say. I'm not so sure of it." She reflected a moment. "Except James Summerlin." She might have snickered, just slightly. "I'd trust him more than Bob Mills."

"I might too," her father admitted, "but his presence reassures certain adults. Summerlin's not going to stay with him though, is he?"

"He has family in Miami." Kris assumed that his friends—her friends—would be welcome in their homes too. "I'm not sure how he's getting there though. The boy can't drive!"

Tom Greene chuckled. "That might be why he needs to travel with friends."

Possibly. Jelly drove, to be sure, but she was still up in the air about it all. She wasn't really sure Jam couldn't drive, was she? She just knew he didn't have a license.

That came to much the same thing. "Ronnie drives, of course. She still plans to go."

"Not in that toy car of hers, I hope," said her mother.

"Hey, it's as big as mine, Mom! I need to go change."

"William?"

"Yep." They were used to Will coming by now. Best they didn't know how serious it had become. She went to her room. Bathing suit? Might as well take one—hmm, the green one—but she wouldn't wear it under her clothes this time. It was unlikely they'd get in the water. It was already going on evening. That one-piece culottes affair? She hadn't worn it since school let out. It was a dodge the girls had employed to wear the forbidden shorts to school without technically wearing shorts. She slid into it.

Ronnie—her friend had asked her advice on birth control. That she was embarrassed Kris could tell but the girl managed to brazen through it. She hoped she had the pills she needed now. If she needed them. Best to be safe about that, wasn't it? Maybe Ronnie was thinking—or even hoping—she and Alan might happen. Half-hoping maybe.

But Alan had turned down the notion of going to Miami with her. "He says he's going to use that week for a long surf trip since I'll be gone," Ronnie had told her. "One of his surfer friends is going with him." She had seemed a bit perplexed as she added, "Grubby Rhein of all people. That means he won't be coming along either."

Kris had sensed that something else had been on Ronnie's mind, something that had happened, something she didn't want to talk about. She wouldn't pry. It might come out on its own in time.

"I don't think those two would be running around together if it wasn't for us. Despite both being surfers," she had said.

Ronnie had agreed. "They certainly weren't buddies in school."

But Alan and Will had been, and Kris had not been aware of it. Where was Will? Shouldn't he be here by now?

And would they be able to have sex this time? Since first coming together they had managed to do 'everything but' in her car or his truck. Will did seem uncomfortable with oral sex. His upbringing, maybe? He might see it as unnatural.

Or maybe it just seemed a bit tawdry, doing it on the front seat of a car. She was willing to overlook that but Will might not be. Will was a romantic at heart. She had figured that out.

"There's Will," called Donny.

Kris reached her boyfriend before he was halfway up the sidewalk. "Let's go in your truck this evening," she said.

"Sure." Should she kiss him? She'd never done that in front of her parents. Or even their house. Oh, it could wait until they were in the truck.

Will had other ideas as soon as they settled on the bench seat. "I have something to tell you before we take off. I've decided against taking the scholarship offer." He let that statement sit there a few seconds before going on to explain. "I'm never going to be a great athlete. I'd do well enough at a little college but why waste the time on it when I should focus on my studies?"

"So—A and M?" She hoped that was the choice. Will would at least still be in Florida.

"Maybe." He seemed reluctant to add more. "It's going to be impossible to stay together, isn't it? No matter what, we'll be going off in different directions anyway." Will turned to stare through the windshield. "Soon."

Soon. She didn't like to hear him say that. "You could go to Edison, and then Florida International in a couple years. That's in Miami."

"It would be less expensive," Will admitted. Not with much enthusiasm. It was likely he had considered that choice. "Or Florida Atlantic. That's what Alan is planning after community college."

"Oh, Surfer U!" They both laughed at that. FAU had a reputation. Will cranked the engine of the Ford. A 'big six' he had informed Kris at some time, not that it meant anything to her. Guys would talk about things like that.

"So where to, ma'am?" he asked.

"A motel room?" She knew it was a stupid suggestion as soon as she said it. There were too many difficulties involved and it only made them think of the difficulties they already had. "Never mind. Let's just go down to the beach right now."

He did so without comment. Thirteenth, just south of the pier. A pretty public sort of place to park. In any sense of the word. Maybe that was Will's intention.

"There are places along the beach that are pretty private once it gets dark," she said.

"Not private enough."

"Oh, you think some midnight beach stroller would trip across us?"

He only smiled at the thought. Kris actually felt it might not be a bad solution. They would need a blanket, of course. Making love on the sand was only for the movies.

Some other time she would come prepared. "Want to walk out on the pier? We've never done that together."

Will considered that and nodded. "Maybe it is time we did."

Chapter Forty-seven
Joey

"Oh, come along. I need someone to keep me company."

"She might not come unless you do," Jam added. "And *I* need her to drive."

"I'll see if I can swing it," was all Joey was willing to promise. She could, of course; neither her mom nor Wayne would raise an objection. Chances were, they thought she was living a wilder life than she actually was. Partying with those rich kids again!

"That makes four of us then," said Jam. "I understand this Mills is bringing along a couple more."

"Young Republicans all," chirped Kris. "You'd better make them ride in his car."

"We're not sure we're going to be able to use the Electra yet."

"Oh, I'll take care of that," Jelly assured him. "The alternative is Joey's Corvair."

"Heaven forbid. Here's a map of Miami," he said, spreading it on one of the tables. They gathered to look at it but Joey noticed Ronnie seemed to be avoiding Jel. Or maybe it was the other way around.

"We'll drive over on the Seventh, early. That way we'll only stay in Miami one night. The convention is out here on Miami Beach." He pointed toward it and then moved his finger to the western outskirts of the city. "Robert Mills has reserved some motel rooms far out from the beach. Practically halfway back to here!" Very much an exaggeration but it sounded good.

"Our aunt in Coconut Grove knows to expect us," Jam continued, pointing further south. "There should be room enough for anyone who wants to crash."

"But not Bob!"

"Yes, Kris, not Bob."

"Um," began Ronnie. "My parents insist that I stay with him in the motel."

There were sympathetic noises. "How do we get around once we get there?" asked Joey.

"I suspect we'll have to take the bus. Even if we could drive out to Miami Beach, there's no guarantee we'd find anywhere to park."

Jelly smirked. "At least anywhere we could afford. Hey, wouldn't it be great if I could take the Vespa? I'd love to ride up Lincoln Avenue on it."

"And down too, I imagine."

Joey was reminded these two inhabited a different world from the rest of them. She had let that slip from her mind this summer, forgotten the gulf between her and the twins. It was something she had been painfully aware of when younger. Something Jelly had sometimes gone out of her way to remind her of.

From the corner of her eye, she noted a car pulling in at the curb by the Summerlin's lawn. Probably just a beach-goer. They'd be filling in on both sides of the avenue on this Saturday morning.

"Daryl?" breathed Ronnie. She turned to get a better look. Sure enough, that was Daryl Sterne's deep blue Falcon. Sandy Penn leaned out a rear window and waved, then pushed at someone in the seat ahead of her, eager to exit the car. The someone was her brother, Russel.

Sandy burst out as soon as she was able and ran up to the group. "Here's Russel!" she announced, apparently to James.

"He was interested in going over with us," was his explanation. It was doubtful any of them would have asked for one.

Russel was the same Russel of a couple months ago. On the other hand, had Daryl let his hair grow? How un-Daryl like!

"Russel," said Jam, extending a hand. "Pleased to meet you. You know everyone, right? Except my sister, Angelica."

"I've heard a lot about you," said Russel. "You can guess from whom. This is Daryl Sterne." There were nods his direction. Jelly gave him somewhat of a long look, one eyebrow cocked. What was in that girl's mind now?

Oh, of course. Ronnie—or someone—would have mentioned him to her. Jelly was just the sort to remember a name or pretty much anything else she heard.

Daryl shook with Jam too. "Are you thinking of joining us?"

"No. Just giving rides today." There was a quick sidelong glance at Ronnie. Did he wonder where her boyfriend was? Oh, stop creating scenarios for yourself, Joanna Varney, she told herself. Life isn't a novel. But maybe Jo Varese could turn it into one! She almost laughed aloud at the thought.

"We've talked over the logistics," James told them. "It's mostly a matter of showing up quite early on the Seventh. Wednesday."

"Here?"

"No, at the Greyhound station," said Kris. "You'll have to pay your own way."

Russel seemed momentarily taken aback. "She's ribbing you, dummy," his sister told him.

Jam tipped his head at the girl. "Oh, your sister is almost as nice to you as mine."

"All you guys deserve far worse," maintained Jelly. Sandy might have nodded just a little too eagerly.

James got back to the question at hand. "Yes, our rendezvous will be here. Two cars most likely."

What was Kris sketching? Joey went to where she could glimpse it without looking over her friend's shoulder. Sandy. That surprised her. A caricature, all sharp angles, big eyes, a toothy grin. That surprised her even more. She moved quietly closer and then crouched beside her. "I didn't know you had that sort of thing in you."

"Neither did I. I don't think I'll show it to her."

With that she closed her sketch pad. "Hey," she announced, "I should make some signs for you guys. My work could be on national television!"

"Nothing too inflammatory," said James.

"Aw, how will I attract an audience that way?"

"Something like 'Peace Now,'" suggested Daryl.

"Make that 'Pieces Now,'" Jelly told her. "Or 'Chill the Figs!'"

"Hmm, I'll have to think about," Kris decided.

"I don't think we have anything more to talk about. Meeting adjourned," intoned Jam. "The revolutionary cell will meet again next week but the location is a secret. Who's hungry?"

"Is there any ice cream left?" asked Kris.

"I imagine so but we're not going to trust you near it." He gave Jelly a stern look. "Nor my sister."

"Wait until her boyfriend gets here. I think he ate as much as the two of us combined!" Then, "Hey, I have a brilliant, brilliant idea! So brilliant! I should let Kris and Will have my room while we're gone."

"I believe that might scandalize the parents just a little, oh sister mine."

"Not to mention Sylvie" said Kris.

"The full moon would be shining in," murmured Ronnie, and then blushed for some reason.

"Yeah, the moon will be full!" crowed Sandy. "You can demonstrate all night."

"All the TV cameras go to bed at Eleven," Joey told her. "And I'm going down to the beach right now before it gets too hot and crowded."

"Best idea I've heard this morning," said Kris.

Chapter Forty-eight
Ronnie

"Russel wouldn't look that bad if he lost a little weight. And those glasses!" It was the first time Angelica had spoken directly to her since that morning in her room.

Ronnie nodded in agreement. The awkwardness between them had largely faded away, once they were again in proximity. She wouldn't have expected that even yesterday. "Russ was bullied a little in school," she said. "More when we were in junior high."

"Russ, huh? I'll call him that from now on."

"If we haven't scared him away permanently." Both laughed at that. Angelica went to where her brother sat conversing with Russel. Maybe she wanted to practice calling him Russ.

'We' she had said. We may have scared him away. Ronnie had made herself a part of this group of friends, a group that extended beyond the little triumvirate that had so long been central to her life. Oh, of course it still was. And in a month? It might all melt away, these friends of the summer. And the friends of twelve years? She didn't know.

Daryl sat by himself at a table beyond Russel and James. Maybe she should go over and talk to him. What about? That was as much a problem now as when they had dated. Never mind. James had gotten up, leaving Russ to talk to Angelica. Now she would really like to know what those two could find in common.

Oh, James was coming over here. He took a seat beside her on the grass. "Jel told me what went down between you two. She feels really stupid about it."

"People do stupid things. You and me and Angelica and President Johnson."

"Me? I am outraged, young lady!"

"Why should you be any different?"

"Why indeed? Then you're okay?"

She was. She thought she was. Ronnie had not mentioned her

encounter with Angelica to her friends and felt that had been a good choice. Of course, she was seeing Sandy with new eyes now. This was best not mentioned either. Not even to James.

She wondered if Angelica had. "I'm okay," she said.

These past days, she had tried to rationalize it all as Angelica's impulsive nature. At first. But was she really impulsive? She wasn't like her sister, who would go off somewhere on a whim. Angelica was the sort who let things build up before acting on them. That kiss hadn't been spur of the moment; as she had said at the time, she was 'horny and frustrated.' That didn't happen all at once.

And she had let what had been friendship—yes, she was sure that was all Angelica had intended at first—become, well, something more. Maybe it could go back to where it was; not exactly the same but working all the better for having been tested. Oh, you sound like some pop psychologist, she told herself. Just let things go as they will.

James had been watching her woolgathering. For just a moment, she felt a little embarrassed, a little self-conscious. "Have you and Russel been discussing theology?" she asked.

"Folk music, actually. He's quite knowledgeable." Another glance toward Russel. Angelica had abandoned him. "You were aware he and Daryl performed, weren't you?"

"I never had the slightest inkling of it."

"It's odd how little we sometimes know of the people we know." His attention went to the street. "Your boyfriend can't find anyplace to park. He's gone up the street and back." James got up and waved to him, then gestured for Alan to follow him. Ronnie decided she might as well follow too.

He went to the little gravel drive that ran behind the garage and removed the chain that blocked it off. "In you go, sir. Please have your ticket ready for the valet when you return."

"Do we have to tip you, Jam?" asked Will, riding shotgun.

"A small gratuity is customary, sir. You might wish to give your driver something as well."

"From this tightwad?" asked Alan, emerging from the other side. "Thanks for letting us park here, James."

"Sylvie's already gone home. You won't be in anyone's way."

Alan retrieved his guitar case and waved to her. He stood looking at the wagon for a few seconds. Deciding whether to lock it up; Ronnie knew him well enough to recognize that. He shrugged and headed their way.

"Nothing worth stealing in it, is there?" she asked.

"Only wet towels and lumps of surf wax." Their lips met briefly and they joined the others in the yard. "Not much going on," he whispered to her.

"We were all waiting for you. The life of the party!"

"That is definitely a new role for me." He stopped cold. "Russ Penn? And—that's your old boyfriend, isn't it? Daryl."

"Yes." What was wrong? "You don't mind, do you? I thought you were old friends."

"Friends? Hardly. They were a part of my life for years and I don't want them to be now. I'm—I'm just fucking sick of their sort," he hissed. "Phonies." Ronnie stepped back in something close to shock. She'd never heard Alan use language like that. She'd never seen him so vehement about anything.

And maybe she understood him. "But they are here and we have to behave."

He settled down almost as quickly as he had blown up. "Yeah, I know." He gave her a smile. She did love those sweet smiles of his, didn't she? "I have to be a phony too. I'll be nice to everyone." A snicker. "As nice as usual."

"Oh, you can do better than that!" Both were still laughing when they joined the group clustered around the tables.

Russel was the first to greet them. "Alan! You're part of this bunch?" Then he apparently noticed his arm around her. "Oh!" There was an embarrassed sidelong look at Daryl. Daryl pretended he didn't see it.

"Yes, Alan is part of our group," Ronnie told him. "A founding member!" They both had to chuckle a bit again.

"We're all members of the Sophisty-kate Club," Joey added to this. She did like to trot that out.

Russel was more bewildered than ever but tried to make the best of it. "Are you going to Miami too?"

"Not me. My family is all for peaceful protest but going off to

Miami and waving a sign seems a little too—active to us."

"Oh." He looked past them. "Booth?"

"How y' doing, Russ?"

Russell looked from William to Kris. "Fine. Um, yes, fine." He grinned then. "My sister has been telling me quite a lot about some guy named Will but for some reason I never connected him with you."

"Didn't she tell you how strong and handsome he is?" asked Kris. "How could you fail to recognize him?"

"I clearly see my mistake now," he said, composure regained. That was one thing Russel was good at. He could always get himself back on an even keel.

Ronnie and Alan strolled on toward the rear of the property. Ronnie saw no reason to question why; she was just as willing to go as to not. "I apologize for earlier," he murmured. "I had sort of a high school flashback."

"You didn't like high school."

"Hated every minute of it. Hated every minute of school from the first grade on. I didn't need to be reminded of it this afternoon."

"But you're going on to college."

He stopped and gazed into her eyes. "Honestly, if it weren't for the draft I don't know if I would. Maybe I'd just, oh, build surfboards." His head lifted and he looked toward the Gulf. "Or sail off someplace. Not forgetting the girl in my home port, of course." He leaned down to linger at her lips.

"Want to go play music?" she asked, when they parted at last.

"Not really but I'm willing to."

"That's the spirit, boy."

"Hmmph. Careful or my inner curmudgeon will come out to play again."

"You keep him pretty tightly tied up most of the time."

Alan had no answer to that. James and Angelica both had their guitars out and were tuning. Maybe they should do the same.

"You guys play, right?" James asked Daryl and Russel.

"Daryl is the player," Russel told him.

"I don't have my guitar with me."

"Here, use mine." He handed over the Gibson. Daryl was clearly impressed. He took a few tentative strums and smiled more broadly than Ronnie could ever remember.

"'Tom Dooley'?" he asked Russel. A nod and he launched into the song, singing harmony while Russel carried the tune. Nothing fancy, fairly simple and straightforward strumming. Daryl wasn't really that good—not even as good as she was—but it was folk music, after all. A little raggedness was acceptable. She sometimes disliked the precision of Alan's bluegrass-inflected playing.

"What do you think of Russel's voice?" Alan whispered in her ear.

"Not terrible. Certainly not in James's league. Yes, not in yours either, so don't pout. But loud, isn't he?"

"He does project," he admitted. "Hey, you two," he said to Kris and Will, standing next to them, "I heard—eventually—what you were up to in my tent." Will looked just a teensy embarrassed. "You know, if you need it again, just let me know. Okay?"

"But where would we pitch it?" asked Kris. "I don't think we could impose on the Summerlins again." She giggled. "Not without them getting suspicious!"

"Joey's yard," Ronnie suggested. "On top of the sand spurs."

"Yeah, sure. We'll try to think of something. Hey, Jam."

"Why don't you go over and show them how it's done, Alan?" James asked.

"Um—ah."

"We all know you don't like to insert yourself. But you're among friends."

"Damn right," said Will.

"Double-damn right," added Kris.

"What the heck does that mean?" her boyfriend asked.

"Better than single-damn but not as good as triple-damn."

"Oh. I reckon that makes sense."

"You two done?" asked Ronnie. "Forget being among friends, Mister. You don't like those two. Go show 'em up."

Alan only shook his head and did as instructed. Will and Kris followed him.

James watched them for a moment. "You and I have yet to practice anything together. We could certainly give them a run for their—

hmm, not money. I doubt they've ever made any money."

"Shall we stand on a street corner somewhere and busk?"

"I have, just for the hell of it," he admitted. "The way I do most things. Alan's playing."

Yes, he was.

Chapter Forty-nine
Kris

Had the end of whatever she had with Mackie led to this complicated relationship with William? Would they ever have had sex if she hadn't felt, deep down, just a little betrayed?

But it had begun before then, before she knew. That night up at the pass? Or maybe long ago when that little shy boy came to school with his doughnut. She had liked Will from the start, more so than her friends.

"I'll need to get on my bike soon and ride home," she told him. "Alan will take you home, right?"

"Uh-huh. He won't try to hurry me. That's not Alan's way."

But he would drop hints if he grew impatient. That *was* Alan's way. "Daryl would give you a ride if you asked," she said. Or had he left already? "Or Jelly!"

"Show up at my house on the back of a little red scooter? I'd never live that down!"

"Oh, you know everyone would be looking at her. They wouldn't even notice you or what you were riding."

"Yeah. They'd be saying old Willie has traded up! Hey, don't hit me, woman!"

They sat quietly for a moment, watching the stars appear in the darkening sky. "But they don't really know about me, do they? Your family."

"About as much as yours does, I'd reckon. They haven't laid eyes on you but Sylvie Cooper is a source of information." He chuckled softly. "Of gossip might be more accurate."

"She lives in your neighborhood?"

"No, no. All we black folks don't live together, Miss Greene." His voice grew softer, more serious. "Even though some people think we should. People of both colors." Will didn't add to that for a few seconds. "Sylvie attends services at our church. Might be there right now, in fact."

Kris knew the cook had Saturday afternoons off. Sunday mornings too. "Our tent was pitched right about here. We could pretend we're in it again."

"And everyone could pretend they don't see us?"

"Oh, you would bring up a little detail like that." She leaned her head on his broad shoulder. "I want you, Will Booth. There has to be someplace here. Oh." Inspiration hit her.

"You've thought of something." Will sounded wary. Well he should!

"Come with me." They rose, hand in hand, and walked back toward the house. A few curious eyes followed them as they went on around the front of it. Let them imagine what they will, she thought.

"Alan's wagon?" asked Will. "He left it unlocked."

"Something better. And more private."

Yes, better. She imagined that luxurious white upholstery. "We're going to sneak into the garage and use the back seat of Mister Summerlin's Cadillac!"

He stopped in his tracks. "You're not serious, are you?"

"Completely."

"If he knew we'd never be able to come here again."

"You're going to tell him?" She giggled. "And Sylvie isn't around!"

He hesitated and then followed. The door to the garage was locked. Kris felt like screaming. "Damn," she muttered. "Damn!"

"Triple-damn?" asked Will.

"It's not funny!" She gave the door a kick. "Well, maybe it is, just a little. But disappointing."

"That it is."

It was dark and private here, in the dense shadows of the tamarind trees, shielded from the street lights, from the big house. She looked up through the branches. A faint glow in the second story windows. Was that Jam's room? No, his was the dark windows over to the left. His parents' room. She'd been up there a couple times, years back, before the twins had largely disappeared from Naples.

"Let's pitch our imaginary tent right here." She wrapped her arms around her lover. "Oh, you've already pitched a tent. I can feel the pole!"

The noise Will made was hard to interpret. Laughter and embarrassment and lust all rolled into one. They wouldn't be able to have 'real' sex—once again—but she was going to make the best of what they did have. Oh, they *could* do it, of course. She imagined herself with her back against the garage, Will entering her. No, no. That wasn't what either of them wanted. Not a rushed coupling here.

She unfastened his shorts. Will responded quickly, as always. "Do your part," she whispered. He would. She'd just distracted him for the moment!

His mouth found her, his hands caressed her. Her own hands found his erect shaft. Hard as a rock. A soldier at attention. Other cliches. Stop that, she told herself. Pay attention to the work at hand! She kept herself from giggling, not that Will would mind. He might not even notice.

Oh yes. He had deftly unhooked her bra, under her blouse. His fingers slipped beneath it to cup her breasts, stroke the nipples. Kris knew she had nice breasts. She sometimes was bothered by their size. They got in the way of things.

Guys certainly didn't mind them. They liked large breasts. Ha, they liked all breasts. She had to admit Will's manhood was not so large. Pretty average, going by her admittedly limited experience. The fact was, Will did not rival Grubby Rhein in this department. She couldn't help comparing them, could she? And he was so much better in every other way!

Maybe she should just masturbate him. Her hand slid up and down, the thumb caressing the head each time she reached it. He would come this way. That she didn't doubt. "Oh, that's the way," she whis-pered as Will's own hand slid down her stomach, slipped into the front of her shorts.

"Silky," he murmured, fingers stroking her thatch of pubic hair.

"Lower," she demanded. Then she slipped her own left hand in beside his, directed him to the right spot.

"Ah. Ah." Oh, the boy was getting near, wasn't he? She should finish him off properly. Gently, she guided his hand out of her pants and knelt, her mouth engulfing the throbbing shaft. It didn't take long.

Her own left hand had remained in place. It didn't take long for her either. Both breathed deeply for a few seconds.

Kris wondered if there were tell-tale stains on her shirt, her pants. Will's pants too. It was too dark to tell. "Let's go get under the outdoor shower." Their friends might be able to guess why or they might think she and Will had taken a dip in the Gulf. It didn't matter and she could ride her bike home wet. She wouldn't mind at all.

And Alan would just have to put up with Will dripping on his car seats.

Chapter Fifty
Joey

"Russel thinks you are all too frivolous. Yep, that's the word he used!"

"Oh yeah? There are a few words we could use to describe Russel."

"I'll bet!" Sandy's laugh would have been louder if her face wasn't buried in her towel.

Pompous. Pretentious. At least as annoying as his sister. Joey was not going to actually voice these. "So he's not coming with us," said Ronnie. She certainly didn't mind. Her boyfriend seemed to dislike Russ for some reason. Not that any of them were particularly fond of the guy.

Five girls all in a row, lying in the sun. Why did they do it that way? They could have been at any angles to each other. She rolled over on her side, got up on one elbow to look down the line.

The Triumvirate might have temporarily expanded but it would never become a Gang of Four. Much less Five! Not with Angelica, not with Sandy. Ronnie was at the far end, Kris beside her. A temporary separation. Another was coming, maybe permanent. Tomorrow was the start of August, the last month of their summer in the sun.

"Did you hear about Carter Jones?" asked Kris.

Carter? An older boy, a friend of Will or his family. That's probably why Kris had news. He'd shipped off to Vietnam earlier that year and had been mostly forgotten by those who remained in Naples. It was easy to forget the world here, especially on a morning like this. "What happened? He isn't dead, is he?"

"No, thank God. But he came home with one leg."

"That sort of thing is why I'm going to Miami," declared Ronnie.

"Isn't it why you're all going?" Sandy asked.

Was it why she was going? Or Jelly? Joey certainly disliked that stupid, wasteful war, but she had no claims to being an activist of any sort. She couldn't see herself marching through any streets anywhere. No, she was just going to be a pretend journalist on this trip.

You pretend too much, she told herself, and turned over. "I sort of remember a month ago Jelly was the one eager to go and Jam was reluctant. You seem to have switched."

"Don't expect consistency from me and my brother," yawned Jelly. "I'm more curious than anything else. I want to see what's going on."

"And visit one of those clubs your sister wanted to take us to?" Ronnie asked.

"I doubt we'll have the time. We should go up to New York and demand she take us clubbing there."

She was glad the two seemed on friendly terms again. Maybe she'd never know what had happened between them, not that she couldn't imagine all sorts of things. She could try writing one of them up as a story. More than one of them.

Maybe something about Kris and Will too. They had fooled no one on Saturday.

"Does your brother go to clubs?" Sandy was asking.

"Oh, he's a terrible stick-in-the-mud. My father is forever holding him up as an example to me. I hate him, you know!"

"Yeah, sure," muttered Joey.

"Well, maybe a little, anyway."

That was believable. Sort of the way she felt about Jelly herself. "He has to behave himself if he's going to be ordained."

"Like my brother," interjected Sandy. That seemed to be all she intended to say but then she blurted, "I think James scared him. He's so smart!"

"And frivolous," Kris reminded her.

"Yeah! You're all the smartest, most frivolous bunch I've ever met."

They hadn't been before hooking up with the Summerlin siblings. Just three moderately bright girls living pretty ordinary lives.

But all exceptionally attractive, of course! She sat up, resting her arms and chin on her knees, looked out across the placid Gulf waters. Swim? Not right now. She turned to the row of sunbathing girls again. Reasonably attractive, in honesty. No one would call any of them ugly. Not even skinny little, knob-kneed Sandy. Jel, to be sure, was out of their league.

Was Jam? Forget the priest thing, for now. He was a great looking guy. She'd like to see him on the beach in his bathing suit more often. She also might like him not to treat her like another of his sisters. The one he confided in. Jam was not one to confide in anyone, for the most part. She should feel honored, right?

Joey reclined on her towel, the sun shining down on her, on the last day of July.

AUGUST

Chapter Fifty-one
Kris

What was on Will's mind? He looked so preoccupied, so wrapped up in something. She could wait. It would come out sooner or later.

It did, all at once. "I signed my enlistment papers this morning. Marines. I have to report in three weeks."

Kris could only stare at him.

"You know I've been putting a lot of thought into it. I had to decide something and I decided this. It seems the best choice."

Not the marines. She felt like screaming it. Was it too late to change his mind? "You could end up like Carter Jones." Or worse. Far worse. She didn't want to think about it.

"Guys like Carter are one reason I joined up. I'm going to be a medic. I can help. Make a difference—oh, you know what I mean."

"I don't know anything." The shock was turning into anger. She didn't want to be angry with her Will.

"I've been assured of training as a medic," he continued, "assuming I can pass all the tests. It might be useful when I get out. I might even go to medical school."

Doctor William Booth? William Booth, MD! "Oh, Will." She couldn't hold back the tears any longer. "Oh, you idiot!" She buried her face in his chest. "Can we go some place this evening and talk?"

"I'm sorry, Kris. Things I have to do. Tomorrow. I promise. I want to be with you as much as I can until—until I can't."

"Me too." She raised her lips to his. Who cared if the family saw anything now?

Kris watched his truck till it turned at the corner. It was done. She didn't want to accept it but she would have to. At least he wouldn't be shooting at people. That would make him a little safer. And who knew whether this mess in Vietnam would continue much longer?

Her mom was waiting right inside the door. She was the only one home this afternoon. "William has joined the marines," she told her immediately. That would simplify a great many things.

Marge Greene's mouth opened and closed. The preemptive strike had been effective. "I'm sorry."

She hoped her mom would have enough sense not to say anything about it being for the best. Even if it was likely she was thinking it. "I'm going to go out a while. Maybe ride the bike somewhere."

"The Summerlins'? Your father intended to stop by there this afternoon. Something about the trip your friends are taking." She toyed with her necklace beads. Mom always wore jewelry of some sort. "I'm glad you aren't."

Kris ignored that. "Maybe I'll see him." She hadn't particularly planned to go there but now—why not?

Sure enough, there was her dad's car when she came around the corner. Didn't they have offices for this sort of thing? According to Ronnie, Preston Summerlin's was very comfortable. Her father's looked more like a fast food place. She rode on up into the lawn and deposited her Stingray at the porch door.

Jelly stepped out onto the porch. "Hey, come join the party. Your dad just got here."

"Why the heck did he come here?" she asked, following the girl into the house.

"He brought that Mills guy to make the final plans with James. And Daddy, I suppose."

They passed into the living room. "In the library," said Jelly. "Let's wait for James. He's still upstairs."

She was in no hurry. Not to see the three men in the library nor to say anything about Will to her father right now. He'd hear of it soon enough. Maybe she should just go back outside.

Too late. Jam was coming down the stairs. "Taking part in the conference?" he asked.

"I'm just an innocent bystander!"

"But I might put a word or two of wisdom in," said Jelly. "If needed."

All three entered the library. The men seated around the room had clearly heard them coming. Probably heard what they had been saying. "My son James," said Summerlin to a lanky young man sitting upright in one of the chairs. "And my daughter Angelica. This is Robert Mills."

"Bob," said the man, rising and offering his hand to each in turn. Jam took a seat on the couch but Jelly remained standing in the doorway beside Kris.

"You know my daughter," added Tom Greene. "The innocent bystander."

And she wished he didn't. She only nodded in his direction.

"There's not a whole lot to finish hashing out," her father said, apparently taking the lead in this. He'd coordinated things between Jam and Mills from the start.

"We meet here at Five AM on Wednesday," said Bob. "My car and yours?" Jam nodded. "Do we go across the Trail or take Alligator Alley?" The Alley had opened for its entire length earlier that year.

"We don't have to travel the same route," James pointed out.

"But it would be best if you did," her father said.

"Alligator Alley then," said the young attorney. "It's the quickest way to the motel I've booked."

Jam shrugged in acquiescence. "Not a battle worth fighting," Jel whispered in her ear. The girl probably didn't care whether anyone could hear her.

"The motel's the best place to coordinate from once we're there, too," Mills continued. "You're staying in Little Havana or something?" His distaste for even having to name the neighborhood was evident.

"Coconut Grove," came Preston's deep, authoritative voice. "With relatives." She wondered if Jam could sound that way. Oh, but he wouldn't have the accent.

But she must ask him to try it sometime.

"It would be sensible," agreed Jam. "You have a straighter shot toward Miami Beach. Even if your motel is rather far away from it." Mills gave him a quick and not very friendly glance. He might have made a remark if the boy hadn't started up again immediately. "We'll show up there as early as possible on Thursday morning for the second day. The big day. I'm doubting we'll get much done on Wednesday but we can try to get near the convention."

Mills only nodded this time.

"There's not really anything else to work out, is there?" asked Greene. "Just little stuff you'll have to handle as it comes." He looked from Bob Mills to Jam. "I'd advise you not to get into fistfights over any of it."

"They can just defer to me," announced Jelly. "Totally impartial!"

"And totally random," said Jam.

A few laughs and the visitors were ushered out the front door. But Robert Mills gave Jam a clearly disapproving look as he passed. Maybe the long hair. The look he gave Jelly held no disapproval at all. Kris would have liked to slap his face for it but Jel pointedly ignored him.

"I do not like that young man," stated Preston Summerlin when they were gone. "Do you know much about him, Kris?"

"Just that he's a newly-minted lawyer, as my dad would put it, working for one firm or another in Naples. Not a partner. Not married. Not much else." She racked her mind for any gossip she'd heard. "Oh, and never served in the military. He'd had some cocka-mamie excuse for a medical deferment. Not sure what."

"That's quite a bit to know, young lady."

"I also know I don't like him either. And he has a hideous haircut!"

"No argument there," said Jelly. "One can excuse many things in a man but not bad haircuts."

Mister Summerlin shook his head. "That sounds more like your sister than you, Angelica."

"That's because I stole it from her." She turned to Kris. "Now what's troubling you?"

Jam added, "And don't pretend something isn't."

"Oh, damn it, guys. Why—why—" Suddenly, unexpectedly, she began crying. She hadn't meant for this to happen. It wasn't why she'd come over here. "Will has gone and joined the marines," she choked out between sobs.

"Ah. How soon does he leave?" asked Jam.

"Three weeks."

He turned to his father. "We'll have to have a farewell party. Here."

"Absolutely," said Preston Summerlin.

We'll have to have sex too, Kris told herself. Anywhere! She was going to make that boy's last month as a civilian memorable. She managed to smile through her tears.

"Thanks. Thank you to all of you."

Chapter Fifty-two
Ronnie

"Oh, I think Joey is going to see you about that job you mentioned. And you aren't allowed to back out now."

Howard Deerfield looked up from the paper. "Wouldn't have considered it. I was serious about being able to use her."

"You know she'd have to fit it around a college schedule."

"Um-hmm. No problem." He turned his eyes back to *The Daily News*. "Your mom's latest column is in here."

"And Alan is outside. Bye!" She wasn't going to wait around for her father's analysis of it.

As soon as she slipped into the front seat of his wagon, he asked, "Have you heard about William?

She nodded. "Kris phoned me about it. She didn't say much, just let me know. And that there will be farewell party at the Summerlin house. How did you know?"

"Will told me." He might have hesitated just slightly before saying, "Before Kris. He'd sort of been discussing it with me anyway. The sounding board bit." He cranked the engine. "Not that he would take my advice."

They pulled out of the shell drive. "I don't understand why he chose the marines. Why not the army?"

"Lots of men go after the medic thing in the army. Too many, and more than a few of them are conscientious objectors of some sort. They know you're serious when you apply for it in the marines."

"So he's more likely to get what he wants?"

"That's the way Will saw it. Or the way his recruiter presented it to him. Want to go straight over to the Summerlin house or stop somewhere first?"

"Summerlin. Kris is there."

It turned out she was not. "She's somewhere with Will," James told them on arriving. "I suspect they'll come by here eventually. They always do!"

"So do we, it seems," said Alan.

"As much as you want," came the completely serious reply. "As long as summer lasts. After that?" He spread his arms. "Only God knows. Hey, come with me, will you? I think my sister wants to talk with your date in private."

Ronnie watched the two stroll away. Alan knew nothing of what had passed between her and Angelica. He never would. That was the past anyway. She and Angelica were on good terms now, weren't they?

The Summerlin girl came and sat down across from her at a table. "We are going to have to talk about some things eventually."

"Are we? Things have smoothed out okay, haven't they?"

Angelica was not to be deterred. "Then I'm going to have to talk. I'm not so okay. I—feel a need to explain myself."

"Oh." She hadn't really given much thought to how Angelica had felt about it all. "Then we will talk." Whether it made her uncomfortable or not.

"I've always had trouble putting boundaries on my friendship. Maybe that's why I don't have many friends."

She thought to protest. No, she didn't know Angelica well enough to say.

"I guess I look for something more. Another sort of connection." A sudden little smile came, a smile that held its share of sadness. "I put the moves on Joey once but she didn't recognize it for what it was. That was a long time ago and I was just beginning to fumble with my sexuality."

"That is not something I am going to ask her about."

"She would just say Jel had been annoying her again. Playing her stupid tricks." Angelica sighed and then just looked at her for a moment. "It's not really about sex, you know. That's easy and there don't need to be any strings attached."

"Like with Grubby?"

"I might have known that would get around. Yes, like with Grubby. He's rather physically attractive." She appeared to be considering that fact. "Yes. But that's not so important. I, um, am not really all that attracted to you physically, Ronnie. It's the truth. I had not been lusting after your body or anything like that. I was—looking for that deeper bond, I think. A way to be closer."

"And sex seemed like the way?"

"Why not? I'm fully aware it's not necessary. Friendship is enough to share. Like you and your Triumvirate." She sighed deeply. "I'd give anything for what the three of you have." Then she snickered. "But of course I was quite horny when I made my pass at you."

Ronnie could only shake her head. "So—like too many things came together all at once. You let your dam burst."

"Damn, you understand my dam!" Angelica chuckled and then stopped to give her a long serious look. "Your dams are pretty strong. I hope they don't all crumble one of these days."

"Maybe some of them should." Had she said that aloud?

"Be careful if they do. Just remember I really am your friend, okay, and I don't ever want to hurt you or—or make you go away. And I need to remember you're my friend, don't I?"

"I am." Ronnie meant it. She was not completely clear about every-thing Angelica had shared but maybe Angelica wasn't herself. The young woman had been trying to work some very complicated things out in words. "And if I were, um, the sort to be into that kind of thing, I'd be all over you." She surprised herself with that but hadn't be able to resist adding it.

It started as a giggle and broke into a full laugh. Ronnie giggled just a little herself. "I don't believe that for a moment, Ronnie. You even keep Alan at arm's length."

"I do?" For some reason, she felt less comfortable talking about this than all that had gone before. It brought up too many unresolved questions of her own. "Oh, maybe. So does he."

"I've noticed. Now what in the world is this?"

A bike of some some sort, emitting a high pitched rattling whine, made its way up the street. Sandy Penn was astride it, grinning and waving.

They walked over for a closer look. "Is that a Solex?"

"Yep. It was Russel's but it's been sitting in the garage forever. He never rides it anymore."

"A scooter?" asked Ronnie. It didn't look much like one.

"A moped," Angelica informed her. It seemed to be a wide-tired bike with a tiny motor perched over the front wheel. "I don't think it will be able to keep up with my Vespa. Even if you pedal hard."

"It will if you stick to the speed limits!"

"Me? I've always considered those nothing more than suggestions."

"I can vouch for that," said James. He and Alan had come over as well. "Are you joining us this afternoon, Sandy?"

"Nope. Have things to do, you know? But I had to show this off! See you later!" She reengaged the motor by some sort of lever arrangement and headed back down the street.

"She'd have been better off with a normal bicycle."

"Maybe I would too," said Angelica. She turned to Alan. "So you're going on a trip of your own?"

"Leaving the same day as you. I'm not sure how long we're going to stay but there's some chance of a tropical storm toward the end of this coming week. With any luck it will stay well offshore and just send waves our way."

"I'd think a storm is a good reason to drive the opposite direction!"

"I might say the same about a political demonstration." His tone and his smile suggested he was not serious. That didn't mean he wasn't. "You two take good care of this poor naive girl, okay?"

That was about as far as Alan was likely to go in expressing concern. His easy-going tolerance and general unflappability did peeve Ronnie some. It was something he put on, assumed, to cover his introverted personality. Just as she had her own ways of dealing with the world.

He did care though. He was concerned. That couldn't be hidden. She *had* been keeping Alan at arm's length. Maybe it was time to change that. After they got back from their respective trips, yes. She loved Alan, didn't she? Enough to move to the next level of their relationship?

A level she'd never reached for before. She'd been thinking about it. She was on birth control now. Was Alan ready? Even their making out had been pretty tame. Their hands had remained well-behaved. But, as her mom had said, boys can be encouraged.

She wasn't sure she was quite up to encouragement. Oh, there was Kris's Beetle. It was about time she and Will got here.

Chapter Fifty-three
Joey

"Everyone's here," said Ronnie.

"And waiting for us." She turned her Corvair around in a dark driveway and brought it to the curb ahead of the two cars. The Summerlin Buick and something else this Mills guy must drive. A Mercury with an ugly vinyl roof.

It would be safe to leave it parked here. For one night, anyway. She had removed the surfboard racks at Alan's suggestion. A target for thieves, he claimed. The girls gathered their bags. "Just throw those in the back of the Electra," Jam told them. "Not on top of Kris's signs, maybe." He slammed the tailgate shut. "You both riding with me? Or with Angelica, I should say."

"I—"

"Shotgun!" rang out Ronnie's voice. "Ha, I beat you for once."

That was okay. She'd as soon sit in the back with Jam. "You should meet our fellow travelers," he said. "Bob Mills at the helm." The tall thin young man only gave them a nod. "And his trusty crew of Young Republicans, Donna and Mike."

"Hi Donna! Wanta ride with the cool kids?" She knew Donna Forrester. She'd graduated Naples High a couple years before them.

"I'd rather be in the back seat with Mike," she replied, hanging on the guy's arm.

He wouldn't be bad to snuggle with in any back seat. Kind of cute in his clean-cut way. The sideburns helped. Donna had clearly punched above her weight with this one.

"Okay then, let's get going," said Bob. A minute later, the two vehicles were heading east, out to where the Alligator Alley toll road cut across the Everglades. A sleepy-eyed attendant took their quarters and they rolled on.

"Whoa, did I fall asleep?" It was light out. She remembered darkness a few seconds ago. James only grunted something. Maybe he'd been asleep too. It was good that she had been able to, after lying awake all night.

The radio was tuned to news. "Hey, isn't there any music we can listen to?"

"Hush," said Jelly. "This is important."

She leaned forward to listen. Some sort of march in Miami. "That's not near where we'll be, is it?"

"These sorts of things have a way of spilling over into other areas."

When did Jel become so astute? Oh, yeah, sure, Joey knew the girl had it in her. "We're still following the Republicans?" The Mercury was just ahead of them.

"Yeah. He drives too slow but I figured it would be best not to go whizzing past him. What's with the turn signal?"

A tail light was flashing. "It's the halfway rest area." Not really halfway but why complicate things? "I hope Bob knows there aren't any facilities on this road." They followed his sedan in. "But lots of places to pull over and fish."

"Oh, you still do that?" asked Jam. "We could have fitted your pole in here easily."

"This would be a great car for a fishing trip! And you've invited me now, remember. I guess we're all going to get out and stretch our legs."

"The mosquitoes should have gone to bed," said Ronnie. She stepped out onto the pavement, yawning and stretching.

Angelica turned to the rear seat. "James, hand me up the pee can, will you? And everyone give me some privacy. You can use it when I'm done, if you need."

Maybe she would. Joey had urinated into more than one coffee can on expeditions like this. Or she could wait for the restrooms at the next toll station. She got out and walked back and forth a bit with her friends. Donna and Mike came over to join them.

"My god, that guy is a pain to ride with," was Donna's greeting.

"We've listened to his complaining the whole way," Mike added to this. He gave them a friendly grin. "Like about being roped into having to babysit a bunch of hippie kids."

"By his boss." Donna snickered. "Who happens to be my dad."

Joey knew Mister Forrester was an attorney. Undoubtedly a friend of Tom Greene. So Mills worked in his office, huh? That cleared the picture a little. Hmm, Mike was even cuter in daylight. Donna? She should ditch the bouffant hairdo. At least it wasn't very high. Her heart-shaped face was nice enough aside from the jutting pointy nose.

Angelica slid out of the Buick and discreetly dumped something beneath it. It must have required some gymnastics to pee there in the front seat. Guys could do it much easier. They didn't even have to pull their pants down.

"Let's go," called Mills. Shortly, they were headed east again. Wetlands spread on both sides of the road, grass mostly with the occasional cypress stand. A canal ran in parallel, the source of the fill on which Alligator Alley was built.

"Hey, Mony, Mony!" Joey sang along as Tommy James came on the radio. She was glad someone up front had switched from the news.

"You have a dreadful voice," Jam informed her.

"And a captive audience!" But she kept her mouth shut after that. It was awfully cloudy. There might be bad weather this afternoon. She had not signed up for standing in the rain. Once they exited the Alley —more quarters paid to get off—both cars turned on Twenty-seven, following it south toward Miami. Going straight ahead would have taken them into Fort Lauderdale and who would want to go there?

"Mills is going to find his motel first, right?" asked Jelly.

"That's what he said," came Jam's reply. "It's too early to check in."

The Seminole Inn proved to be in Hialeah. "We'll all be Seminole Inn-dians," Bob cracked as they piled out of their cars. Joey had to admit it was a little funny. Only a little and maybe not in the best of taste. He and Jam went into the office.

"We need to wait an hour," the boy announced on their return. "I have to admit, this is not at all a bad location." He looked the unprepossessing two-story building over. "Maybe not the best motel though. I wish you would ditch the Republicans and come with us, Ronnie."

She shook her head. "I promised. And you know it would get back to my parents. Mills would be sure to tell."

"Not much they could do about it after the fact," said Jelly. "Oh, sure, I know you wouldn't break a promise."

The others came over to them, Mills followed by the couple.

"There's a restaurant right over there." He nodded toward the street. "How about walking over and having something to eat while we wait?"

"Sounds good," said Angelica. "Get what you need, kids, and I'll lock up the Electra."

Bob's eyes widened just a tad and then went to Jam. Maybe he had expected the boy to take charge.

James was more a planner than a doer. He might have worked all this out but it was his sister who was likely to act as the leader. They crossed the rather busy highway to a little diner. Too many for one booth though Joey wouldn't have minded if the party separated at the door. Everyone settled around a table.

Was it time for a late breakfast or an early lunch? Decisions! The waitress informed them either was available, took their orders, disappeared again.

"Once we get into our rooms, we can plan for the afternoon," said Bob. "If those niggers don't cause trouble." Joey could see Donna roll her eyes. Mike's face showed no reaction of any sort. "You don't have to get to your place early, do you?"

"We can roll in anytime," came Jam's answer.

They were interrupted by the arrival of their orders and ate in silence for a minute or two. Then Ronnie looked up from her grilled cheese and asked her, "Are you going to stay with us or go with James and Angelica?"

Bob jumped in. "We should know that when we check in. There should be room for a third girl."

Damn. Joey knew this decision was coming but had ignored it. She didn't want to desert Ronnie but crowding into a motel room with her and Donna? And they'd see each other the rest of the time.

"Aunt Tina is expecting you," Jelly informed her.

Maybe she should flip a coin. "I'll go to Coconut Grove," she decided and then told Donna, "and you make sure to get Ronnie back to me in one piece."

Chapter Fifty-four
Kris

"I am afraid Alan took his tent on his camping trip," said Will.

"We could always buy our own. Our first house together!"

"Yeah. Ha, I'm liable to be sleeping in a lot of tents the next few years."

"We promised not to talk about that. Only the here and now."

Will sat looking toward the rec center for a while before answering. The couple sat on one of the benches by the shuffle board courts. No one was sliding pucks around this afternoon. "We have to promise something else. We have to promise not to wait for each other. It's going to be too long and we're going to be too far apart."

"Oh, do we have to talk about that? Can't we just enjoy the little time we have left together?"

"That's what we should do. Make the most of it and then—things are going to change so much we can't make any predictions."

"Or promises. I know that, Will. But I won't stop loving you."

"And I'll always love you."

"Promise?"

"Oh, girl." He shook his head and then kissed her. But William Booth did not promise anything.

Would she wait for him? Through her four years at college, his four years in the military? And maybe college for him somewhere then and grad school for her and if he was at all serious about becoming a doctor, even more years. It was—overwhelming. If she let it be.

"I wonder what Ronnie and Joey are up to."

"They would be there by now, I would think. I hear there is some trouble over there."

"I wonder if Alan knows about it."

Will shrugged. "No telling. He's too far away now for us to mount a rescue mission."

"Cocoa again?" Wasn't that where he'd taken her friends?

"I think so. He said something 'bout maybe going further north.

What was the place? Flagler?"

"Flagler Beach is up the coast a way. We drove through it once when I was a little girl." Not so little. It was only two or three years ago. But then, she was still a 'little' girl! "I think it's a beach destination for students at the University of Florida."

Will acknowledged this with a nod but did not seem all that interested. "Things might get rough in Miami. People, um, around my neighborhood have family over there. In Liberty City and places."

"And there is nothing we can do about it."

"Isn't there? We could have been out making ourselves heard, too. Like your friends."

"Our friends, Will. Our *family*."

There was no answer to that. She hoped Will would always believe it was true, no matter what else went down. What the heck was that noise?

Both turned around to see Howard Macklin slowly dribbling a basketball.

"I've heard things about you, Doughnut," he said. "Joining the military?"

"It's true."

He came and sat beside them, occasionally bouncing the ball as they talked. "I can't say I think it's the best choice. But it's your choice." He looked at Kris but said nothing.

"Shoot, Mackie, I don't even know if it's the best choice."

"You had to do something."

"Right. There's never a perfect choice, is there?"

They lapsed into silence.

"You'll have to come to the farewell party," said Kris. "At the Summerlin's on the Twenty-third."

"There is no way I'd miss it. Even though I'm supposed to show up at Ohio next week for an early start on football."

With Jeff? Best she didn't pry into that.

"In the mean time," said Mackie, "how about one last time on the basketball court?"

"I would enjoy nothing better than defeating you again," Will replied. "My cheerleader will taunt you every time you miss a shot."

"Depend on it!" said Kris.

Chapter Fifty-five
Ronnie

The afternoon had been a bit of a bust. They hadn't even had a chance to wave Kris's signs. But they had made it out to Miami Beach, all of them in the station wagon. Nowhere near the convention center. Streets were crowded. Streets were blocked off.

And it was worse on the drive back. There might be a curfew tonight. In some parts of the city, anyway. They were pretty far from the trouble here. There had been tear gas and things thrown and vandalism. It felt unreal to Ronnie. She'd never been close to anything like that before and wished she were back in Naples.

Or that she was on Alan's surf trip instead of Grubby. The others were gone now. The 'Three Jays' Joey had dubbed them—Joey, Jam, Jelly. A new triumvirate. If Donna wasn't sitting across the room she might have cried. She just felt so awful this evening.

She'd be sharing this room with Donna. Though she and Mike were apparently a couple, the arrangement was the two girls together, the men in the other room. The four of them had just come back from dinner at that same restaurant on the other side of Twenty-seven. Ronnie could hear the highway's traffic even over the air conditioner. The room was on the second floor, opening on a covered walkway, only one flimsy door separating it from all that was going on out there.

"What are you going to do this evening?" she asked Donna. "I'm sure you'd rather be with Mike instead of me."

The young woman put down her magazine. "Mike *is* my boyfriend. I'm sure you figured that out."

"Joey did and made sure everyone else knew it."

"Joey. I remember her from Naples High. And you were one of her friends. There was a close-knit trio of you, wasn't there?"

Yes, there was. "That's as good a way of putting it as any. Mike's not from Naples though." It was half a question, half a statement.

"No, I met him at UF. You're going there, right?" Ronnie nodded and the girl went on. "Mike Dobson. We're both going into law."

Donna didn't mention it but she probably knew Ronnie had plans along that line.

"He seems like a nice guy." Not very talkative but then neither was she. And good looking in a masculine, grown-up sort of way. Dobson's hair was dark and short, though combed forward as a concession to current fashion. His sideburns were pretty long too.

"I lucked out with him. He must have been attracted to my intellect!"

A knock on the door. "Okay to come in?" came Mike's deep voice.

"Sure. It's not locked." Donna turned to her. "It probably should be. We'll have to remember tonight."

Mike came in and sat on the bed beside his girlfriend. "Mills disappeared," he reported. "He said something about needing a drink."

"You can take the boy out of the frat but not the frat out of the boy," said Donna.

"Hey! You know I'm in a fraternity." He leaned in and gave her a rather self-conscious little peck.

"One of the well-behaved ones." She got up. "Let's go out too, but only as far as the pool. Did you bring a suit, Ronnie?"

She shook her head. It had never occurred to her. "No matter. I doubt anyone will complain if you swim in shorts and a tee."

"Why not?" She was already wearing them, having ditched her more dressed-up clothes when they returned from eating.

"I'll change and be right with you," said Donna, who promptly vanished into the bathroom.

"I'd better too." Mike went out the door. Ronnie went out as well and leaned on the metal railing, looking down on the parking lot. It was pretty full. Why were all these people here? She doubted any had any connection to what was going on at the convention center. Business travelers? Tourists? One could be headed anywhere from here. To the beaches. Maybe down to the Keys.

"I'm ready," announced Donna, locking the door behind her and handing Ronnie one of the motel towels. The picture of modesty, she wore a dark blue one-piece suit. Her hairdo was protected by a bathing cap. Ronnie resisted the urge to tell her she looked like her mom. Mike joined them and they went down the stairs at the south end of the building. Only a few swimmers, a few more lounging beside the pool.

She looked back at the parking lot. "Mills's car is still here."

"I think he walked to a liquor store," said Mike. "Let's forget him and get in the water. Whoa, it stinks of chlorine."

It did. She could tolerate it. Ronnie backstroked the length of the pool a couple times. It was a pretty good length. Not Olympic size but all she needed. It felt good to get the kinks of car-riding worked out of her. She lay down on one of the poolside lounges. No. Her wet clothes felt uncomfortable. It was even a little cool with the overcast skies and evening coming on.

"Can I have the key?" she asked Donna. "I need to go change."

It was handed over without comment.

Ronnie unlocked and entered. I'll change and go right back out, she decided. A blouse, dry underwear. At least she'd thought to bring a change of that! No need to go into the bathroom. She peeled off her tee, started to unfasten her bra, when she heard the door open behind her. Had Donna come up?

She turned to see Bob Mills leering at her. "Go ahead an' take it off," he said. His eyes went up and down her form.

What did he want? "Get out," she managed to squeak. The man only laughed and pushed the door shut behind him.

"Don't you want a real man, hippie girl? Not like that pansy you came over with." He fumbled with his belt buckle. She could see the bulge in the front of his pants. "I know about you freaks," he growled. "You'll do anyone."

The pants dropped. Ronnie had never seen an erect penis before. She started to back away but there wasn't much room. She was right against the bed. Maybe she could jump up on it and across to the bathroom. Lock herself in, away from this—this horrible man.

He had his manhood in his hand, shaking it, stroking it, as he took a step toward her, a bit clumsily with his trousers around his ankles. "C'mon baby. Suck me. Y' know y' want it."

It was too much. Ronnie screamed as loud as she was able. Louder than she would ever have thought she could. Surprisingly quickly, Mike burst into the room.

"What the hell?" He took it all in and grabbed Mills by the collar. "Get out of here!" He gave him a push and the man tripped, sprawling on the floor.

Donna stepped around him. "Come on," she commanded, and threw a towel about Ronnie's shoulders. "Bring our stuff." She escorted her into the other motel room.

A laden Mike joined them in a couple minutes. Ronnie stared at the two, unsure what to do. "Thank you," she choked out and began to cry.

"You go call us a cab," Mike's girlfriend told him. "I'll get Ronnie ready to go."

"Where?" Ronnie managed to ask.

"To your friends."

Chapter Fifty-six
Joey

It was dark outside. The full moon hid behind a blanket of clouds.

"I believe Ronnie has a certain spiritual yearning. She knows nothing of religion but is seeking it. Unknowingly maybe."

Joey thought she had seen it. It just took Jam to put it into words for her. Ronnie was attracted to James, wasn't she? She'd seen that too. Maybe her friend didn't even realize it, but she seemed drawn to both his physical and spiritual sides.

That was not at all a good idea. Even if Jam didn't end up as a priest he was an elusive target for anyone's love. She knew. She'd had her own crush on him. Crushes. They had come and gone.

Ronnie should just get serious with that perfectly good guy she already had. Oh, what did it matter? In a few weeks, she would be in Gainesville. Maybe what she had with Alan couldn't survive that anyway.

She had to share a room here with Jelly. That *could* be survived. For one night, anyway. Jam was sacking on a couch in the living room but all three of them were together in the bedroom right now. It was a nice little house, very Mediterranean, all white stucco with the obligatory red tile roof. The Summerlins' aunt and uncle spoke Spanish to each other. She was Maria's sister? Joey thought she had that right.

Their Aunt Tina stood in the doorway. Tia Tina. Joey was already calling her this. "There is a taxi out front. Is it friends of yours?"

"I wouldn't think so," said Jelly, but she got up anyway. They followed her and the older woman to the front door, where Jelly put her eye to the peephole. "It's—Mike? And Ronnie and Donna. Oh, Ronnie does not look well at all!" She threw open the door and rushed down the walk.

Joey was not far behind. "What happened?" she demanded.

"Inside," said Donna. "Let's get her into bed first."

Ronnie seemed almost to be sleepwalking. She complied with everything they asked of her and was soon resting in a darkened room.

Sleeping? That Joey didn't know, as she pulled the door almost to.

"So now," she said. "Let's have it."

"Bob Mills assaulted her. No physical harm but psychic? I don't know."

"He never got the opportunity to touch her." There was a touch of adoration in Donna's eyes. "Thanks to Mike."

"If I'd been there he would never have touched anyone again!"

"Or me," said Angelica. They all adjourned to the living room, a circle of concerned friends.

Joey most definitely considered Donna and Mike friends now. Tia Tina hovered nearby but did not join them. The Summerlin's uncle was snoring somewhere upstairs and had missed it all.

Jam started it off. "Give us the whole thing, will you?"

They did, a few words about Bob going out, them hanging at the pool. "With Ronnie in her room and Mills gone, we thought we might, um, appropriate his room for a few minutes." Donna might have reddened a little as Mike told them this.

"So we were right next door. It's a good thing or we might not have heard her," she said.

"Honestly, he may have been too drunk to, um, physically harm her. In any sexual sense."

"He barely had it up," she added.

Mike gave her a raised eyebrow. "You noticed something like that?"

"Well, where did you expect my eyes to go?" Good point. They all would have looked.

"But he could have hurt her otherwise," stated Jelly. "Frustrated men use their fists when they can't use their cocks."

Donna rose. "May I use your phone for a long-distance call, ma'am?" she asked the aunt. "Collect, of course." She turned to the room. "I'm going to tell my father everything that happened. Robert Mills is not going to work in Naples again."

Joey got up too. "I'm going to sleep in Ronnie's room. Even if I have to do it on the floor." For a moment, Jelly looked like she might have something to say, but only acquiesced with a little nod. Joey had seniority as Ronnie's friend. She recognized that.

But she didn't sleep when she lay down on the other bed in the little room, but lay there in her clothes, on her side, her eyes on the dim form of her friend. There was far, far too much on her mind. She wished there was some way to have Mills arrested. No, there just wasn't enough and Ronnie didn't need to have her name brought into anything. They would have be satisfied with the man's misdeeds being known among his associates.

Even though he might go to some other job in some other town and assault some other woman. Joey rolled over to stare at the ceiling for a while and then checked on Ronnie again. She seemed to be sleeping soundly. Tia Tina had offered sleeping pills but they didn't seem to have been needed. Except by her!

She sat up on the edge of the bed. "Can't sleep?" came a soft voice.

"No, Jel. That's nothing new." The girl was a shadow framed by the doorway.

"Me neither. May I sit down?"

"Sure."

The two sat side by side and watched their friend sleep until dawn stole into the skies.

Chapter Fifty-seven
Ronnie

It seemed no more than a bad dream now. And she certainly wasn't going to let it get in the way of having a good breakfast. She munched on toast, thick with guava jelly, while James listened to the news on the radio. Ronnie did love guava jelly.

Everyone else seemed to still be asleep. Angelica and Joey were sprawled on the bed next to hers, snoring, when she awoke. She hadn't bothered them.

"Things have gone totally to hell. Even if any of us had wanted to stay—"

"Which none of us do," she assured him.

"It would have been impossible to go anywhere or do anything. Everything's blocked off. They may call the National Guard in."

"That won't be a problem if we go home via the Trail, will it?" she asked, spreading more jelly.

"Not at all. I guess there's no great hurry to hit the road." He looked at her for just a moment, but said nothing more.

Appraising her. Of course, he was concerned. She understood that. They all would be. "Donna and Mike are riding with us?"

"Uh-huh."

Then the big question. "I don't suppose there's any way Alan won't hear about it."

"I wouldn't think so. But not any details."

Ronnie nibbled her toast. "So he may just think the guy made a clumsy pass at me. In fact," she said, "that's pretty much what he did. The official story."

His eyes narrowed. "You aren't, well, trying to pretend nothing happened, are you?"

"Hey, he never even laid a hand on me. I've been pawed by guys. Nice guys, supposedly."

"Okay." She could tell that didn't satisfy him but James was not going to pursue it.

Whether it satisfied her, she wasn't at all sure. The image of Mills with his pants down, dick out, would stick with her. Not haunt her; that she did know.

"Would you take me to church sometime? I could ask Joey but she's —" How should she put it? "Too familiar with me." And she wouldn't necessarily trust her explanations about what was going on.

"She would probably be there if you went to Sunday mass with me."

"Not if you went later. I know you two always go really early. Before I get up!"

"Hmm. How about the Saturday evening service in a couple days?"

"I thought Kris went to church, I mean temple, on Saturdays."

"We Catholics like to get an early start on Sunday."

"Okay. If Alan doesn't want to go out then. I'll remind you later."

"Do that. Ah, the first of our sleeping beauties."

"Hi, Donna."

"Good morning to you both. I'm glad to see you feeling well this morning, Ronnie."

"Oh, I was just a little under the weather." She couldn't help bursting out in laughter. "I was exposed to something!"

Jam groaned. "I'm not sure anyone else should hear that joke."

"Probably not."

Donna seemed to take all this with complete equanimity. She had even smiled slightly at the joke. The kind of businesslike person who got up and dusted herself off, as the cliché had it, and who might expect others to do the same. Ronnie wasn't really like that but she was willing to give the impression this morning. She didn't need anyone feeling sorry for her.

Yesterday had just been too much, she told herself. The whole day! It was no wonder she'd crashed last night

An unshaven Mike followed Donna in after a while. He would have a considerable beard if he let it grow. It would practically cover his whole face, leaving his eyes to peer out from their hiding place. Not the best look for a lawyer! Angelica and Joey finally.

The uncle again did not make an appearance. Maybe he was shy. There were farewells to their Aunt Tina. Tears in Angelica's eye? In

Tina's anyway. Then they were on the road.

The long way across Florida, back to Naples, while Miami seethed behind them. Ronnie hoped she would never go there again.

Chapter Fifty-eight
Kris

Ronnie was subdued, yes, but seemed all right. Subdued was fairly normal for Ronnie. She hoped it didn't cover anything else. Her dad had filled her in on what happened. Leaving out some details, no doubt. She had passed on even fewer details to Will.

She watched Ben Forrester drive away, with his daughter beside him and her friend in the back of his Lincoln. He'd been waiting, as had she.

Ronnie and Joey finished stowing their stuff in the Corvair before coming over. "So, did you miss me?" asked Joey.

"Oh, no. We've been busy fucking our brains out while you were gone." She wished.

"Sorry we didn't get to wave your signs on national television," said Ronnie.

"We watched some of it. It looks like Nixon will get the nod this evening, to my father's chagrin."

"At least he's better than that idiot Reagan," felt Joey.

"Mom calls him an air-head."

"Do you know if Alan is back?" asked Ronnie. The question was probably aimed at Will. Kris didn't keep tabs on the surfer boy.

Will only shook his head. "He's been too busy fucking his brains out to notice," said Kris. "I told you about that."

"But not in any Cadillacs."

"Shush. That's our secret fantasy."

"Yours. Not mine."

"What's this?" asked Jelly. Jam was carrying on a conversation with his parents but his sister had wandered over to join them. "I want to hear about *all* your fantasies."

"She wants to make love in the back of your father's car."

"Blabbermouth." She didn't really mind since it was never going to happen.

"Hmm. That does sound delightful. With the top down, cruising around town?"

"Jelly! I'm shocked." Unfortunately, she could envision it. It might even show up in her dreams now.

"Hey, it was your fantasy. I just punched it up it a little. Want to come in and eat something?"

"We'd better get to our homes," said Joey. "Worried parents and all that, you know?"

"Yeah. You guys—just be okay, huh?"

It seemed a bit uncharacteristic of Angelica. They said nothing until Joey's Corvair pulled away. Then Jelly turned to them. "Ronnie doesn't seem to want to dwell on it so we won't either. Understand? All right, then. There's ice cream in the freezer."

Will leaned in and whispered as they walked toward the house, "She can be as bossy as you."

"Just remember I'm *your* boss and we'll be okay."

Preston and Maria Summerlin were already in the kitchen with their son. Sylvie, too, busy at something at the sink. Kris had no doubt she was making sure not to miss any gossip.

"Dreadful goings on," said Mister Summerlin, as they entered. "You and I were right about that fellow, Kris."

"None of them should have been allowed to go," asserted his wife. "They are too young."

"All adults, dear. We should be pleased they even bothered to ask. And—" His already grave voice became more so. "It was we who failed, trusting a man we shouldn't. Forcing him on them, despite our misgivings."

"You know I would have clouted the guy and walked out of there," Jelly informed them. "Is it too close to dinner to have ice cream?"

"Ronnie's more vulnerable than you." Kris thought she should say that.

"In some ways. In others, she's tougher than I'll ever be. No, Sylvie?"

"I'll have the meal on in less than an hour, Miss Angelica," the cook replied. She looked at Kris and Will. "Will there be guests?"

"If they wish to stay," Preston told her.

"I think not, sir. But maybe just a little bowl of ice cream for the road."

"Anytime, miss, anytime. And—I'm proud of you boy," Sylvie said to Will. "We're all proud of you."

Approval at last.

"If you two can have a little, so can I," said Jelly. "Out on the porch. I'll bring it to you."

"She's training for a career as a waitress," Kris informed her parents.

"They've been waiting for me to choose something. Shall I fix you a bowl too, James?"

Jam only shook his head. He seemed preoccupied. Nothing new there.

In a couple minutes, Jelly emerged onto the porch with a tray and three bowls. She gave them a look and snickered. "Chocolate and vanilla."

Kris had to shake her head at that. So dopey and maybe even sort of racist.

"The best combination," said Will.

Until it melts.

Chapter Fifty-nine
Ronnie

"The rain sent us running home. It wasn't too bad our first couple days. Even some decent waves." Alan had arrived home only a couple hours ago. He might not have come over at all if he hadn't heard about what happened to her.

Will told him, of course, not that he knew half of it. Nor was Alan going to learn any more from her. He wouldn't ask. Alan didn't pry.

But she could tell he knew. "You look worn out," she told him. He was leaning on his wagon, in front of their house, his surf board still in the roof racks.

"I suppose I am. I haven't even stopped at my home yet. Just let Gordie out at his place and then ran into Kris and Will." He didn't have to tell her where. "And over here."

"Gordie?"

"He doesn't really like being called Grubby much. Maybe that's, um, a name he's outgrown."

"Like Doughnut becoming Will."

"Exactly. You know Grub, er, Gordie's folks are nearly as wealthy as the Summerlins."

She hadn't exactly known but she was aware they could buy him nice things. Gordon was maybe a bit of a spoiled child poster boy. "They don't live in as nice a place."

He shrugged. "Not as nice a location but bigger and more luxurious. Swimming pool and all that."

"Darn. Maybe I chose the wrong rich family to be chummy with!"

"I'll introduce you." Then came the solicitous look she had been expecting since he drove up. It just took Alan time to get to it. "Are you all right, Ronnie?"

"I'm getting asked that a lot and yes I am all right. Nothing actually happened to me, you know. It was just, um, a scare." That was a good way to put it. She should have thought of that before. "Now you go home and rest up and I'll see you tomorrow and make demands on you!"

He chuckled at that and kissed her goodbye and drove off. She really would have liked him to stay. He smelled so good, of saltwater and adventure. But the boy was dog-tired, as her dad might have put it. She could see that.

Well, she wouldn't have to call James to tell him she wasn't coming. Should she take the Simca or ride her bike? Oh, she'd rather be dressed up. Drive. My god, what should she wear? This was even worse than going to Preston Summerlin's office!

She imagined what her folks would say if she told them she was going to church. Nothing maybe! Dumbfounded! Ronnie could imagine it but didn't intend to test it. Slacks? Women wore pants to church, didn't they? Catholic women? Maybe not some of the Protestants, the more conservative ones. No one would give it a second thought if they saw her in slacks and a blouse. She should have some bells like Angelica. Big ones! Striped!

But black was okay this afternoon and a pale purple cotton blouse, short sleeves. No one with any sense would wear long sleeves in August, even if they were running from one air conditioned space to another. She didn't know whether she'd go anywhere after the service. After mass. A little brooch pinned at the top button. Flowers on enamel.

"Bye Mom," she called. "Not sure when I'll get back. Maybe early!" Maybe not. She was leaving too early. She would end up sitting in the church for half an hour before anything started. That wasn't necessarily bad though, was it? She could get the lay of the land. Ten minutes later she pulled into the parking lot behind Saint Ann Church. Work was progressing on the new building just to its north. She sat there and surveyed it all for a couple minutes, the homely little box of a church that had stood here as long as she could remember, tan stucco, tall arched windows of frosted glass.

And there was James on his black bicycle. She got out and approached him as he chained it to a railing at what must be a rear entrance. He looked her up and down but made no comment. James was probably at about the same level of dressiness she was. That made her feel better about it. "Just do pretty much what I do," he told her.

"Or do nothing but sit if you prefer. No one will care about that." Then he grinned. "But don't improvise."

"No dancing along the tops of the pews?"

"We save that for Easter." In the tall wooden double doors. One side of the tall wooden doors, that was. A few people were scattered through the church already, most sitting, a couple kneeling. James dipped his fingers in something by the door and made the sign of the cross. That Ronnie recognized. I'd better not try, she decided, and followed him to a pew maybe two-thirds up the room—the nave they called it, right? He went down on one knee and then slid in. She attempted a genuflection too. That was harder than she would have thought. A good exercise but one would have to use both legs equally.

James folded down some sort of little padded rest and knelt on it. She emulated him. "How long do you kneel?" she whispered.

"Until my knees get tired." She sat back when he did. He folded the knee-rest thing away. "Mostly you can just stand when I stand and so on," he told her. "Here's a missal if you want to look at it." The little books were in pockets on the back of the pews. "I've memorized all the mass."

Maybe a priest would have to. She looked around the interior. Statues on either side of the altar. She had seen them before, once when she had come in here with Joey, after school. Years ago. They were the same statues, polished brown wood. She liked them. That was Mary, right? And the guy on the other side? "Whose that?" she asked James. "A saint, right?"

"Saint Joseph. See the carpenter tools?"

The statement meant nothing to her. A boy in a black and white— what? She wanted to call it a dress but it was unlikely anyone else did. A boy in black and white lit the candles on the altar. Flowers. There were lots of flowers in here. Catholics had better not have allergies!

The priest entered, the boy in his wake. Everyone stood up. Good, he was speaking English. She had heard that Catholics didn't do the Latin thing anymore but had been a bit unsure about all of it. Ronnie tried to find her place in the missal. James reached over, turned a couple pages, and pointed. "I could just tell you what's going on," he whispered.

Good idea. She put the book away. "A greeting, some prayers," he went on, very close to her ear. She hoped people didn't think they were necking in church. "And now we confess what sinners we are." She tried to listen to the words, to make out what everyone was saying. Focus on the priest. He was the loudest.

The church had filled up pretty good. Far from crowded. "Now we listen to some readings and a sermon." This was better. They could sit. Was the priest Italian? He looked Italian. The accent was mid-western. One heard all sorts of accents in Naples. Standing again. "A profession of what we believe," James told her. And sit. Catholics got up and down an awful lot.

"Now we get to the theatrical part," her guide whispered. "The offering of the gifts. The washing of the hands." She could follow that. It really was sort of like a play. And she understood now why the kid was called a server.

"Won't there be any singing?" she asked.

"Not this time. We'd have to go to a later mass on Sunday. The ones where everyone is awake. Up we get."

And then kneeling. James looked very solemn during this part and didn't say anything. The priest held up a little round piece of bread. The host, right? Then a goblet which she assumed held wine. Was this when they were supposed to change or something?

"It's time to go up for communion. Not you," he whispered. "I'm all for offering communion to anyone who wants it but the official church frowns on it." She sat and waited for James to return. There wasn't much more. It had the feel of winding down. Up and down a couple more times. The priest left, the boy came out and snuffed the candles and carried off the cruets they had used earlier.

James sat back. "And that's a Catholic mass," he said, "in about its most basic form. I hope you got some of what you wanted from it and, uh, you know you can ask me anything you want about it, anytime. It's still light out, being summer and daylight savings time, to boot. Want to come over to the house?"

"I'm kind of dressed up," she said.

"Ha, then you could take me out to dinner!"

James wasn't serious, was he? "Some other time. Thanks for coming with me."

She watched from her car as he rode his bicycle away. Then she drove home.

Chapter Sixty
Joey

Jelly, by herself? Joey went up and slid into the pew beside her. "Isn't James coming this morning?" she whispered.

"Went to the Saturday evening mass. I don't know why."

And Joey didn't know why Angelica was there. Twice now. Most uncharacteristic!

She might as well stay here beside her even if she didn't like being so far forward. "Maybe he wanted a change of pace." Or maybe he was avoiding her? There wouldn't be any reason for Jam to do that, would there?

The two walked outside together after mass. "No scooter?"

"No point in making all that noise early in the morning. Especially a Sunday morning."

"Wow. You've become considerate, Jelly."

"I manage occasionally, between the acts of selfishness."

"Seriously, don't think I haven't noticed. We'll make a decent woman of you yet."

"Walk home with me?"

Pushing her bike all the way. Oh well. "Sure."

They crossed Third Street at the corner and started west along the sidewalk, beneath the towering dawn-lit palms. It was just starting to be noticeably a little darker, these early mornings. "Have you spoken to Ronnie these last couple days?" asked Jelly.

"A little. She seems okay to me. Not that I know anything." Oh, she shouldn't tack that disclaimer onto her statements so often. Even if it was true.

"I think she's okay too. She was only shaken. She's already gotten over it." Jelly paused a few seconds, thinking through something. "Mostly. I think I did worse to her and she seemed to get over that too. I'm not sure I did."

"I thought something had happened between you two. Hasn't that blown over?"

"I guess so. Or maybe not. I don't know."

"That clears things up. Do you want to tell me what happened?" Now you've let yourself in for it, girl. Ah, consider it material for a story.

"I made a stupid pass at Ronnie. She's put it behind her but I don't know whether I still feel guilty or frustrated or what."

"Oh, like you did to me that one time?"

Jel turned to her, obviously surprised. "You knew I was coming on to you?"

"I pretended I didn't. It seemed the easiest way to deal with you. At least when I was fourteen."

'Maybe it was. I never bothered you again, did I?"

"Um, you went off to boarding school and never had the opportunity." Jelly probably had loads of opportunities at those schools. She would not ask about that, even if it would be good material too.

"Good point. The worst thing is that now I'm afraid Ronnie will always see me and Robert Mills as two sides of the same coin. Hell, I may see myself that way."

"Guys hit on girls all the time and no one thinks anything of it. You didn't attack her, Angelica. You didn't wave your pecker at her!"

"Maybe I would have if I had one. How do I know?'

"I don't believe it one second. You wouldn't want to have a pecker anyway. I happen to know you prefer them attached to men."

"I do." Jelly smiled a little to herself. "But in spite of all that, I'm still a virgin."

"Really?" It wasn't so astounding. "So am I. We should find a couple of guys to deflower us."

"I've been telling myself that forever but every time I start with a guy, something tells me 'this isn't the one' and I end up giving him head or something. And then avoid him."

Damn. That wasn't so unlike her own pattern. Not identical. Almost to the Summerlin house. "But—you like girls too?"

"It seems that way. I don't know what I am, Joey, or what I'm looking for."

"I'm still looking for that guy to deflower me." A little humor could only help. This was all becoming a bit too much.

"Ah, Joey. We'll have to start searching at once. Any specifics?" Jelly stepped back and looked at her. "You're blushing! You thought of someone, didn't you?"

Joey heard herself saying, in a rather small voice, "Your brother."

"Oh, him. Join the club! James is assuredly not a virgin, despite his talk of sanctity and all that. Girls like him and he's made the most of it." She reflected a moment. "Not this summer though. Maybe he's maturing."

"I think I'm one girl he's not interested in."

"Maybe. Maybe not. Want to come in?"

Joey took a long look at the Summerlin house. "Not right now. Maybe I'll come by later."

Right now she felt more like riding. Riding fast and far.

Chapter Sixty-one
Ronnie

He was reticent. Ronnie could see that and understand it. Alan thought he would be taking advantage, that maybe she still was troubled by what had happened. She would have to convince him otherwise.

But if she tried too hard that would just further his doubts. Make him nervous, fearful of doing some sort of harm. She shouldn't have waited so long but she, too, had become comfortable with the pattern they had established.

That was going to change soon, whatever the two of them did. "There won't be many more of these gatherings," she said. "There won't be much more summer. Let's make the most of it."

"How?"

"Make like Kris and Will?" Oh, that had been too much. Alan got that wary look again, right away. The look like he was afraid of moving for fear he might break something.

"We can skip nights in a tent. Unless—" Should she say it? "You would still like to take me on a surf trip some time." She decided to plow on, having gone this far. "I might like someone to come and whisk me away for a weekend of camping when I'm stuck in Gainesville."

Ah, that worked better. She had moved it all into a nebulous future.

"I think I might like that too." He nuzzled her ear. "Anything sooner?"

"Just this for now," she said, and raised her mouth to his his. Yes, that was what she wanted from Alan. All she needed at the moment. She let one hand come around to rest on his buttock. Tight. She was tempted to give it a little squeeze. "Let's go see what everyone's up to."

Hand in hand, they walked across the lawn. Yes, she would go slow for now but there was so little time left. She had no illusions about Alan actually running off to Gainesville to take her surfing.

"Raining again," he said. "Everyone is moving onto the porch."

"There isn't much of an everyone here." It started coming down harder. "Run!" A few seconds later they were under cover, watching a sheet of water run off the eaves. "This reminds me of our first date."

Any hopes of rekindling those memories disappeared. "Alan!"

He turned. "Gordie. Hey." There was a note of—maybe not quite surprise in his voice but perhaps a bit of a question. His surfing friend was sitting next to Angelica.

James was over there. No one else around? Oh, Joey and Sandy were coming out of the house. The younger girl should be flying later. Sundays, right?

Gordie was coming over to them. "Man, I thought Jelly had been turning a very cold shoulder to you."

Gordie snickered. "She says she doesn't like Grubby but she's okay with me. Crazy, huh? Still—I don't think I'm going to get any repeat performances."

Ronnie saw Alan's jaw tighten. He didn't like him talking like that around her. For some reason she was reminded of her savior in Miami, of Mike busting into a motel room where—no, that's done. No reason to think of it.

Maybe Alan needed a Donna, someone with a firmer hand than her. "I'm going to go talk to James," she announced. She'd leave the surfers to amuse each other.

James looked up as she took a chair beside him. "Hi, Ronnie. How have you been doing since our clandestine rendezvous?"

"Oh, all right I guess." She wasn't going to air any of her frustrations. "I've been doing some religious reading." Some before, some since.

"Those fantasy novels you like are sometimes close to being religious readings."

"They are, aren't they?" She would have to suggest that to Alan. "Tolkien, right? I got some of his, um, themes."

"They're rather Catholic themes."

"Really? Huh. I'm not sure I recognize a Catholic theme."

He only shrugged. "That's not important. Good writing can just let you absorb ideas."

"With a minimum of pain. What are you reading there?"

He held up a book in something other than the familiar Latin alphabet. "Cyrillic? No, Greek, right?"

"Right indeed."

Joey was hovering above them. "Is he flaunting his learning again? You know he can't really read it. He just pretends to impress girls."

"Well, I have three lovely girls around me right now so I guess it works."

Sandy made a rude noise. "Have you been giving that girl lessons, Joey? Corrupting young minds!"

"She's just learned to see through your bull like the rest of us, dear Jam."

There were times Ronnie resented her friends and this was one of them. She'd been having a serious talk with James. And this too seemed something to hurry with, picking the boy's mind, before he disappeared. Before summer disappeared. "I'm going to go reclaim my boyfriend," she said. "I suspect he and Gordie are having a secret affair."

"Ah, you've found out. We've all been trying to keep it from you."

"Yeah, sure, Joey." She got up and looked around for Alan. By himself now, looking out through the screen, the lawn shimmering in a half-light as the sun tried to break through the clouds.

"It's let up."

"Let's walk outside." She wanted him by himself. No distractions. Maybe they shouldn't even have come here.

The grass was soaked. She kicked off her sandals and went on bare-foot. "Good idea," said Alan, doing the same. He was in flip-flops. Alan wore those a lot.

"Ah, I'm finally getting you out of your clothes. A little at a time!" He did not respond to that, as humor or anything else. "You have something on your mind?"

"Oh, all sorts of things."

"I hope I'm one of them."

"The most important of them all."

They walked on, almost to the west end of the property. "We were so awkward just a couple months ago. Less than a couple months. But we became comfortable with each other right away, didn't we? I'd never—had that happen with a boy before."

"Me neither." He chuckled. "I mean with a girl."

With a boy too, she was pretty sure. Alan did not warm up quickly to either sex. He still didn't but he had made new friends this summer. Friends he shared with her. All her resentment toward Joey evaporated. She almost wished she were standing there with them right now.

Almost! She wrapped her arms around her boyfriend. Her man. His response felt—cool. But tender. Alan was still being tentative, careful. Still worrying about hurting her somehow. "Kiss me, you stupid surfer boy."

That was better. A long kiss. And some tongue. That he had been willing to put into their kisses from the start, more than she had. She'd warmed to it. As Ronnie had told her friends, Alan was a pretty great kisser.

She needed more than kisses from him now. Encouragement time? She felt clumsy, trying it. Squeeze his ass? She did let her hands slide across his buttocks and up the back of his tee shirt. Stop thinking. Just —just try to do whatever came natural. It was in her. Surely it was in Alan.

She pulled her lips away from his. "Lower. Kiss me everywhere." Ronnie arched her head back, exposing her neck in a clear invitation. Yes, he got the message. Now keep working down! She let her hands slide back down and into his shorts. She'd never touched a man's ass before. He shivered but kept on task. Use your hands too, she thought. Anywhere.

Maybe he would have. The rain began to patter on the leaves, on the hibiscus around them. Alan straightened up. "We'd better get inside."

Ronnie sighed and they headed back to the house.

Chapter Sixty-two
Kris

"I wonder what Grubby wants?" He was clearly headed their direction.

They had just stepped out of her Bug into the rain-swept street. It looked like the weather might be clearing now, but with a tropical storm moseying along the east coast, they couldn't count on it. "Call him Gordie," said Will. "That's what he prefers now."

Damned if she was going to. She'd gone to school with Grubby, dated Grubby, had sex with Grubby. She didn't know any Gordie. Kris looked at the man beside her. She hadn't known any Will either, had she? Okay, she'd try Gordie

He came right up and started in without a word of greeting. "Alan has told me of your difficulties. Just a couple more weeks, Will? That's hard, man." His eyes flickered to Kris and back to Will. "Hard on both of you. Anyway, here's the thing—we have a nice, unoccupied guest house at my folks' place. They call it a pool house. Same difference. And when I explained the situation they said you could use it."

That was an astounding offer to come out of the blue. Forget Grubby. This Gordie was a great guy!

"They aren't bothered by, um, me being black and Kris being white?"

"And not married, to boot?"

"Nope. Surprised me! Anything for our soldiers, said Dad. That might have been a hint for me to enlist! And Mom's a sucker for romance. My step-mom. I don't know what the other one would think." He probably gave the question more thought than it deserved. "She might just be a little sour on it."

"For how long?" she asked.

"How long would you need it?"

"We have twelve days now. Right Kris?"

"Thirteen nights if we count this one."

"Oh, right. The nights are important."

"I'll say," agreed Gordie.

"But not overnight. I'm—I'm not quite ready to flaunt our—well, sexual relationship in front of my parents." Even if they were almost certainly aware of it by now. "Except the last night. I want to be with you every minute of it, Will."

"You know where I live, right? Oh, of course you do, Kris."

Having had sex in his bedroom, yes, she had a pretty good idea. It was a canal-front home, a little further south than where she lived.

"We can go over a little later and I'll give you a key. Come and go as you want but, you know, be discreet, right? And it's too bad if you're in a hurry 'cause I want to go talk to Jelly some more." He turned away and then back. "I forgot! Just a sec." He ran to the Mini-Moke, parked across the street and, retrieved an envelope. "This is for you, man. Maybe you'll want to look it at now and again when you're, um, wherever you are!" This time he was gone for good.

Will opened it and slid out a large glossy print of Kris in her bikini. She crowded in to look at it. Not too bad. The girl and the picture! "Borrow Gordie's Polaroid when we get to the pool house and you'll be able to take some reeeally sexy pics," she told him. "Now put that away and let's go up to see our friends." She wondered if Gordie had any other pictures from that day she could see. Not that she would want Will to have photos of her friends in their bathing suits. No sir!

Pretty much everyone was on the porch. No rain fell at the moment but the grass and outside tables were too wet for comfort. Jam greeted them as they came through the screen door. "A spooky sort of light this evening, isn't it? Hamlet's father might come sauntering out of the shadows any moment now."

Sandy might have taken a quick glance outside before breaking into a grin. "You don't believe in ghosts, do you?"

Jam only shrugged but Jelly jumped in. "Hamlet did. That was all the play needed."

"Oh, didn't everyone believe in ghosts back then?"

"The appearance of ghosts in Shakespeare's work proves only that the audience was willing to believe in them for the length of a play. After leaving the theater, some would have believed and some would not, just as today."

Gordie gaped at her, baffled maybe, but clearly impressed.

"Ah, maybe so, sister mine," answered Jam. "But as the bard said, all the world is a stage. Do we believe enough to keep this play going? For it to make sense?"

"Don't start talking about sound and fury," she told him. "I'm just going to enjoy the show."

The best of advice, thought Kris. And what a show there would be tonight!

Chapter Sixty-three
Ronnie

Ronnie was frustrated. She wouldn't deny that. Some people were still treating her with kid gloves. Whatever those were. Some kind of leather, right? She didn't see the connection. No matter. It had been a whole week since—since what happened in Miami. It would be tomorrow, anyway. It already felt like ancient history.

"Hi Ronnie. By yourself?" James immediately chuckled. "Well, obviously."

Yes, by herself. No triumvirate. No Alan. She had ridden over on her bike this morning, not sure why but at loose ends. That was another expression she wasn't so sure about. "How about you? Are you by yourself too?"

"Pretty much. Dad's at his office, Mom's playing tennis, I believe. Oh, Sylvie's in the kitchen but she'll ignore us if we don't bother her."

"Angelica too?"

"I'm pretty sure she went down to the beach. I am not my sister's keeper."

"Even I recognize that as a religious reference."

"That has become a cultural reference." He didn't seem very interested in the subject. "Going to go down and join her?"

"I don't feel much like it this morning."

"Then come in. I can make coffee." He held the door open for her. "Or are you a tea drinker?"

She giggled, despite herself. "Iced tea, maybe."

"There's always a pitcher of that in the fridge for Dad. Your friends tend to guzzle it when they come over. Lin did too."

"Wouldn't it be bothering Sylvie if we helped ourselves?"

"Oh, not too much. I'm her favorite, you know. She likes me much better than my sisters."

Ronnie was willing to believe it. "Have you heard from Lin?"

"Very little. You might ask Joey. She probably gets more news than I do."

James led her into the kitchen. Sylvie did not seem very busy. A little radio played gospel music. "Good morning, children. Do you need anything, James?"

"We'll just help ourselves to a little iced tea." He lifted a large, full pitcher out of the refrigerator. "And drink it in the library. Don't worry, Sylvie, we'll be sure to use coasters."

"Mister Summerlin will have your hide if'n you don't," she good-naturedly warned. "Here's glasses for you."

They settled on the leather couch in the library, mostly because there was a low table for their glasses. James was true to his word and made sure to place cork-lined wooden coasters beneath them. They sipped the drinks without saying anything for nearly a minute.

"Have you been doing more reading?" Jam asked.

"Oh, sure. And thinking deep thoughts."

"I'll have to hear about them." He waved an arm toward the book shelves. "There's a whole lot to read in here. It's not all law books. In fact, most of it isn't. Dad keeps those at his office."

She didn't have much interest in the books right now. Ronnie leaned back. Would it be wrong to put her feet up on the table? She was leaning against Jam too, a little. He felt solid. She needed solid this morning, maybe.

And he wasn't pulling away from her, like some people. "I like it in here," she whispered. "I like being in here with you." She surprised herself by leaning over and giving him a kiss. Just on the cheek. Sisterly, almost.

He did not seem at all that surprised. But he did draw back.

"I'm sorry. You don't need me doing things like that."

"It's not a problem, Ronnie." His smile was reassuring. "I like you. I've liked you since you first showed up here. Before Alan was even in your life. But he is now."

"Only part way. I don't know if I can ever get anything more from him."

Slowly, almost reluctantly, James told her, "I've noticed that."

Ronnie leaned over against him. Maybe she snuggled. It wasn't important what you called it—especially once James put his arm around her. He had been attracted to her all along. That's what he had said, wasn't it? And she knew she had been drawn to him.

This time the kiss was on the lips, where it belonged. More followed and she found herself halfway on top the boy, her hands here and there. Oh! She drew back suddenly, having felt his erection.

James was breathing a bit heavily. Not that she wasn't. She reached forward, intentionally this time, to touch the front of his shorts. Her fingers felt the outline of his manhood, traced it through the fabric. What did it look like? It—it would be beautiful, wouldn't it? Like James himself.

"May I—" She fumbled with the zipper, her hand shaking.

He gently removed it. "Not here."

Was he going to reject her? She stared into his face. "Come on." James took her hand. They stole out of the library and up the stairs. His bedroom. She was going to be in James's bedroom. There was one large bed. The morning sunlight spilled onto it, into the room.

James quietly shut the door behind himself. Behind *them*. "Are you certain of this, Ronnie?"

She nodded. Doubts could wait until tomorrow. Then she was in his arms again. James wasn't going to handle her with gloves of any sort! "Let me undress you," he murmured.

Undress her. She was going to stand naked before James Summerlin, with her too-ordinary body. Her too-ordinary self. Why would he want her at all? Slowly, deliberately, he unbuttoned her blouse, a sleeveless white cotton affair she had thrown on this morning when she decided to get on her bike. As ordinary as the rest. She shrugged it off as soon as all the buttons were undone.

"My turn." Not that one could get very creative with a tee shirt. She slid it up as slowly as she could make herself, her hands gliding up his smooth, tanned skin. Then off over the head. She had seen James without his shirt lots of times but this time was different from all the others. Her lips found his chest, lean and sinewy, but not overly muscular. Oh, those broad shoulders! She let her hands slip into his shorts.

His own hands were behind her. Her bra. He was undoing her bra. Quite deftly. She felt the hook release and shook herself so it fell forward, the straps slipping from her shoulders. She'd have to let go of him to get it off entirely and she didn't want to.

She had no choice when his mouth found her breasts and she arched back. The bra fell to the floor, forgotten. "We don't have to go further," James whispered. "You know I'm not going to force anything."

The last warning. Her last chance. She could still hold back from going all the way. Maybe James would like oral sex. Ronnie had never done it before but she was willing to try. Her only answer was to undo the button on his shorts.

She slid them down. His erection was clearly to be seen inside the white briefs. "Now it's my turn again," said James. Her shorts had just an elastic waistband. No bother at all to kick them off after the boy slid them down. He stepped back to give her a look. Ronnie felt another wave of self-consciousness. Not embarrassment. There had been none of that this morning, not since she first impulsively kissed him. But the body he was scrutinizing now, the not-so-large breasts, the soft stomach, the skinny legs. There was nothing there James could be attracted to, was there? Maybe nothing any man could be attracted to.

But Angelica had been attracted to her. Why not her brother? Hell, why not Angelica someday! James came close again, embraced her, kissed her, here, there, the lips, the shoulders, the breasts. She slipped her hands into the top of his briefs and began to work them down. "Together," laughed James, as his hands found her own panties. Then they both stood regarding each other with their pants around their ankles. They must look so silly!

And James looked so good, so desirable. Ronnie kicked her panties away, even as James did the same, and wrapped her arms around him. Wrapped herself around him, with his erect penis pressing hard against her abdomen. She had to look at it again, leaning back and peering down. Was it ordinary? She had no way of knowing, nothing to compare it with. Oh, she had seen pictures. There was something different. She touched the tip with one finger. "Oh, you're not circumcised."

James chuckled. "Mom doesn't approve. Do you?"

She approved thoroughly of this rod, this dick, this penis. Ronnie let herself glide down his body, to allow her lips to brush against it. "No." What was wrong? She looked up at Jam. "I won't have you on your knees. Come." He reached down, pulled her up to him.

With one motion, he threw back the spread on his bed. Then they were entwined on the sheets, lips, hands, discovering each other and at last James entering her, thrusting, her entire body responding to his rhythm, filled with it, both gasping with ecstasy. She felt him relax.

"Did you make it?" he whispered. She wasn't sure how to respond. "I take it you didn't." James lowered his lips to her crotch, as she bucked with almost unbearable pleasure, used his tongue to bring her to completion, leaving her gasping, spent.

She gasped for a different reason when he raised his head.

"What?"

"You have blood on your face!"

"Your blood, Ronnie. I believe I popped your cherry."

There *was* quite a bit of blood on the sheets. James had known she was a virgin, hadn't he? He slid up to lie beside her, embraced her tenderly.

"I am going to have to slip down to the utility room and wash these on the sly," he said.

"Does Sylvie do the washing?"

"No way. We have a housekeeper in twice a week." He looked the bed over again. "I'll do something. No problem."

Was there regret in his voice? James's hand slowly glided up her torso, to rest on one breast, his fingers idly fondling the nipple. His mind seemed somewhere else altogether.

"No problem," James repeated. "But you and I—I don't know if that's a problem or not. Not that I wouldn't do this all over again."

"Not right now, I hope!"

"I'd do it all day if you asked it of me."

"All night too?"

"I need *some* time off." He kissed her brow and rolled out of bed. "We had better clean up." A peek out the door. "Coast is clear. You can have the bathroom first."

Ronnie did have to give that beautiful body, that beautiful boy, one last lingering look before she slipped out of the room.

Chapter Sixty-four
Joey

"Sit down," ordered Jelly, "and let me just say this outright. James had sex with Ronnie."

That was an unusual way to be greeted. It took a few seconds for the statement to sink in.

"I don't know how it happened but I think it's eating him up," Jelly continued. "Both of them, maybe."

"And you know this how?"

"I had just come back from the beach and was changing in my room when they sneaked up the stairs. I'm not a voyeur but the walls are not sound proof." There was a trace of Jelly's typical mischief in her voice as she went on. "At least not if I go into my parents' room and put my ear against them. And—there were the sheets."

"Sheets?" What did that have to do with it? Beds could be remade.

"Soaked with virgin blood. I saw James stuff them into the garbage can later."

Joey had known Ronnie hadn't been with a guy before. She just hadn't thought about that aspect of it. "So we know they went—"

"All the way? Yes." There might have been a sort of smirk. "I won't bleed, of course. I've never had a dick in me but other objects have found their way through my hymen."

"Ooh, gross, Jelly."

"Grosser than a piece of meat?"

She wasn't going to argue that point, but Jelly had not objected to those pieces of meat on other occasions. In other places.

"Damn," she said. "James."

"Yeah."

"And Alan. I don't think they've broken up."

"Maybe they won't. I'm sure it was a spur of the moment thing for both of them. Best forgotten and never repeated."

"I'm not sure Ronnie could do that."

"She might be better at it than any of us." Jelly turned her attention to Joey now. "Don't pretend this doesn't effect you, Jo-jo. You just got finished confessing your undying love for my unworthy brother."

"Aah, you would bring that up. But remember, I only said I'd choose him to deflower me. Just like Ronnie has done."

Jelly nodded. "Valid point. There's nothing we can do anyway."

"Right now. We will not mention this to Kris. Understood?"

"She has enough on her table."

Things could change. They *would* change. And she did not intend to say a word to anyone involved in this mess. "I've been receiving missives from your sister."

"Wow, missives! She only sends the rest of us letters." The mocking tone softened. "Sometimes. Almost never, in fact."

"They're just gossip. I may have become her long-distance diary."

"I'd bet gossip from the New York publishing scene is just as boring as any other."

"Her scene, anyway. I wouldn't want to be in that world. Books, maybe."

"Sounds good. And when you're a famous, fabulous author, the firm of Summerlin and Deerfield will handle any legal problems for you!"

"Deerfield?"

"Oh, yes. We're going to have a famous, fabulous law office, with loads of flunkies we can mistreat."

This, she might ask Ronnie about.

"I guess I'll go down onto the beach. What I intended when I rode over here."

"Instead, I handed you a bag full of drama to keep you awake at nights."

"Like I needed that. Oh, I recognize that awful sound."

She turned to spy Sandy on her moped. "She's been following me around on my scooter. I usually let her keep up." Jelly waved to the girl. "And sometimes I'm mean and give her the slip or just speed away from her."

Joey waved too. "We're going down on the beach," she called. "Wanta come along?"

"Sure do!"

"Are you certain you want to befriend her?" whispered Jelly

"Why not? We may be the only two left here in a couple weeks."

Chapter Sixty-five
Ronnie

"News," she reported to Alan as she climbed into his wagon. "I've decided for certain to go to Gainesville for college."

He looked puzzled. "I thought you were already committed to UF."

"I'd been giving a lot of thought to attending Edison. To be with Joey and you."

He put his vehicle into gear and backed out. "I think you made the right decision. I'll keep an eye on Joey for you."

Darn, he would say something like that. Alan would make this hard. No second thoughts anymore. She and Alan would be going different ways. She had to make him see that. "The signs pointed that direction."

Signs. Maybe it had been a sign. Not that Ronnie believed in signs, not the way some people meant when they talked about them. God hadn't tapped her on the shoulder and pointed. It was more like one of those by the roadside that read 'caution' or even 'stop.' It was time to stop. There was no point in going forward; not on this road.

"Damn," he said, and put on the brakes. "You're breaking up with me."

So oblivious at times and so able to see right through things at others. She could only give him a little nod. She felt her eyes misting.

"Is it because of Miami? Because I wasn't there for you?"

Ronnie was astonished. It was something that had never entered her mind, but it explained much. Alan had been feeling guilty when they were last together. Guilty of abandoning her.

Now it was her turn to be filled with guilt. "No, not Miami. That has nothing to do with it." But she could not tell him why. Just that it wasn't going to work with them going different directions and that was true, wasn't it? He'd be hurt and maybe not completely understand.

Alan started forward again. "We're still going out tonight. We can talk about it over a meal. If you want to."

She wouldn't talk about it. Not really. She would only give him obvious reasons, the ones she had at the ready, the ones that even made some sense. Not all the confusing stuff behind them.

Oh, she had felt confused about many things. She still did. She hated herself some for betraying Alan. But she could convince herself she was not his future and he wasn't hers. Nor was James. She did not think there would be a repeat of what had happened between them.

But she did not regret it in the least. That she did know.

"Would you have sex with me?" she asked.

"I—I'm not sure that's a good idea considering what just happened."

"Exactly. Neither am I. We shouldn't have sex and it's probably a good thing we never did. We're not going to be together, Alan. You can see that, can't you?"

"Honestly, I thought I could see a way to it." He turned left at Gulf Shore but she didn't think he had a destination in mind. He was just driving to drive.

"Then you see more than I can. Maybe you can see dreams but all I see are obstacles."

They cruised along the palm-lined street. "Do you resent that?"

"I've loved it and I've resented it. I've loved how good you can be and hated how you can—can live in another world. One I can't get into."

"I know that's true. Too often, I'm just lost and afraid of making things worse. So I—pull away."

"Oh, Alan. I know you would never intentionally hurt anyone. You're about the best person I know, when it comes to that."

"There isn't someone else, is there? You know I wouldn't mind if you traded up. Just be—be honest with me."

"No. No one else." She was sure of that. But being honest with him? She didn't even want to think about that. "Where the heck are we going?"

They had just passed the pier.

"I have no idea. Shall we drop in on Kris and Will?"

Despite all this serious talk, all the burden she felt, Ronnie had to giggle at that. "I wouldn't mind driving by and taking a look. You've been there?"

"Only to pick up Gordie and bring him back after our trip." He took a left, then a right, and cruised south a tad further before going left again. "Down the street." The pavement curved, with large houses on either side, deep well-maintained lawns leading to canals that communicated with Naples Bay. Alan slowed down. "This one."

"I don't see Kris's Bug."

"Probably not there this early, but they can park around where we couldn't see it anyway. That's the pool house peeking around the corner of the main place. Hey, your dad didn't design this one, did he?"

Ronnie had no idea. They went around a cul-de-sac and back to Second Street. "How about a sundae at the Rex-all?" he asked.

The scene of their first date. Not subtle at all. But it didn't matter. "Sure."

Back downtown, a shared snack at the counter in the drug store. No visits to the book store this time. No kisses in the arcade.

No kiss when he left her at her house. Only tears when she was again in her bedroom.

Chapter Sixty-six
Kris

"More Polaroids?"

"As many as I can get. Of course, I'm going to pass them out to all the guys in my company."

"Oh! Then I'd better do my part for our boys. How's this?"

"Whoa! I'm liable to forget about taking pictures and jump on you again." Whirr.

"And who is going to complain?" Kris struck a different pose.

"Niiiice. Hey, arch back a little so your breasts come up and—yes." Whirr.

Whirr and whirr again. She was pretending to be into it but Kris was getting a little bored with Will's picture taking. She fully intended to let him take every picture he wished until he couldn't anymore.

They were, as suggested, being discreet. They mostly came and went to this guest house at night, and used Kris's modest little Volkswagen. The neighbors—if they noticed it—might think she and Gordie were back together!

Will sat looking at each snap as it developed. Instant cameras were a godsend. He wouldn't have pictures of her to take with him otherwise. Not the sort of pictures he was taking now!

"I'm gonna put some clothes on," she announced.

"Don't need to do it for me, girl," mumbled Will, distracted by the four pictures lying on the table before him.

"I think the Summerlins would expect it. And we can come back here and I'll take them off again for you."

Will stood up. "Sounds good. It's still a little light out."

"Just scrunch down in your seat, like when we came." She slipped on her shorts and came over and kissed him. "I hate having to sneak in and out."

"You mean sneak me in and out. I'm willing to put up with it to be with you here."

"Oh, sure, I know I'm worth it." And it would be for only one more week. Then Will would be gone. She fastened her bra and pulled a tee shirt on. "Ready?"

In five minutes or so they were pulling in at the Summerlin house. Not much more than a week left for visiting this place. One week. Next Friday they would be showing up for Will's farewell party. There would be other farewells for him, sure. His family, his community. But those who came here, the core of them, were Will's family too, now. The triumvirate and the Summerlins and Alan and even Gordie. Maybe Gordie.

Not that others wouldn't show up. Mackie had promised. She didn't doubt some of Will's old teammates would come too, and maybe bring dates, and others would just hear about the party or wander up off the beach! She hoped there would be a huge turnout. Her Will deserved it.

Okay, turn it down a notch, she told herself. You're getting silly. It was nothing but that family this evening. Some of them. "Alan and Ronnie aren't here yet," she told Will.

"Oh. Um." He was decidedly hesitant to say what seemed to be on his mind.

"What? Spit it out, Will."

"They've broken up. Alan told me."

"And you didn't see fit to let me know?"

"He didn't say I could. I figured Ronnie would talk to you anyway."

"She didn't." She didn't. Why not? "Do you know what went wrong?"

"Alan sure doesn't. That boy is hurting, whether he shows it or not."

"Hey, guys!"

She waved to Jelly. No sign of her brother. Joey staring into space while Sandy went on about something to her. No guys at all, except her Will, and she didn't intend to share him!

"Did you know about Ronnie and Alan," she asked as soon as she was close enough.

"Joey told me a few minutes ago. She'd stopped by the Deerfields and Ronnie told her she wasn't coming. And why."

"The why of that why is what I wonder."

Jelly shrugged. "Who knows?"

Kris had a suspicion the answer to *that* question was Jelly. Maybe Joey too. No point in prying. She would talk to Ronnie, though. Sooner or later.

They went on over to Joey and Sandy. "What are you two going on about?" asked Kris.

"James! He's being all distracted and moody and stuff. You know? We're trying to figure him out," claimed Sandy.

"You're trying to figure him out. Jel and I gave up long ago. Hi, kids, and welcome to the gloomiest party of the year."

Kris sat down beside her friend. "I know what you like to do when you're like this. Move! Let's go walk the beach like we used to." She glance toward the house. "Maybe we can even get Jam to join us."

"I'll ask," volunteered Sandy, jumping up and running inside.

"Some of James's pot might be just as good," said Jelly.

"After we get back. Ah, she actually managed to drag him out into the open."

Jam ambled their direction, Sandy hurrying along ahead of him. "Hey, James," called Will. "Whatcha been up to?"

"We've all be burning to know," Joey added

"Not much. I'm just sitting around thinking too much again. The usual stuff, my vocation or lack thereof. My sinful nature!" Jelly and Joey gave each other a meaningful look when he said this. Meaningful to them, Kris assumed. She couldn't figure it out.

"Well then, think while you walk. We're going to go all the way from one pass to another."

"And back? That's like fourteen miles, isn't it?"

"Okay. Maybe that would be a bit excessive. Let's go south," suggested Joey. "And we won't trick you this time."

"These nights will turn cool before we know," he said as they reached the sand and turned toward the pier. "Before you know. I suppose I'll be off studying."

"You're not the only one leaving town," his sister reminded him.

"Yeah. You're out of here next weekend, right Will?"

"I have to report on the Twenty-sixth. I'll be on a bus most of the day before. Leaving Saturday evening, in fact.

"For Le Jeune?"

"Uh-huh. Even medics have to undergo basic training."

"Pretty tough, I hear."

"So am I!"

"This softy? He still has to sleep with his teddy bear."

"As long as that teddy bear is you." The kiss that ensued was long enough they had to run to catch up.

"You guys are scandalizing Sandy," Joey informed them.

They probably were. Kris wondered if the girl had a boyfriend. Not one that she'd ever brought by. They were about to pass under the pier.

"Let's walk out to the end. It may be last time we—we ever do it together." How she wished Ronnie were there too.

As if all of the same mind, they climbed to the decking, walked westward, toward the great expanse of Gulf that stretched between them and Mexico. Will and Kris came last, hand in hand, not speaking, only sharing the glorious sunset that lay before them. Even Sandy was silent. A few fishermen cast or dangled lines. Others walked, some east, some west, or leaned against railings.

The end. One always reached the end, the point where one could walk no further, go no further. It would be dark soon; already the evening star shone.

This end was only the tip of a pier, a structure of wood and concrete. They could turn around but would they arrive at quite the same place they left? No matter. Their friends would be there and they would eat or even smoke some of Jam's rumored pot. Better get rid of Sandy first!

Then she and the man she loved would return to their retreat.

Chapter Sixty-seven
Joey

Howard Deerfield's office was a little space between the Trail and Tenth, not that far from his home. Not far from her home either. Cluttered. Two drafting boards, two desks.

"I can't give you a job description," said Howard Deerfield, leaning back in his swivel chair, "because there isn't one. You'd be a this-and-thatter."

"A girl Friday?" suggested Ronnie.

"Or whatever day works best with her schedule!" Deerfield chuckled at his own joke. "Okay, if I'm the boss you have to laugh too," he told the girls.

"I don't know my schedule yet," admitted Joey. "I'm going to try to concentrate as many classes as I can into two days a week. Maybe Monday Wednesday, maybe Tuesday Thursday."

The architect considered this. "Why?"

"If I ride the free bus I have to spend all day at Edison. I might as well make the most of my time there."

"That's pretty sensible."

"I've been rubbing off on her, Dad," claimed Ronnie.

"It only took twelve years," Joey said.

"Twelve years. Darn." He seemed to think about that long enough to make them a little uncomfortable. "Twelve years. It's hard to believe but I know it's true. That's a long time to be friends at any age."

"Even when her parents stuck her in another school," said Ronnie.

"I remember." He looked up at Joey. "Saint Ann, right? My little girl was quite indignant about it. I'm surprised she didn't go over and give them a piece of her mind."

"I was sending them bad vibes."

"They were making enough of those themselves," Joey said. "So, I'd be like filing or answering phones or typing or making coffee?"

"All at the same time!" He leaned forward suddenly. "I'd be more likely to have you running errands. On your bike, if you prefer. Picking things up here, delivering things there."

"My dream job!"

"I'm glad to hear it. If you want to do more, we'll see. You can even learn to draft, if you'd like. Apprentices come and go here, some of them future architects or kids who think they'd like to be. Some just interested in learning how to draw up house plans." He swiveled to face Ronnie. "I let Daryl try his hand at some simple drafting when he came over." He shook his head. "I think the boy might have done better to stick with his engineer career path. He's not, well, very creative." A swivel back, recline again. "I'd bet your Alan has more natural talent for this kind of work. He's the sort who makes things."

"He's not my Alan any more. He's—" Ronnie burst into tears and left them without another word. She didn't quite run outside.

"Shit," commented Joey.

"Did that boy hurt my daughter somehow?" demanded Deerfield.

Joey was uncertain how to answer that. Was honesty the best policy? "She was the one who hurt him, sir." She shook her head. "And he doesn't even know about it."

Ronnie was waiting outside, equilibrium restored. Neither of them said anything about what had happened. Joey hoped Howard Deerfield wouldn't when Ronnie got home. But of course he would tell his wife. She'd be more likely to bring it up.

Nothing she could do about that. "Let's ride over to my house." The two mounted their bikes and pedaled slowly in the direction of the Trail. At this busy time of day, the sidewalk beside it would be their safest path. "I got a letter from Lin yesterday. She's writing to my address now."

Ronnie gave a distracted nod. "James is gone."

"Gone?"

"Left Naples. Off to his school." There was not much emotion, one way or another, in her voice. "Angelica called yesterday to tell me. She —she thought I should know."

She could have let Joey know too, couldn't she? "He didn't even wait for Will's party?" The party Jam had planned.

Ronnie only shook her head and began to sob again. "You're thinking you drove him away. Don't believe it."

"Huh? Do you—do you know—"

"About what happened between you. Yes. And Angelica. She was in the house at the time."

"Oh."

"James was going to go anyway. Your encounter only sent him on his way a week or two early."

Ronnie nodded slowly. "I guess I knew he was never going to stay."

Joey considered saying something about Alan and then reconsidered. Best to let that lie. "Here's the turn." A couple minutes later they were in front of her house.

Chapter Sixty-eight
Ronnie

Alan was going to be there. She wasn't going to let that bother her. He had a right. He was Will's friend. She doubted she would be able to speak to him.

Ronnie brushed her hair. It had gotten noticeably longer over summer. Lighter too. She thought she'd like to keep it that way. But these days spent in the sun were ending and there might never be another summer like this one. It hadn't been a bad summer overall, had it? An eventful one! Alan's image passed through her mind again, to be superseded by that of James.

Was his hair still long? Did those beautiful locks end up on the floor when he went off to his school? She couldn't exactly picture him without them. And in vestments like the priest wore when she accompanied him to church. Maybe she would go back on her own some day. Or with Joey. Why not with Kris, for that matter? Jews, Catholics—she knew about as much about the one as the other.

Poor Jam. He couldn't be Jewish without being circumcised. Ronnie did not at all like the idea of someone taking a knife to him. Ready. Shorts, a nice blouse. She looked okay and it wasn't her night, after all.

"I'm heading out," she told her parents as she passed through the living room. She was glad Mom hadn't quizzed her about Alan. Not that there weren't a couple of clumsily-veiled questions.

"Give our best to that boy," her father called after her.

"I will!"

She didn't hurry to the Summerlins. Instead, she pulled over at one of the beach accesses and looked at the water for a while. The surface was only a little choppy from the afternoon sea breeze, sparkling in the sun. No rain would interrupt this farewell party. Back around—always pretty easy in this little car—and out onto Gulf Shore, down to that blocky old beach-front house, the one with the tall, graceful coconut trees and almost more memories than she could handle.

Still plenty of places to park. Smoke rose from the barbecue grill. Was Mister Summerlin himself going to man it tonight? This wasn't just for young people. A smattering of adults stood around. Yes, yes, they were all adults. Except Sandy over there. She had dragged her brother along, hadn't she?

Ronnie waved to the girl and hoped she wouldn't come over. No such luck. At least Russel didn't follow her. "Is the guest of honor here?"

"Nope. Alan says he'll be along shortly. He was just with him."

Alan. Her heart jumped just a tad, ached just a tad, when she spied Alan. No date. She hadn't expected one. Alan was no more likely to hook up quickly with someone new than she was.

Sandy had stepped back, her face clouded. "Shit!" she said. "I'm such a dummy talking about Alan to you."

Ronnie had to laugh. It couldn't be helped. "There are far worse things in the world than hearing Alan's name," she assured her. "It's too bad James isn't here."

"Jelly says he's having another crisis of faith." The girl giggled. "She says they come regular, like periods."

She could imagine those words coming from Angelica Summerlin. "I suppose she's around somewhere." With James gone, this was pretty much her show. With Sandy as her trusty aide, maybe. His leaving didn't seem to have bothered Sandy any. But of course her crush hadn't been on him.

"If you, um, really don't mind me talking about him, Alan kind of took over as the guy in charge. Along with Mister Summerlin, of course."

"Okay. Then I know where to lodge any complaints."

No Joey either. Nor her Corvair but she might have ridden her bike. She and Angelica could be hiding out here somewhere. The two of them were pretty thick lately.

Macklin. No sign of the boyfriend. Not the guy next to him, beer in hand. He'd been on the football team at Naples High with Will and Mackie. And he'd probably brought the beer with him.

There came the guest of honor at last, chauffeured by Kris. Will stood up in the convertible VW, like someone in a parade, and waved as they came up the street.

She had not the slightest doubt Kris had told him to do it.

Chapter Sixty-nine
Joey

Jelly stood watching Russel Penn mingle. "Maybe I can get Russ out of his pants. I'll make it my quest! And no, Joey, he's not going to be 'the one.'"

"I wouldn't think so."

"Hmm, maybe someone else? I am horny this evening. I'm willing to admit it." Her eyes fell on Alan. "Hey, Alan doesn't belong to Ronnie anymore. And I do like the boy."

"So do I, Jel. Please don't bother him."

"Bother, you call it? But okay. Hands off Alan." She surveyed the crowded back yard again. "You don't leave me much to choose from."

"There's always Gordie."

"Considering what followed the last time he'd probably ask me to marry him if we did it again."

"He does come from money."

"I intend to have my own. Even though Lin is going to inherit way more than me and James." Joey didn't bother to ask her about that. Lin was a Salas and that was where Maria Summerlin's money came from. "Anyway," Jelly went on, "Gordie's going to be a photographer. I doubt he'll make much doing that."

"There is something to be said for doing what you love."

"No doubt an independently wealthy person told you that. Hey, have you seen the photos he took of you guys on the beach? He had to show them to me."

"Not yet. Hey Alan!" She beckoned to him. "You need to stop pacing around keeping tabs on things. You make people nervous."

He settled down beside them. "That's only fair. People make me nervous."

"You two are both going to college in Fort Myers, right?" asked Jelly. Double nods. "Do you have to commute every day? It's like, what, forty miles?"

"Not quite," Joey told her. "Still a bit of a drive."

"I'll probably ride the bus up to Edison," said Alan. "It's a lot cheaper than driving."

"Me too. But we'll be stuck there all day. I'm hoping to arrange my schedule to work with that."

"Yeah. If we can't swing that maybe we could car pool some days."

That was a pretty good idea. "We'll have to coordinate our schedules. Chances are we'll be taking a lot of the same classes anyway."

"Or you could pitch your tent on campus," suggested Jelly, "and live there all semester. There's going to be a speech or some other idiocy." She got up and sauntered toward the group gathered near the grill.

"The last farewell," murmured Alan. "I'm going to miss him." He sighed. "And I already miss Ronnie."

"I think we're both going to be missing lots of things soon," Joey told him.

Laughter came to them across the dark lawn.

Chapter Seventy
Kris

The dimmest of light filtered through the curtains. Will. Beside her, asleep.

Kris rolled her nude body over, lazily, to look at the clock. Seven. They still had some time together. Should she wake him? She hated to waste even a minute of what was left.

She could just jump him right now. That would wake the boy up! But he would probably need to pee. For that matter, so did she. She found her way to the bathroom. Ugh. I'm a mess after last night, she told herself after a glimpse in the mirror.

Kris urinated, splashed some water on herself. Better. Oh, why not get in the shower? With any luck, sleeping beauty might awaken and join her. First she looked at herself again in the full length mirror on the back of the door. What did Will see in that little girl?

Get the water right. That's a good temperature. In she stepped. Ah, let the stream's warmth melt away the little aches, the tension—but not all the cares. Those would remain with her. She would be losing Will in just a couple hours.

"Need your back scrubbed, ma'am?"

"I need more than that." He slipped into the enclosure. His dark skin glistened where the water ran down, down his muscular torso, his powerful legs. Maybe some would not be so impressed with William Booth, call him short, call him stocky. Kris liked short!

"Let's make sure we get this clean," she said, lathering his cock. "We might need to use it later."

"And get all sweaty again? So why are we getting cleaned up now?"

Neither had an answer to that. They didn't have many words at all. Dried off on the luxurious bath towels—Gordie's parents went for the best—they returned to the bed. The bed that had awaited them last night after the party came to its end, after all the best wishes had been wished and all the farewells had fared away. And they had made love as long as they could, as passionately as they could, until sleep could be held off no longer.

Our last time, thought Kris, as they came together. Tomorrow the man she loved would be already far away, traveling to whatever destiny he had. But now, she was his only destiny, the grail at the end of his quest, ready to be filled.

"Who's on top?" she whispered.

"Let's arm wrestle for it."

She jumped on his left arm, put all her weight on it. "I win!"

"Your choice then."

He lay sprawled on his back, his manhood only semi-erect. She'd have to fix that. Kris lay down atop him, her cunt at his face, his penis in her hands. She slowly licked the shaft, watched it respond, thicken, stiffen, engorge. "A nice piece of candy," she said, running her tongue up it again.

Oh, there was Will's tongue. It had been hard to get him to be willing to do that sort of thing. He was pretty halfhearted about it at first, some ingrained taboo about oral sex he had in him. She'd fixed him, she was pretty sure. Oh yes. Oh, man! Will was just the right size. They fit together so well. She got up, turned around, straddled his penis. Up and down. Do your part, Will, my legs will get tired. He bucked violently once, twice, but then settled into the rhythm she had set, the two moving together. She fondled her breasts as she rode him. He liked to see her do that, she knew, tweak her own nipples. A shudder as he came, pulsing once, twice, three times before relaxing. She reached down to her cunt and followed him into orgasm.

"Now we do need that shower," he said a couple minutes later.

"What, we're not going to do it again?"

"Oh, girl, I wish—" He pulled her to him, stroking her hair. All at once, she found herself crying. Not just a tear or two. Bawling. It was all going to end now, he was going to leave this house and she might never see him again.

And neither had any words for the other. None would do.

Mackie was going to come and pick Will up, take him to his home so he could pack what he needed and say goodbye to his family. It had been good to see Mackie last night, to talk with him a while.

They remained in each other's arms a few more minutes. Then Will kissed her tenderly, lifted her arm from his body, went to clean up. Kris slipped into the clothes she'd left on the floor last night. She could shower anytime. A single honk.

Will went to the window. "It's Mackie. Time I go see my folks."

"And then you'll be gone."

"Yes. Don't come to see me off. Let this be our farewell." They had already agreed to this. Maybe he felt it needed repeating.

Will took Kris in his arms. They kissed long but could not kiss forever, and then he went out into the morning.

"Don't throw your life away, Will Booth," she murmured. "Don't throw your life away."

Chapter Seventy-one
Joey

"Jam left his bike behind. I might as well use it."

"Saddle up then and we'll ride over to Ronnie's place."

"I've never been in any of your homes." Jelly straddled the black three-speed. "No, wait. I'm pretty sure I went with my father to the Greene's house when I was little."

"You remember an obnoxious little girl being there?"

"Ha, do you mean me or Kris?" They peddled across Gulf Shore. Joey preferred to take less traveled streets on her route to her friend's house.

"I filled Kris in on Ronnie and Alan and Jam. I figured it was time she knew. But she knows not to bring it up around Ronnie."

"But she knows that you all know." Jelly shook her head of long dark hair. "What a curious bunch you are."

"That's the pot calling the kettle something. Speaking of pot, have you heard from your brother?"

Across Second. "I did. He called to tell my parents he had safely reported to his destination. Then he talked to me and told me had he detoured to Chicago to demonstrate at the Democrats' convention. Our parents do not need to know this."

"Damn. I hope he's okay. It looked pretty rough there on the news." Brutal, even. "Maybe Ronnie doesn't need to know it either."

"I would agree. Oh, past the school. Such happy memories!"

"Not for those who attended with you. Let's cut through it."

"The nuns will hunt us down if they see us riding our bikes down the hallways."

Out the front of Saint Ann School, down Lake Drive and across Fifth Avenue. They wove through the Naples streets, left here, right there, but moving north overall. "The Penns live right over there." She waved an arm to her left.

"I wonder if Russ is home. I missed my opportunity with him."

"I suspect he snuck out the back door when he saw us coming."

And finally, a halt in front of the Deerfield house. "How grand!"

"You should see mine. Hi, guys." She waved. Ronnie and Kris were both at the front door.

"It really is rather nice," Jel whispered before they reached their friends. "I like all the trees around it."

"Me too. Hey, can we fit all four of us in your bedroom, Ronnie? It's only triumvirate-sized!"

"And that triumvirate kept getting bigger over the years," said Kris. "Some members more so than others."

"We can fit four in the clubhouse," felt Ronnie. "It might be tight if we added Sandy."

"She's not very big. We'd hardly notice her."

"Hey, she's taller than me," protested Kris.

"We hardly notice you either," Joey pointed out. But Sandy was built like a sheet of paper.

Perhaps it did feel a little odd, four reasonably large, more-or-less adult women sitting around a bedroom with a pink bedspread like schoolgirls. This too might be something that would be left behind.

"How soon do you all have to take off?" asked Jelly. She perched on the edge of Ronnie's little vanity, while Ronnie and Kris took the bed. Joey had settled in the chair.

"A couple weeks for me," said Joey. "Not that I'm actually taking off. You two have like a week longer, don't you?"

"Uh-huh,' agreed Ronnie. "I'll be going up a few days before classes start. Get into my dorm. I'll have a roommate, I guess. Damn, I wish it was one of you guys!"

"Even me?" asked Jelly. The smiles around the room held a tad of embarrassment. "Hey, I'd behave!"

"Yeah, sure," said Joey. "What about you, Jelly? Have you decided where you're going yet?

"Why, the University of Miami!" She sat down beside Kris and gave her an exaggerated hug. "Kris and I are going to be very bestest friends on campus. Very, very bestest!"

"You're kidding," said Kris, disentangling herself.

"Nope. Music major. Sorry Ronnie, we may not be lawyers together after all."

Ronnie didn't seem broken up about it. "You were able to get in this late?"

"They kind of wanted me. I'm like a star football player except prettier! And when I study composition, I'll name my first symphony the Triumvirate and base each of the movements on one of you."

"I'm the *vivace* one," declared Kris.

"Obviously."

Joey didn't much want to think about what kind of music she'd be. Maybe a funeral march.

Jelly flitted on to a new subject. "Daddy's having his Labor Day barbecue on Monday, of course. For adults and we should all refuse to be one for a couple more weeks. I guess I will have to make an appearance anyway. The last Summerlin child standing!"

"Jam will be back sometime, won't he?" asked Kris. "Lin too?"

"I don't think we can get rid of them. Maybe next summer." Next summer. It seemed far away. "Maybe even some weekend or another. You know you can always show up on the weekends."

"It won't be same if none of you are there."

"Oh, don't worry about that, Ron. You know Daddy likes you." She looked around the room. "The rest of you, not so much!"

Preston Summerlin might have hoped his own daughter had ended up more like Ronnie. No, that was unkind of her to think. He certainly loved Angelica.

"Just a couple days till September," said Ronnie, to no one in particular and to no particular point. "Fall."

"Not really. September is just a word anyway," Kris told her.

"And a word isn't a real thing. It's just an idea, like James tried to tell me." Her voice trailed off a little.

"James tries to tell lots of people lots of things. I just know you can't have a story without words and that we still have a week or two to lie on the beach before we go our ways. Let's all ride there right now!"

Why not? They did have some time left but it would be only an echo of what had come before, the three months since she and Ronnie and Karen had marched across a graduation stage.

Summer was truly over. Its story had been written. Their story.

New words, new stories, would come but Joey wasn't ready to pick up her pen right then. She and her friends went out into the sun.

SEPTEMBER

Epilogue
Ronnie

Darkness was falling on Naples, on the beach, on the streets. The street lights should flicker on soon. Nature's own lights would begin to shine in the sky.

The three of them pedaled slowly along one of those streets. They had no real destination in mind. The beach probably. Third Avenue probably. Their favored spot not so long ago. It was Joey's spot, wasn't it? She was the one who started them meeting there.

Never mind that. It was their spot. It belonged to them in a way the Summerlin house did not. Would they ever lie in the sand behind that house again? It was close to the pier and they would surely go there sometimes. Wouldn't they? Wouldn't the three spread their towels beside it, walk out on a sunny day, not minding that the boys ogled them in their bathing suits, maybe buy a drink at the snack bar and watch tourists and fishermen and pelicans?

She didn't know. It wouldn't be the same anyway. Nothing would ever be the same. The world changed. Naples changed; it couldn't be the Old Naples her father went on about.

Third Avenue. Sure enough, Joey was signaling to turn here. They rode on to the beach but remained straddling their bikes as they looked out over the dark water. A little rough this evening. Not enough to surf. She wondered if Alan had found time to surf, found the waves he desired.

"Lots of phosphorescence," Joey noted. The waves tumbled around the pilings in a light show of pale greenish luminescence. It was as satisfying, it its way, as the fireworks display they had watched from the Summerlins' yard. Not as noisy!

"Walk?" she asked. "Or ride a little further?"

"Let's just ride," came Kris's answer. Joey nodded. Back to Gulf Shore, south in parallel to the Gulf. She counted the avenues.

"Lots of lights," Joey stated. The Summerlin house was lit up for their Labor Day party. Strings of lights again stretched around the eaves and from tree to tree, and a crowd filled the lawn, eating, drinking, talking of little things, maybe just enjoying a summer night. The last summer night.

Jelly would be there somewhere. The girls rode up the street, past the gala, turned at the beach and rode back. Back toward their own homes, their own world.

Three girls at the close of a summer in the sun, the same as at the beginning.

Afterword

I have endeavored to be accurate on events both in Naples and the world during the time this novel is set. However, the characters are not intended to be accurate, nor even inaccurate, portrayals of anyone. They are quite fictitious and any resemblances to actual persons are, as they say, coincidental. They are as much inspired by people I have known since as by anyone in the Class of Sixty-eight.

Nor is any character, major or minor, in any sense the author—except that my own memories of that time and place underlie the story. I did attempt to be true to the town itself. As many others of the 'old' Naples, I did not like the way the town grew and changed. Yes, I too grew and changed, as do my 'triumvirate' of young women. That is what the story is about.

Will there be another novel to carry the story further? I promise nothing but I do hope to return to Naples in time.

Sienna Santerre

www.ingramcontent.com/pod-product-compliance
Lightning Source LLC
Chambersburg PA
CBHW030526030726
47495CB00004B/873